JUNIPER

Rafa
and the
Real Boy

a novel
Emily Juniper

JUNIPER

SOCIAL ISOLATION PRESS

For you.

JUNIPER

TW:
This book alludes to sexual assault. Though not explicit, it may be triggering for those who have a history of trauma in this realm.

JUNIPER

He looks at me in horror, still clutching his throat. Then, for no reason I can explain, a wave of calm washes over him and he's no longer suffering. Ash touches my cheek again, then pulls me in and kisses my forehead. His lips are icy, but they soothe the white-hot wound on my temple, like aloe to a burn. Electric sparks permeate from the place where his lips meet my skin. I close my eyes and soak up as much of him as I can, as much as I'm allowed. I angle my chin up toward him, wanting more, my body taking over once again. But I feel him slipping away, as if he's fading into the background, dissolving like watercolors while I remain acrylic. Then, just as our lips are about to meet, the sparks disappear, and so does he.

JUNIPER

Chapter 1

I never believed in God or the supernatural, or anything beyond what I could see with my own eyes. I've never bothered with luck or fate or even karma. I am not a physicist and I'm no cynic–just a girl who's seen enough of the world to know that *I* control what happens to me. So when Mom said that I was going with her, that I didn't have a *choice,* that the courts would remove me from Dad's place in Boston and ship me (hands held by a state social worker if necessary) to Minnesota if I refused to go on my own, my beliefs about self-determination were virtually shattered.

In the end, I packed my room into boxes and hauled it piece by piece into the moving truck. Mom drives the new Subaru, I ride shotgun, and Benny sleeps in the back, diligently staining the beige upholstery with beagle drool. There was no kicking or screaming, no threats of running away, no tears. I accepted my fate and decided it was better to go quietly than to cause any more trouble for Dad. He and Mom avoided eye contact when we left, but he held my head between his large, rough hands, kissed my forehead, and said *I'll see you soon, Rafaela.*

Whatever "soon" means.

Were the ride under more favorable circumstances than the permanent separation of the two people I love most, I might enjoy it. We drive through mountains in upstate New York, then past the great lakes. They are beautiful–vast and crystalline–but they make me feel even more insignificant than I already do. At one point, Lake Erie creeps up so close to the freeway it threatens to swallow us whole, never to be seen or heard from again. I think I might be okay with that.

I give Mom the cold shoulder until well after the *Welcome to Minnesota* sign, and I'm pretty impressed with my endurance. Until this point, the only words I've spoken aloud are "I have to pee," every few hours. Eventually, though, I realize that no amount of silence will turn the car around, and I'm starting to get tired of my broody Spotify playlist.

"So, you're talking to me again?" is her response when I ask how much longer the drive will be. I hate having to answer obvious questions, especially when I'm in a sour mood, so I say nothing.

"About four hours." she says after a pause, strumming on the steering wheel with her fingers. "Four hours and change."

Still, I say nothing.

We drive the next three and a half hours in deafening silence. I'm not giving her the silent treatment anymore, but after we cross into Minnesota, I feel a sudden flutter in my chest. It's as if I'm chock-full of angry, trapped butterflies, which makes it hard to breathe, much less focus on conversation. Over the past few weeks I have spent so much time and energy throwing my belongings into cardboard boxes and fuming at Mom for leaving Dad that I haven't had time to consider my own future. I haven't Googled my new high school, investigated my new classmates on social media, or looked at the online listing of the house we're moving into. All I know about Minnesota is that people say "eh" a lot and wear cheese on their heads. Or maybe that's Wisconsin. I don't know, it's all the same.

By the time we pass the reflective green sign that reads *Esko–30 miles,* we are deep into moose country. As in, we've actually passed a few signs for moose crossings. Trees line the roads in straight, tight rows, like tall soldiers staring us down, and the six-lane interstate dwindles into two bumpy lanes. I see more roadkill in two hours of driving through Minnesota than I saw in seventeen years in Cambridge–deer, coy dogs, porcupines–and I wonder with unease what type of meat Minnesotans eat. There's a thick dew coating everything as if it has just finished raining, and the road grows darker and greener the further north we go. For the second time today, I feel like the universe is preparing to swallow me whole.

Our house is down the last turn of a dead-end street. Mom calls it a *cul-de-sac,* but dead-end seems more fitting. We pull into the cracked driveway after driving straight through the night, and Mom jumps out of the car with more enthusiasm than I can even pretend to muster. She's about three espresso shots deep and wired on caffeine. I'm wired too, but for a different reason.

Anxiety has been creeping up on me little by little since we got off I-90, but as I plant my feet on the fissured pavement, I am wracked with one powerful adrenaline surge after another. It's like cross country when I'm steadied at the starting line, inches away from runners on either side of me, waiting for the gun to go off. I am a fast and confident runner, but the ten seconds in between the "ready" and the air gun blast nearly kill me every time. I can never decide if I'm going to pee my pants or vomit, but right now I feel like doing both. I stare the foreign house in the face and every nerve ending in my body ricochets, igniting my fight or flight response. Unfortunately, even if I wanted to, I have nowhere to run so I concede to the fight.

"What are we supposed to do with all this house?" I say it under my breath, but loud enough for Mom to hear. She normally ignores my mumblings, but she must be desperate for conversation.

"Wait till you see it. It's *beautiful* inside."

I have to digest the massive exterior before I can even think about what's in the house's belly.

"How did we go from living in a townhouse to… *this?* Are you in the mob or something?"

"Don't be so dramatic, Rafa. With the same money, you can buy a lot more real estate in Minnesota than you can on the east coast, and I told you, we got a good price because the previous owners were in a hurry to move out. And now we have a little extra money to put toward our vacation." She winks at me.

I roll my eyes. I have always wanted to go to California, but Mom is using it as a bargaining chip to win

back my affections and right now the only place I want to
be is in Boston. In a huff, I storm off.

The house is quiet, but not peaceful-quiet. Eerie-
quiet. Ivy crawls up its stone skeleton and spreads over
the roof, much like the norepinephrine presently invading
every crevice of my brain. There are cornflower blue
shutters and window-boxes full of crisp, dead plants that
haven't been tended to in ages. The fissures in the
driveway are home to blades of grass poking through—an
act of rebellion against their lifeless surroundings.

"It looks just like a storybook," Mom says in awe.

Yeah. A Tim Burton one.

I take a deep breath and walk up to a heavy door,
reaching for a macabre knocker. God. I can't believe I live
in a house with a *lion's head* knocker. I push open the
unlocked door and take the first step into my new home,
though I refuse to acknowledge it as such.

There is a mahogany staircase in the entryway that
splits at the top, a rounded archway, and too many rooms
to count. Cables skirt up the walls like veins, and a brick
fireplace is the sole inhabitant of the living room. The ash
in the firebox is the only evidence that this house has been
inhabited anytime this century. On the mantel is a small
porcelain animal, sculpted by tiny hands. I pick it up and
find one of the legs is missing, and it is hard to tell if it's
supposed to be a deer or a dinosaur. On the belly of the
creature are the letters *AG*. I wonder who it belonged to
and why it was forgotten. Was AG forced to leave her
childhood home too, so quickly that she forgot a part of
her menagerie? Had she also been an innocent bystander
to a crime we call divorce?

My daydream is interrupted by a loud slam from outside, as the movers start unloading our furniture from the U-Haul that pulled in behind us. They carry in our old green couch, Mom's desk, and the few other pieces of furniture we have. Seeing all of our belongings piled in the middle of the cavernous living room is depressing. I wonder how we will ever fill it with enough things to cut the emptiness.

I carry in a few bags to look busy. A green and white canvas satchel with a loopy "R" initialed on the front holds a stack of journals, ranging from pristine to disintegrated. Seeing the leather-bound one on top forms a knot in my throat. Last year, when things weren't going so well for our family, he surprised Ollie—my little brother—and I with a trip to the Harvard bookstore to pick out a book. Ollie picked out the third Harry Potter book —he was just discovering the series— and the leather journal was my selection. I hug it to my chest and lug the bag upstairs into the first room on the left, claiming it as my own.

This room is not the largest, but it has a bay window and I'm immediately drawn in. Ever since I saw *Peter Pan* as a little girl I'd wanted one, and my mouth curls into an almost smile when I imagine myself sitting there late at night reading with a flashlight. I brush off the window seat with my palm and the dust makes me sneeze. The room with the bay window is in the back of the house and has a perfect view of the yard, which is the size of at least three football fields. I sit down and gaze over my new kingdom for a few moments. And it *is* a kingdom.

From my old bedroom window—my bedroom at Dad's—I could observe the bustling city. In Cambridge, the streets are wide, and the walkways are alive with commuters. There was always something to look at, something to wonder about. In contrast to the concrete of the city, here, there is only vegetation—threatening and wild as though no one had bothered to cut it since the seventies. There is an old swing set, which I might have enjoyed had it not been covered in rust and were I about eight years younger. Adjacent to the swings is a shabby doghouse, which Benny will scoff at. He's used to sleeping in my bed curled up near my toes and would never entertain such a primitive idea. There are also the remains of what used to be an in-ground pool, but it has been filled to the brim with rich, red dirt. Next to the hole lays a discarded diving board, some pool noodles, and a deflated raft. Probably for the best—I'm a horrible swimmer and even my Puerto Rican blood doesn't stop my skin from frying like worms on hot concrete in the summertime.

Beyond the yard is an endless forest brimming with evergreens thick with the sound of nothingness. No commuters, no cars, no whistle of a midday train in the distance or airplanes taking off. No bustle of any kind. Only emptiness, like the feeling in the pit of my stomach and the void in my heart where happiness lived a year ago.

I gaze out at my new surroundings for a while, but when my thoughts become too dark to sit with, I open my journal, curl up in the bay window, and begin to write them out onto pages no one else will ever see.

Chapter 2

"Rafa!"

"Rafa, it's time to go!"

Mom yells up the stairs, and I roll over to see it's only 7:01. Seven a.m. is way too early on any given day, but it is especially too early on the first day of what I'm now referring to as my apocalypse.

"Rafaela Amelia Torres!"

"I'm *coming"* I snap. Waking up one minute late is no reason to use my full name.

I sit up and instinctively think to go wake Ollie, who always slept in too late, but remember he isn't here. My stomach sinks. I should be used to him not being with us, but in those first few seconds of consciousness it's easy to forget. I push away the longing for my old life that is bubbling below the surface of my skin and throw my wavy, chocolate hair into a messy bun.

October in Minnesota coaxes goosebumps to the surface of my skin, so I throw on my favorite hoodie I got at an *Andrew McMahon* concert last fall and briefly wonder how the Esko music scene is. Probably not great. I highly doubt a town with more trees than people can draw much of a crowd to anything. I slip into a pair of skinny jeans and a brand-new pair of olive-green Vans that Dad gave me as a parting gift. He knows me well.

I pocket my iPhone and earbuds, scarf down a candy bar, and run downstairs to find Mom is already waiting in the car.

"Are you ready?" She asks, cruising through town at fifteen miles per hour over the limit. She has always been a bit reckless behind the wheel, yet somehow, she's never gotten a ticket. It is a running joke in the Torres family that Mom could talk her way out of death if she wanted to. Beautiful and confident with pool-blue eyes and an ever-present smile, she would never understand the struggle of entering a new school all socially awkward and gangly and pale as a vampire. Or a naked mole rat. I may have inherited my Dad's eyes, hair, and demeanor, but I definitely got Mom's melanin. Or lack thereof. She's paler than I am, but she has blonde hair, blue eyes and a rosy complexion, so it looks a little more natural on her.

"Can't wait." I say under my breath.

"Aw come on Rafa, it won't be that bad. Your grandmother used to move us around all the time when I was little. One year here, another there."

I roll my eyes. It is so easy for her. She can walk into any room and find a friend, whereas I can't say my name without choking on my own tongue.

"What time am I picking you up?"

"You really don't have to, I can take the bus."

"Nonsense, I'm off today. What time?"

"I dunno, five I think. I'll text you." I keep the syllables to a minimum, focusing all of my energy on keeping my breakfast down.

We drive a few blocks, stopping for crossing guards and lines of children making their way to school. Mom feels my energy and sighs.

"Are you ever going to forgive me?"

I know that holding a grudge against Mom over the split is unfair, but I miss my old life and my old home and our family before it was broken and I'm not quite finished feeling bitter over it.

"I'm sorry," I say, sounding terser than I mean to. "It's just really quiet here. And I miss Dad. And... Ollie. A lot"

"I know you do sweetie. I miss home, too. And even Dad sometimes, funny as it sounds." I roll my eyes. I don't say it, but if she really missed Dad she wouldn't have left him in the first place. I wait for her to mention Ollie too, but I know she won't. I should be used to it by now but it hurts all the same.

"It'll be Thanksgiving before you know it and you'll get to spend a whole week in Boston. And anyway, you'll love it here soon enough. We finally have peace and quiet. And *space.*"

That was a passive dig at Dad. She always hated the townhome, but Dad refused to give it up. She thought it was cramped, but I miss the closeness.

"I never had any problem with the space we had before," I say.

"And we'll have so much more money." She adds, ignoring my disdain. Her new job as head trauma nurse at

St. Marcy's is a big step up for her, but I don't see why the money even matters. We were never rich, but we never struggled. It wasn't as if she *had* to take this job. It was her way of running away from the tension that had plagued her and Dad for the past year and a half. I could understand if she wanted to move to a different city, but *Minnesota?*

She pulls up to the curb and I clamber out, pretending not to hear her say "good luck, sweetie."

As soon as I'm out of the car I see a hundred things that make me uneasy, most of them adolescent human beings. They're scattered across the courtyard, waiting for the bell like clucking pigeons waiting for a stray French fry.

One of the groups is clearly the jocks, which will absolutely not be my crowd. They're in blue and yellow letterman jackets flanked by a group of pretty girls who laugh loudly and with their heads thrown back every time another one of them speaks. There are a few kids playing Nintendo Switch on the ground, speaking a foreign language only known to gamers and coders. There is a group of girls who look like they must have been homeschooled until eighth grade–braids, no makeup, and shapeless jeans. The groups serve as a reminder of how hard it's going to be to make friends as a newcomer in October of Junior year. It wouldn't have been so bad if we'd moved here at the beginning of Freshman year, when high school was still shiny and new, but by now all of these people know who their friends are, and nobody goes out of their way to be seen with the new kid.

I scan the courtyard looking for somewhere–anywhere–to hide. I take a few tentative steps toward the brick building and feel like I'm walking down a path lined with blind, gaping eyes. Anxiety tells me everyone is staring, judging, talking about me; but pessimism tells me nobody notices me at all. I muster the courage to make eye contact with a freckly red head sitting by herself, but she quickly averts her gaze. She's probably just shy, but I take immediate offense. My cheeks redden and I look away as well. Until I can establish myself in one way or another people are going to treat me like a leper, or worse. At least lepers get to be part of a colony. I am too average–it's likely I'll drown in a sea of mediocrity.

Glancing at the people around me I weigh my options. I am not going to fit in with the jocks or the popular girls, which rules out half the student body. The Switch kids would probably let me sit with them, but I am not going to have that be the first clique I get in with.

Finally, I see a table with only one girl sitting at it. She has a small, boyish frame and a blue pixie-cut that I could never pull off, and she's lost in a book which I instantly admire. I work up the courage to sit down next to her and introduce myself, but she just gives me a blank stare and returns to her book.

Ouch.

I take out my journal and will myself to become invisible, while the anxious heat radiating from my body slowly melts the October frost.

Chapter 3

"So your first class is down this hallway, and then Art is upstairs just through the double doors. If you get lost, it's a big block, so if you just keep walking, you'll end up where you began. And all of the offices are down this little adjunct here."

"Okay, thank you," I say to the secretary, whose name has already escaped me. I take the schedule and packet of brightly colored forms from her.

"And remember—that information needs to be filled out, signed, and returned by tomorrow or you won't be eligible to participate in track."

"Right. No problem."

I'm anxious to get going so I'm not late for my first class. The secretary motions me in the direction of an unoccupied locker, assuring me that if I need help throughout the day any student will be happy to point me in the right direction.

"The kids are nice here; you'll see."

I nod my head and hope she's right.

I leave my belongings in the green, paint-chipped locker and look at my schedule. History—good. Might as well get the boring classes out of the way early. The room is just down the hall, easy enough to find, but when I walk in, I am appalled. The only available seat is front and center. I sit between a pretty blonde girl and a pimply boy, both of whom I hope will let me blend into the room. I put down my books and begin filling out the packet of forms from the secretary. I am about to Google "zip code for Esko, MN" when the blonde girl next to me cuts into my bubble.

"55753." She says, obviously spying.

"Thanks," I mutter. She continues looking over my shoulder onto the pink paper. It's a little weird, but it's not like I care if anyone knows I'm up to date on my tetanus vaccine. The blonde leans in closer, squinting to the top of the page where I just finished writing my address.

"You live *there?*" she asks intrusively. I can feel her bubble gum breath on my shoulder. Apparently personal space isn't common knowledge in Esko.

"Sorry," she says "I just recognized the address. I went to some dope parties there last year."

"Oh, cool." I reply, not knowing what else to say. She'll be disappointed to learn that tradition will not be continuing, unless her idea of a party is a sleepover with chocolate chip cookie dough and reruns of Parks and Rec.

"I'm not much of a partier."

"That's okay. We're all lying low this year anyway." The way she says "we're all" makes me think she's one of the popular kids.

"Who lived there?" I ask, making an effort to be conversational. Her tongue blows a giant, pink bubble which she pops loudly with her teeth.

"Some family. I didn't really know much about them except that they always had expensive liquor laying around. Disaronno, Belvedere, all the good stuff. The kid who lived there was really smart, gonna be valedictorian this year or something. His parents were like...neurosurgeons. Or his dad was. Yeah, his dad. He and his wife would travel every other month doing surgeries all over the country and leave the house to the kid. But you know, I don't-didn't-really know him."

"So, the family moved?" I ask, a stupid question. Of course they moved. The girl's face falls, and she looks down at her manicured, Tiffany blue nails.

"Well" –she pauses– "yeah, they moved away at the end of last year. Couldn't handle being here anymore."

"I understand that." I said, too quickly and with little tact.

"What do you mean?"

"Oh, just that, I don't know, there are probably more exciting places to live."

Immediately, I can tell I've offended her. *Smooth, Rafa. Smooth.*

"I'm sorry, I don't know why I said that," I begin. She recovers quickly, cutting me off.

"It's okay. I mean, you're from the city, right?"

"Boston."

"Right. Like I said, *the city*."

"I guess." When people say "the city" back east, they're usually referring to New York.

"We have different kinds of fun out here."

"I didn't mean–"

"I know what you meant." The blonde says. "Anyway, that's not why I said the family that lived in your house couldn't handle being here anymore. The parents moved away because their son *died.*"

My breath catches in my throat, and my tongue doesn't cooperate when I try to form words.

"I'm– s– I'm sorry."

"Don't worry about it," The girl says. "You couldn't have known."

I'm grateful for her understanding. I don't know why, I'm usually not a nosey person, but I can't help but ask her what happened.

"How did he die?"

The blonde looks around like she's about to tell me something she shouldn't. She looks to the back of the room to a group of jocks passing around a Juul. For a moment I think she's not going to tell me, but she lowers her voice and begins.

"Well. There was this huge party at his house. Your house, now. Everyone was there, and I mean everyone. Even the losers and loners."

She looks around again and continues.

"Anyway, the kid–Gable–got really drunk and wandered outside alone, fell in his own pool, and drowned."

"*Jeez.*" I murmur, thinking about the filled-in pool in my backyard. "That's… awful."

"Yeah, well. It was his own fault."

"I guess so." I say, not sure I understand her unfeeling response, but maybe it's her way of dealing with the loss–that I can understand. "I'm sorry."

She shrugs, but it's forced. Uncomfortable, not nonchalant. "It's alright. I didn't really know him, and I wasn't even there that night."

This surprises me, because the way she was talking about the party definitely made it *seem* like she'd been there. She must read my mind, because she chews nervously on her bottom lip and adds, "I had make-up SATs the next morning, so I sat that one out."

I'm trying to come up with something to say when the bell rings brassily above my head, and I nearly jump out of my seat.

"Good morning, class." Says a tall, thin, man who must be close to retirement age. He introduces himself as Mr. Finch and when he does, a little spit flies out of the corner of his mouth and right onto my desk. I heave a little on the inside.

"Welcome to Global 11!"

Finch's introduction is enthusiastic enough, but it's all downhill from there. After the announcements he sits down in his chair, barely visible behind a stack of outdated history textbooks that probably talk about Columbus as if he were a hero. He begins taking attendance, calling out names as students raise their hands and say "here" robotically.

"Hannah Acker?"

A pretty, long-haired girl with a retainer shoots her hand into the air.

"Aiden Fervor?"

The pimply boy to my right raises a chubby paw. "Greyson Kohl?"

A handsome, athletic looking guy with dark hair and one of those blue and yellow letterman jackets raises his hand.

"Taylor Lewis?"

The blonde girl I'd been talking to raises her hand.

"Here."

She glances back at Greyson and gives him a look. He winks at her and looks away, then he directs his attention to me and winks again. I can feel my cheeks redden as I turn around, embarrassed to have been caught studying him.

"Ra-fay-ella?" Mr. Finch calls, getting the accents totally wrong. Clearly he's never seen a Latina name before.

"Oh. Here." My hand shoots into the air. Apparently he'd said my name a couple of times while I was looking at Greyson, because a few kids chuckle.

"You forget your own name?" Finch jokes, chuckling at my expense while I die a little inside. It should be illegal to publicly poke fun at the socially anxious. Punishable by death.

When he finishes the attendance with "Trinn Zimmerman," Finch starts talking about World War I and try as I might, I can't bring myself to care about Archduke Franz Ferdinand given the history I learned about my house a few minutes earlier. I'm wondering all sorts of things about what Taylor told me, but my mind keeps trailing back to a shameful thought that makes me question how good of a person I really am: had that kid Gable not gotten himself killed, I wouldn't be forced to live in his gaping mouth of a house in this God-forsaken town in the middle of nowhere.

Chapter 4

There is no reason in hell that someone like me should try out for a sports team on the first day at a new school. Though I'm a good runner, I'm mostly doing it to keep Mom off my back. At my old school, she had taken to checking in with the guidance counselor every other week to make sure I was "socializing properly." She is so bubbly and outgoing that she can't understand why a teenager would want to spend her lunch periods in the library reading a book and listening to music in a puffy bean bag chair. I, on the other hand, can't understand why anyone *wouldn't* want to do that, especially when the alternative is a noisy, crowded cafeteria that smells of mystery meat.

To be fair, she wasn't wrong. I didn't really have any close friends back in Boston. None close enough to bother checking in with me now that I'm gone, but I can't blame them. I'd been so wrapped up with family stuff last year that I didn't check in with anyone very often either.

I drop my bag in the corner of the locker room and strip down to my bra and underwear. Once I'm in shorts and a tank, I fiddle with my combination lock mindlessly until the majority of girls clear out, not wanting to be the first one in the gym. I give myself a pep-talk to squash the self-doubt that's creeping in, but it's like trying to squash a giant spider that keeps growing every time you step on it. Inevitably, it engulfs you.

The gym is peppered with athletic looking girls, and guys wearing shorts that take the name too literally. Nobody needs to see that much guy-thigh. I notice a handful of students from my classes today, but nobody seems to see me. There's a group on the upper level, stretching and running practice sprints down the fifty-meter strip. The impish looking girl with icy blue hair from this morning is standing alone, but she is giving off serious don't-come-near-me vibes, and since I don't want a repeat of this morning, I don't bother saying hello. I can tell who the popular girls are by their manicured fingers, obnoxious look-at-me laughs, and expensive clothes. Taylor is among them, which isn't surprising. She and her group are flanked by most of the guys in the gym, all of whom are de-facto unapproachable simply because they are the opposite sex. Panic rising, I turn to flee back to the safety of the locker room but I bump into something tall and hard that nearly knocks me off my feet.

"I'm so sorry," says the tall, hard thing, placing a hand on my shoulder to steady me. "You okay?"

"Yeah, I'm–thanks."

"Don't mention it. I'm Greyson, by the way."

I almost say "I know," but thankfully stop myself in case he doesn't remember me from History.

"Rafa. Rafa Torres." I keep my replies short, as it will leave less of an opportunity for me to make a fool of myself.

"That's right, you're in my history class, aren't you?" His smile stretches the width of his face, his teeth a glowing shade of white. Opalescent, almost.

I nod.

"Rafa. That's a pretty name. I've never heard it." He ponders me, smiling like the Cheshire cat, and, as with the Cheshire cat, I'm not sure his intentions are good or purely self-serving.

"It was my grandmother's name, she is–was– Puerto Rican." I try to return the smile but it feels more like the face you make after you stub a toe on the coffee table. He is attractive, and my experiences with attractive members of the opposite sex ended in fifth grade when I threw up on Nick Hellburg at the middle school dance.

"Have I seen you before? Maybe at one of my games?" Greyson asks, squinting his eyes and cocking his head a little. He has to know I'm new here, so I'm guessing his question is just a way to tell me he plays football. As if it's not obvious just by looking at him– his calves are the size of my waist. It also dawns on me that he has no knowledge of my long history with social awkwardness. I decide to at least act confident, even if inside, I'm shriveling.

"I don't know, have you?" I ask, trying to be coy, impressed by how convincing my voice sounds.

"This is a pretty small school, and I would *definitely* know if I'd seen you before." He doesn't break eye contact, and his bright brown eyes bore into my green ones. Is he... flirting with me?

"Well, then I guess you haven't."

Am I flirting back?

"Maybe I'll see you at one soon, though. Right?"

I decide to quit while I'm ahead and make a smooth exit.

"You might." I pause and let the line sink in, then make my smooth departure. "I've got to go..." Shoot. What did I have to go do? I didn't think my exit through "...pee." I finish, unsuccessfully. It had been a fun couple of minutes pretending.

"Let me know if you need help in there." He smirks.

Well that was kind of skeevy.

I smile sheepishly and walk away, but nonetheless, I successfully disguised the fact that I'm a nervous, reclusive wreck. I skip off to the locker room, hardly noticing the dirty looks I am getting from some of the other girls.

Once back in the gym, I join the crowd on the elevated track. I run as fast as my legs will carry me, feeling the blood simultaneously pumping through my thighs and rushing to my head. Within ten minutes, this whole Esko situation has improved drastically. I know it shouldn't mean anything but getting Greyson's attention did make me feel special.

I sprint around the small indoor track, not even knowing how many laps we have to run. The air in the gymnasium is stagnant, but I imagine wind blowing through my hair and stretch my legs to their maximum extension, feeling weeks of stress float out of my body like water slipping out of a sieve. Writing is relaxing for me; it calms my mind, but nothing does for my body what running does.

We run fifteen or twenty laps before the coach blows his whistle and we stand to attention like Pavlov's dogs, minus the salivation.

"Everybody pair up!" He shouts.

My high comes crashing down. I am Icarus, and partner drills are the uninhabitable ocean. Finding a partner for anything is my worst nightmare. I stand blankly and wait for the chaos of the pairing-up ritual to be over, so the remainders and obvious outcasts can have a go. To my surprise, I don't have to wait very long.

"Hey," says a voice, as light and twinkly as sunlight bleeding through a window. "Be my partner."

A statement, not a question. It's Taylor Lewis.

"I just figured you haven't met too many people yet."

"Right, well, thanks." I say, surprised that with a whole gaggle of beautiful followers, she chose me. Do I possess some shiny new girl power?

We start stretching and chat amiably about our days, but Taylor saves the big question for when she has me in a precarious position. I'm on my back with my legs pointing toward the ceiling and she's pushing them toward the ground, over my head.

"So what's the deal. Do you have a boyfriend back home?"

I can tell the question is loaded.

"No."

She pushes down harder on my legs, straining my hamstrings. I struggle to breathe under the building pressure.

"Girlfriend?"

I laugh a little, only because no one's ever asked me that before.

"Also no."

I gulp buckets of air when she lets go and my lungs have space to expand again.

We swap positions, and I get the impression she doesn't like not being in control.

"Well, you should be careful with Greyson."

I'm not taken aback. I had already guessed the conversation was heading in his direction.

"What do you mean?"

"He's a player you know. He's probably just trying to get in your pants."

Our eyes meet, and for a second I think I detect a genuine glint of concern.

"I've never even kissed a guy, let alone, you know...*that,"* I assure her. I could have said that, to my knowledge, no one at my old school seemed interested in doing *that* with me, but I stop myself from offering my outcast status to her on a silver platter.

"Well, all the more reason for him to be interested. You've got that sacrificial virgin appeal. Boys can practically smell it."

Gross.

"I don't have time to think about...*that.* But thanks for the heads up. Really."

"And besides we're...kind of together," she adds, as if I hadn't gotten the hint to stay away.

"Taylor, I'm not interested in him. I swear. I'm just interested in passing Precalc."

I'm being sincere, but she still looks skeptical. I don't know why someone like her would feel threatened by someone like me anyway, she's beautiful. She's blonde and curvy in all the right places, with plump lips, blue eyes, and soft round cheeks. I'm just...average. Average height, thin but not skinny, with boobs and hips never got the memo that it was time to come in. And though I know looks aren't everything, I also know that Greyson is a seventeen-year-old boy. And seventeen-year-old boys can't usually see much below the surface unless it's below the panty line.

The whistle blows and Coach instructs us to take four more laps around the course. When I turn to Taylor to change the subject, she's nowhere to be found. How stupid of me to think she actually wanted to be my friend.

She didn't want to be my friend. She'd just been marking her territory.

Chapter 5

I am grateful to have the house to myself when I get home. In a few hours, Mom will want to know all about my first day—how classes went, if I think I'll make the team, and who I befriended. She'll ask out of concern, but it will feel like an interrogation.

I'll tell her I met a few people with friend potential, and that I like the new school so far. I'll probably toss in some details to make it more believable, like the fact that the popular girl asked me to be her partner at track practice. It isn't *exactly* a lie. Mom won't know either way and it's better for both of us if she doesn't worry about me. She's had enough on her mind lately.

Feeling ambitious in my solitude, I deviate from the usual boxed mac and cheese and dig through the vegetable drawer. I chop up a head of romaine lettuce and plaster it with dressing and parmesan, then sprinkle some of Mom's homemade croutons on top, feeling like I just walked out of the Culinary Institute of America for putting together a Caesar salad. Benny lays at my feet in feigned adoration, but I know he's just hoping for a handout. A leaf of lettuce flutters to the ground and he sniffs it once, then huffs in disappointment and skulks away.

I turn on Netflix to enjoy a well-earned binge after the day I've had. I'm shamelessly addicted to *Pretty Little Liars* and decide to re-watch it for the millionth time. As the show drones on I float into a daydream that involves me kissing a guy in a pub bathroom, and even though I've never been to a pub *or* kissed anyone, I have a pretty colorful imagination. Anxious people are like that. We're so practiced in dreaming up horrible scenarios on the regular that we can imagine just about anything.

Derailing my train of thought, Benny jumps from his pouting spot and begins barking ferociously at the glass door in the kitchen. He has a bit of an overactive trigger finger when it comes to presumed threats, so I usually don't take him seriously. But I have to admit that I'm a little spooked, because he's so deliberate and this is my first time alone in the new house at night. His nose is pressed up against the glass and a fog spreads over the surface like a veil. I try to convince him to come to me, but even a shaving of parmesan doesn't entice him.

"Benny!" I call, but his stance remains unchanged.

"Benny! Come here, boy! C'mon."

He looks at me as if to ask *what's wrong with you, you stupid human?* and goes on barking. It's unsettling that I can't hear any cars whizzing by to remind me that there's civilization outside. Other than his barking, it's too quiet. For all I know the apocalypse happened while I was

caught in my daydream, and my imagination switches back
to its default setting–assuming the worst.

I try to push the bad thoughts out but in the end
the worries win, and I get up to make sure all of the doors
are locked for the third time tonight. Once I check the
locks, I jostle the door handles to make sure they work. I
consider calling Dad, but he's an hour ahead of me and
will have already started the night shift at the construction
company he manages. And even if I did call him, what
could I say? *Hey Dad, Benny's barking and I'm terrified.* He'd
say *Rafa, he's a beagle, that's what they do!* Then he'd worry
about my anxiety and how I'm adjusting. I shake off the
urge to call. I cup my hands and cautiously peer out the
glass door Benny is still growling at, but all I see is
gathering darkness floating through a blanket of green.

"Shh, it's okay buddy. It's okay." I scratch his
favorite spot right above his tail but even that doesn't
placate him. He continues to snarl.

I look out the window once more to be sure. For
a second I think I see movement, but when I look closer
there's still only darkness. A moment of too much silence
passes, followed by another round of barking. My brain
continues to invent a horde of terrible things hiding in the
woods; everything from knife-toting psychopaths to
behemoth, Harry Potter-esque arachnids.

I realize I'm spiraling, so I take three deep breaths
like my old therapist taught me and try to regain control
of reality. In all likelihood, Benny is barking at the wind
and I am making something out of nothing. I resolve to
carry on with my evening and pretend that everything is
okay, which it undoubtedly is.

"Come on Ben. Come lay on the couch with me." Would he actually be able to defend me if someone broke into our house? He's tough, but he's packed into a pretty small body. I try to pick him up and take him away from the door but he's too fat, so I leave him to his barking and go back to the couch and my dinner.

Stopping me in my tracks, I see a flash of movement emerge from the dark and bolt toward the door. A scream slips out of my throat as I grab my phone, realizing in a flash that I don't even know if Esko has a police station. I'm fumbling with the touchscreen, about to dial 911, when my brain finally comprehends what my eyes are seeing, stopping the frantic movements of my fingers.

It's a deer.

An innocent, truffle-eyed fawn. I wipe beads of sweat off of my forehead and exhale a sigh of relief. My heart is pounding a thousand miles a minute and I laugh in spite of myself at the 9-1- staring up at me from my phone. I play out the conversation in my head. *Hello? Yes, I have an emergency. Bambi is trying to break into my house.*

Benny continues yammering, but the deer seems to know he is of no consequence trapped behind the glass. The fawn nibbles at some grass and to Benny's dismay, is soon joined by its mother.

The doe and her fawn eventually wander back to the woods, but they've unsettled me enough that I don't feel comfortable downstairs in front of the naked windows. I go up to my bedroom and flop face first onto my fluffy comforter. The emotions of the day hit me like a tidal wave, and I feel a heavy knot form halfway down my throat. I bury myself in my pillow, sadness creeping over me as I strain to find the familiar smells of home lingering on its case.

At first, the perfume of home clung to my things like a child to her mother's leg on the first day of kindergarten. But after just a few days in Minnesota, the scent is beginning to fade. The citrus of Dad's cologne, the earthy smell of his hands, and Ollie–best of all, Ollie. I hadn't washed my bedding in a desperate attempt to keep the smell of his little head on my pillow, but even that is beginning to vanish. We used to lay in bed on our backs and I'd read picture books to him and tickle him until he cried from laughing so hard. I inhale as deeply as I can and comfort floods me as I detect the slightest hint of my old life, but I know it won't last much longer. I take off the linen, shove it into my duffle bag, and zip it up to seal in the scent. From now on, I'll have to ration it. One sniff a day. I can't let Esko's scent of pine and loneliness take over. I can't let it devour the nostalgia I cling to so desperately.

I wipe my tears on my hoodie and they turn the lavender fabric to a deep purple hue. I think of Mom, a chameleon who blends in anywhere and resent her for it. I wish I could change colors, too. I wish I could change *anything*. I hate it here. I miss Dad, I miss Ollie, I miss our townhouse full of so much love. I miss the noises and the smells of the city, I miss having a say in anything, and I miss not being sad. I feel like I can't even remember what it was like to be happy, which makes me even *more* sad. I plug my headphones into my ears–music is the only

comfort I know at this stage of a cry– and try to imagine
I'm anywhere but Esko.

Chapter 6

On Monday there's a list posted in the foyer of the school with the names of those who made the track team.

I'm not sure if I want to see my name or not, but when I do, I feel a wave of something close to pride. There are a few other names I recognize, including Taylor and Greyson, and Ingrid, the girl with the blue hair. When I tell Mom the news, she acts like I've won a Nobel Prize. She's so ecstatic that she takes me to the local sporting goods store and buys me a brand-new pair of running shoes, though I think part of that is her still trying to make up for separating our family and dragging me to the most unpopulated town on the planet.

On the first day of practice, coach tells us we're doing timed sprint relays and that everyone needs a partner. Not surprisingly, Taylor doesn't race over to buddy up with me. She's hardly paid any attention to me since tryouts, except to throw a shady look in my direction whenever I get within ten feet of Greyson. This time, I'm alone at the end of the pairing-up ritual.

"Ingrid, work with Rafa." Coach instructs. For reasons I don't know, Ingrid looks genuinely pissed off that she has to work with me.

"Hi," I say cheerily as she walks over, but she merely nods in my general direction and says nothing. I repeat the greeting, thinking maybe she couldn't hear me over the buzz of the gymnasium. This time my attempts are returned with a more impatient nod. I don't know what I've done to make her treat me so coldly, but I guess some people don't need a reason to hate the new girl. Maybe she too was a part of the Greyson love club and was angry over the chummy conversation I had with him last week. Although, upon studying her again, I'm sure that isn't the case.

In addition to her blue hair, she has a septum piercing and wears thick eyeliner, dark clothes, and a choker. Her standoffishness extends well beyond me (at least I can stop taking it so personally) and I've yet to see her talk to anyone at all. Greyson, on the other hand, is a walking J-Crew commercial who's always surrounded by pretty people, sneaking hits off a vape pen and talking about the latest party. I doubt that he's ever even noticed Ingrid, and I doubt equally as much that she would want him to.

Somehow Ingrid manages to get through the entire set of drills without speaking to me once. She communicates in nods, body language, and the rare facial expression, but does not open her mouth except to breathe. At one point I ask her if she's okay, and if I have offended her–which I didn't think plausible–but she shakes her head "no" and returns to status quo.

When we're done with warm-ups, Coach tells us we're going on the trail for a long run. We shuffle one by one out the doors at the back of the gymnasium and are greeted by a slap of freezing cold air that can't be forty degrees. I jog out with the group, trying to nestle myself in the middle of the pack in the hope of borrowing some body heat. I blend into the gaggle of synchronized runners when I feel somebody intentionally brush up against me.

"Hey, Rafa," says a voice, smooth as molten chocolate. "Long time no see, eh?"

"Hey Greyson," I chatter through shivering teeth, looking around to see if Taylor is nearby. I'm not interested in being on the receiving end of another unnecessary turf war.

"How's it going?" His stride is swift, and my frozen legs struggle to keep up.

"Not...too bad," I pant, and even though I know I shouldn't, I enjoy the attention. "Howzit..going...for you?"

"Excellent."

By the looks of him, I doubt life is ever going less-than-excellently for him.

"Just enjoying *finally* being single again."

This is bait that I'm not taking, so I indicate that I'm struggling to talk and breathe at the same time.

"What about you?" He asks, ignoring my cue "Have a boyfriend back home? Boston, right?"

"Yes...and...no."

"Girlfriend?" He asks skeptically, raising an eyebrow. I must be putting out some seriously lesbian vibes, as this is the second time in a week I've been asked if I have a girlfriend.

"No," I huff again, my lungs wrestling the frigid air.

"You should hang with me sometime. I mean, sometime other than when we're being tortured at practice."

If it didn't mean I'd be trampled by a stampede of runners, I would have stopped dead in my tracks. Is Greyson Kohl–the most popular Junior in Esko–actually asking *me* to hangout? I'm flattered, but I think back to my conversation with Taylor and I definitely don't want to get involved. At my old school, it was so easy for me to fly under the radar. Why does it seem to be so difficult now?

"I kind of got the impression that you and Taylor... "

I say it without thinking and immediately regret it. It might have been personal. Maybe they were in the early stages, where the boundaries are still unclear. Or worse, maybe they just broke up. Maybe I'd vomited up a secret she had entrusted me with, even if it was in an overly aggressive way.

He scoffs.

"Please. That girl is nuts." He circles his index finger in the air above his head.

Even though she wasn't exactly welcoming, I don't like the way he talks about Taylor. Granted, I don't know their history, but I have been on the planet long enough to know the guys who call their exes *crazy* have usually done something to elicit it. I don't know how to respond, so I don't.

We are deep in the woods behind the school when it hits me how utterly strange it is to send a group of teenagers out to run trails for track practice. At my old school, we ran on an actual *track,* or sometimes the three-mile, well-groomed, cross country loops in Cambridge. This trail is narrow and winding, and anything but groomed. It's cold and desolate and nothing like what I'm used to, but I have to admit it is sort of grotesquely beautiful. There's still a thin layer of frost on the ground, which makes me wish I'd worn my new runners because my old cross-country shoes don't have much traction left on them at all. I can feel my ankles working overtime to steady my legs with each footfall.

"What about that girl you were working with during warmups today?" Greyson asks, forcing his way back into my attention.

"Huh?"

"Is she your friend?" he asks, sounding slightly winded. I hadn't noticed, but somehow we've inched way ahead of the pack.

"Oh, coach made us work together. I don't think she likes me though. She wouldn't talk to me. At all."

"Ingrid doesn't talk to anybody."

"Like...she doesn't...have friends?"

"No. Well, yes, that too. But I mean, she literally *doesn't talk.* She came back from summer break like that. That girl is in serious need of a shrink. Or a locked psych-ward."

"Do you think *all* girls are crazy, Greyson?"

"I don't think you're crazy."

My stomach tightens up. A compliment that's really a backhanded insult to another girl isn't a compliment at all.

"Why do you hate Ingrid so much?"

"I don't *hate* her; I'm just being honest."

"People don't talk about people they like that way," I point out, bluntly.

"Okay, so I don't like her," Greyson admits. "But that doesn't make what I said untrue."

"Fair enough."

"Plus, she's a pathological liar in the worst way. I'd stay away from her," he adds, as if he hasn't made his feelings toward Ingrid clear enough already.

"I don't get that vibe from her," I say under my breath. From what I've seen of her around school, she isn't trouble. All of the teachers seem to go out of their way to be nice to her and she pretty much keeps to herself.

"You can work with me instead," Greyson continues, and I notice it's a direction, not a question. He gives my hip a quick pinch where my shirt has ridden up, and I can feel the sweat from his hands on the goose-bumpy flesh of my torso. A wave of anxiety floods my veins.

"Thanks," I say, shifting my body in the opposite direction, "but I don't think I can keep up with you in the sprinting drills. Plus, coach put me with Ingrid, so I should probably stick with her for a while."

"Hmm," he nods, unconvinced. "Well, if you change your mind, work with me tomorrow. Trust me, you don't want to get mixed up with that freak." The word "freak" drips out laced with hatred.

Besides the fact that I have nothing to say to that, I am too out of breath to continue the conversation. I feel the weight of the ground pushing back under my feet as the trail veers downhill. It's slippery, and halfway down the hill I start to lose my footing. I'm no longer keeping pace with Greyson, whose legs are miles longer than mine. I look back to see we are way ahead of the rest of the pack with the exception of one person struggling to close the gap between us and the rest of the team. It's Taylor. I make eye contact with her for a moment, but she looks down quickly. I feel a flutter of something down my neck. Did she see Greyson touch me? What if it had looked like flirting? Surely, it wasn't.

I turn back around a second too late. Trail running can get really dangerous if you aren't watching the placement of each step, a danger which is exacerbated by the frost and my unfamiliarity with this trail. My left heel catches an ice-glazed root, and I overcompensate by kicking my right leg out faster to catch my weight. I am so focused on my left side, that the sole of my right shoe catches a wet, mossy rock, and my left leg doesn't recover in time to compensate for my second misstep.

I feel myself being dragged down by gravity. My surroundings shift, Greyson turns, and I can see him try to catch me in slow motion. I see the ground come closer and closer, frame by frame. My brain sends the S.O.S. to my arms, but like Jell-O, they flop at my sides and don't respond.

C R A C K.

A deafening noise; the sound of my chin colliding with cold, wet rock.

The muffled sound of someone shouting for help.

Shock particles working to subdue something that should hurt but doesn't.

An oddly comforting icy-hot sensation cascading down my neck.

Finally, darkness.

Chapter 7

I hear hundreds of indistinct noises and panic radiates from all around me, but I have never been more at peace. It is dark and muffled, a soft womb of safety. There is no anxiety here, no wondering if I will say or do the right thing. I lie here, my head cupped in warm, protective hands, and wait.

Chapter 8

I emerge from sleep, one eye at a time. My vision is cloudy, but I can see that a television is on, though I can't hear it. I can't hear anything, not even the sound of my own shallow breathing or the *drip, drip, drip* of the IV fluid flowing through a plastic tube into a bulbous, blue-green vein in my right arm.

I'm not sure where I am or why, so whatever drugs are pumping through me are doing an excellent job of keeping me relaxed. After ten minutes or so of semi-consciousness, my vision creeps back to its usual 20/20 and my hearing returns like turning up the volume on a tv one notch at a time.

I hear the jostling wheels of a cart being pushed down the hallway and some miscellaneous white noise I don't recognize. The air hangs around me and smells of Clorox and fresh linen. I try to piece together what is going on, but I'm struggling. There's a stiff splint on my right arm and a throbbing in my head, though I don't feel any discomfort. I reach up to touch my forehead and find three or four metal staples cloaked in dry, crusty blood, and stitches marching in a line down my jaw. I instinctively call for my Mom, and like magic she appears.

"You're awake!" She darts into the room, her face tessellated with joy and concern. She's wearing teal scrubs, has a stethoscope dangling from her neck, and looks exhausted. *Of course.* I'm at St. Marcy's.

"Mom...what happened?" I ask, struggling to remember how I got here. I remember Greyson...and the trail...the sound of my feet crunching with each stride...another fuzzy figure I can't make out. Someone holding my head.

"You took a little spill."

She feels my forehead with the back of her hand even though there's a thermometer clinging to the wall behind her.

"Still no fever, that's a good sign."

She has a look on her face that I've seen only a few times, but it is recognizable. Another hospital room comes back to me. The same smells of bleach and sheets. Mom, Dad, and...Ollie. My heart sinks a little. She's worried but trying not to let on how much.

"How long was I...?"

"About two days." The concern deepens.

Two days? I slept through two freaking days of my life? The words fail to formulate in my mouth, which is dryer than the tub of cotton balls in the corner.

"You have quite the lump on your head, a sprained wrist, a split chin, and a bad concussion which led to a TBI. When they got to you..." she trails off.

"What?"

She stifles a knot in her throat.

"Mom..." I try to sit up to reach out to her, but my head hurts too much and I fall back into the crinkly pillow.

"You went into sudden cardiac arrest. It's a rare side effect of traumatic brain injury. A freak thing, really." She covers her eyes with her left hand, and I notice something glint in the fluorescence. She's wearing her wedding ring tonight, which she took off the day we left for Minnesota. Strange.

I shelf the observation and try to process her words.

"I don't understand." I croak, my tonsils begging for water.

"The doctor is calling it a 'medical anomaly.' One in a couple hundred thousand. You're going to be okay—but—they had to use the defibrillator. Your heart—it stopped for a minute." Tears roll down her cheeks as she strokes mine. "Leave it to my Rafaela to make track practice a life hazard."

I rub my chest, feeling a newborn burn in the areas where the defibrillator paddles must've collided with my skin. Other sensations are rising to the surface of my skin, too. My head is starting to hurt, and my jaw is stiff when I open my mouth to talk.

"That's a little too much to process." I say.

"I know honey, I know. The doctors have been monitoring you closely, but all of your vitals are good. Your potassium and RBCs were a little low, so they gave you some intravenous supplements, and—"

"Mom," I cut her off. "In English please. Or Spanish, at the very least." She gets a little carried away with medical terminology, forgetting that not everyone is Nurse Practitioner.

"You should eat more bananas is what I'm trying to say." She smiles through drained eyes and hugs me lightly, careful not to touch my injured parts. "Can I get you anything?"

"Maybe some water?" I croak.

"Sure thing, mi amor." She caresses the side of my chin that isn't stitched up before walking out of the room.

I close my eyes, trying to shake myself back to reality. I try to process what I've been told, but I am tired, so tired, and it's an awful lot to think about. My head is foggy and I begin to drift, the lines between dream and reality becoming increasingly difficult to differentiate. I try to wait for Mom to come back with water, but I lose the battle and drift back into an unfeeling sleep.

Chapter 9

I stay in the hospital for three more nights to ensure my brain doesn't swell up and ooze out of my ears, but when everything checks out on Sunday morning, I am more than ready to go home. There are only so many times you can eat hospital eggs and tapioca pudding for dinner and actually enjoy it.

When we get home, Mom tells me to go upstairs and lie down immediately, as if I'm a child. When I promise I'll only get up to go to the bathroom, so she agrees to let me stay on the couch as long as I don't turn on the television.

"Not at all Rafa, not even for one episode of anything. You have a severe concussion and if you strain your brain—"

"I know mom, I *know,*" I stress, not wanting to come off annoyed, but this is the seventh time she's warned me about the risks of screen time with a brain injury. Having a nurse for a mother is great in an emergency, like the time Harper Coome needed the Heimlich at my seventh birthday party after trying to shove ten marshmallows in her mouth at once, but sometimes it's a little much. She knows too much about the human body for her own good.

"Mom, I'm *okay,*" I insist, as she examines my staples for the quadrillionth time. "Go to work, I'll be fine."

"Is your phone charged? Make sure it's charged. I need to be able to reach you at all times. But no social media. Or games. I told Dad if he wants to talk, he has to call you. No messaging. Nada. None. *Zilch.*"

"*Yes,*" I say, holding up my iPhone and portable charger, exasperated. "And I *know.* Don't worry. My phone is here, it's charged, and I won't use it. Pinky promise. My head doesn't even hurt anymore."

"Mmhmm, right. *That* would be the morphine talking," she replies with a "just-wait" smile.

"I'll be home around seven. I can pick up some vegetable soup from that bistro down street if you want. I haven't had much time to grocery shop."

"Sure." I force a smile to appease her, though I don't have much of an appetite.

She kisses me gingerly on the forehead before leaving and reminds me one more time to keep my phone on.

When she's finally out the door, I sift through the messages on my phone. I know I'm not supposed to, but I haven't been able to check my phone in days and it's blowing up. Dad has been texting me nonstop since the incident. Apparently, he almost took a direct flight to Duluth the evening it happened, but Mom somehow convinced to hold off. The three of us in a hospital room wouldn't be good for anyone right now, and he's right at the end of his busy season at work. I text Dad that I'm okay, and not to worry because Mom is waiting on me hand and foot. That will probably make him chuckle; we used to share secret looks with one another whenever Mom got on one of her maniacally overprotective kicks. Secret looks that meant *we know she means well, but God it's annoying.*

I add that I'm surprised Mom didn't hire a butler to wait on me while she's working and tell him I won't be able to use my phone much over the next few weeks. He texts back:

Love you, sweetie. Good luck with mom. I'm here whenever you need me, always. Talk soon.

I obey Mom's instructions and set my phone down on the coffee table. I pick up one of my journals and begin to write, though technically I'm not supposed to be doing that either. What starts off as a play-by-play of what happened turns into a ranting lament about my own life, and when I emerge ten minutes later, I feel a little less sorry for myself. My situation could be worse, after all.

Sure, I have no friends, the most popular girl in school thinks I'm out to get her boyfriend, I'm out of track for most of the season, running for leisure is out of the question too, and I'm sick to death of all the damn trees, but it could definitely be worse. I try to think of all the ways my situation *could* be worse, hoping to convince myself of the fact, but can only come up with a few. Eventually the self-pity makes me tired, and I doze off with my journal splayed open on my chest.

*   *   *

A pleading "woof" from the kitchen interrupts my dreamless, morphine sleep. Benny is sitting by the glass door, staring at me intently. I realize Mom forgot to let him out in between dropping me off and heading back to the hospital, which is going to be problematic.

I wipe the sleep from my eyes and sit up slowly. It takes me longer than usual to come-to, and Benny cocks his head curiously as he watches me. When I'm finally upright, he wags his tail and whines. Mom's warnings replay in my head like a metronome, but Benny looks desperate and Mom won't be home for hours.

He woofs again. Unfortunately, we haven't installed the dog fence yet, and if I let him out on his own, he could disappear after a rabbit. Against Mom's–and my– better judgement, I decide to take him out.

I stand up slowly and pocket my iPhone. I feel fine, and some sunshine will probably do me good.

"C'mon Benny, let's go."

I walk to the mud room to get the leash and feel a slight throb in my temple. It's probably my body adjusting to being vertical for the first time in half a week. I throw a pair of grey sweatpants on over my shorts and a beat-up, old hoodie. Benny zooms around me excitedly and I somehow manage to clip him into his harness with my good arm, my right arm still trapped in an inflexible splint.

The air outside is warmer than I expected, a welcome surprise. It's noon and the sun is sparkling through the evergreens, evaporating the last bits of morning dew from the night before. I haven't spent much time in my own backyard, and I have to admit that it isn't half bad. Much prettier than the dirty sidewalks and obligatory yet out-of-place trees planted in cages every fifty yards back in Boston. The air is cool and fresh, and I find myself enjoying it almost as much as Benny is. I strip down to my t-shirt and leave the hoodie, along with my phone, on a sunny patch of grass near the back door. Today could almost pass as a mild June afternoon, and I can envision myself escaping out here with a blanket, some iced tea, and a book on warm summer days.

And surely I'll have friends to invite by then.

I'm so caught up in my thoughts that I let Benny lead me all the way to the woods line. The grass is taller and bristles underfoot, and I'm tempted to keep going until my senses come back to me. The last time I'd ventured into the woods had not ended well for me. It ended so un-well I'd nearly died. After that pleasant thought, the wood line doesn't look quite so enticing. Maybe I'll save the exploring for another day, preferably when there isn't metal in my forehead.

Unfortunately, my practicality came a moment too late. As I'm about to head back to the house I see something move on the edge of my peripherals, but Benny sees it a second before. He takes off after the deer, almost ripping my good arm out of its socket and leaving my bad one dangling painfully. I try to hold on, but he's strong and his prey drive is even stronger. He howls and lunges, unable to defy a thousand years of instinct even against my wild pleas. I shout and try to use my right arm for support but recoil at the sting of the sprain. I instinctively recoil to protect my injuries, and the leash goes flying into the air, disappearing into the woods behind my dog. And just like that, Benny is gone.

"*Benny!*"

I shout his name over and over again, but I can hear him continue to rip through the woods, on the heels of the bouncing white-tailed. He doesn't have a chance of catching it, but he'll run himself to death in the process. I'd removed his collar when I put him into his harness, and his collar was hooked to his license and all of his identification tags. If he got lost out there, we'd have no way of finding him.

I start after him on foot. If the deer gets far enough away and Benny hears me asking if he's hungry, it might be enough to coax him back. Luckily the ground is completely dry, but roots burst from it like little mountains and I am wary of my footfalls. If I get hurt again, it won't matter what condition I'm in because Mom will kill me.

I keep going. I can't see him, but I can hear muffled sounds in the distance and head toward them. I'm hoping that once Benny accepts that he isn't going to catch the deer he'll come back, following the sound of my increasingly frantic calls. I have no idea what lives in these woods, and I'm not about to leave Benny out here by himself.

I run half a mile or so before I slow to a walk. I feel suddenly winded, and if I go much deeper into the fir trees, I will no longer be able to see the sunlit opening in the distance leading to our yard. My throat is hoarse from shouting Benny's name, and my head is lighter than the air around me.

Probably just from screaming. The justification is weak, but the concussion has completely dulled my hypochondria.

I slow to a halt, unable to carry the weight of my own body anymore. I drop to my knees between two tree roots, right before they buckle underneath me. I struggle to catch my breath, regretting the decision to leave the couch.

What if I die out here?

What if Mom never knows what happened to me?

How can I put her through this after all that we went through with Ollie?

I'm selfish. All I had to do was listen to her this one time, just this once, and I couldn't even do that.

No.

Stop it, Rafa.

You're spiraling.

I focus on my breathing. Inhale, hold, exhale. Inhale, hold, exhale. I can't let anxiety interfere—I have enough issues at the moment. *One problem at a time.* I can sit here quietly until I catch my breath. If I don't find Benny, I'll go home and find the number for animal control. Benny is in a harness and lead; nobody would mistake him for a stray.

But what if somebody finds him, and wants to keep him? Or what if he never gets found and starves? And aren't there wolves now in Minnesota?

Stop.

But what—

The *what-ifs* are an angry riptide of possibilities, and if I'm not careful they will carry me away.

I brush the panic aside and focus on drawing deep, slow breaths, until the tingly feeling in my head subsides. I start humming to pull my mind away from the panic and focus on the sound emanating from my closed mouth, sound waves vibrating my teeth as if they are home to a small colony of honeybees.

For a few moments, my humming is the only noise in the woods, and everything is still. It's so tranquil that I drift off into a momentary sleep, the ground forgiving, the tree roots cradling my injured body.

Chapter 10

I am startled awake by a sound that doesn't blend with the other noises of the wood—the breeze, the rustling of leaves, the honking geese flying south overhead. I orient myself as quickly as my lethargic brain will allow and recognize the sound to be footsteps— steady, and so soft they hardly rustle up the underbrush.

A rush of relief shoots through my, followed by a swift kick of adrenaline.

What if it's not Benny? What if it's a mountain lion?

I don't even know if mountain lions live in Minnesota, but the thought is enough to make me pay attention. I situate myself further back into the crotch of the tree and listen.

Pad, pad, pad. It's coming closer.

"Benny?" I call in cautious voice.

I peer around the trunk of the tree but see nothing. I keep watch, waiting until whatever's approaching comes into view. I can't tell which direction it's coming from, but the *pad, pad, pad-ding* continues. Then, with a final rustle, Benny emerges from the dense thicket with a look of triumph on his face and I exhale a tremendous sigh of relief, but the relief subsides to uncertainty when I see that he isn't alone.

It's a man. Or, rather, a boy. He's tall, but not menacing, and approaches with a relaxed air about him. As he comes closer, I can see he isn't much older than I am. He has sandy brown hair and his skin is warm and bronzed, as if he'd recently vacationed somewhere tropical. He wears a fitted white t-shirt which shows off toned forearms, and he has the slim but muscular build of a swimmer, or perhaps a soccer player.

I've heard enough horror stories to know better than to talk to strangers I meet in the woods, but Benny is usually a pretty good judge of character and he seems to have already made friends. I stand up and dust the moss off of the back of my pants, pull a leaf out of my snarly, unwashed hair, and pray I don't look as disheveled as I feel.

"Is this your dog?" the boy calls from a healthy distance. Benny answers his question before I have a chance to, running straight into my arms at the sight of me. His muzzle is covered in slobber, there are burdocks stuck to his thighs like little porcupine quills, and he's still panting from his fruitless galivant. He presses his head into my chest and whines apologetically.

The boy chuckles. "Well I guess *that* answers the question."

He grins unabashedly and rubs his hands through his hair. Which isn't much less disheveled than mine. He looks even younger up close– maybe a year or two my senior if that. His warm nature and my gut tell me that most likely, he isn't a threat.

"Thanks," I say, cautiously friendly. "He went after a deer and I–I couldn't hold onto him."

I hold up my splinted arm, justifying my inability to contain a 35-pound beagle.

"Whoa–What happened to you?"

"Track accident."

He takes a step toward me, but not too close that I feel invaded. In fact, some visceral part of me– somewhere below the surface of my consciousness– wishes he'd step a little closer.

"You know, Track was a noncontact sport back when I was in school."

So he *is* older.

"Did you graduate from Esko High?"

"Last year was my last year."

His voice is smooth and warm, like butter melting in a frying pan.

"I'm Ash," he says, closing the gap between us by another broad step.

"I'm Rafaela, but everyone calls me Rafa." I follow his lead, this time taking a step toward him. I hold out my uninjured hand, motioning to shake his but he recoils, widening the gap again.

"I, uh, have a bit of a cold," he says, holding his hands up and coughing into his shoulder. "Wouldn't want to give it to you, you look sick enough as it is. No offense."

How could I take offense with all these stitches, staples, and breaks?

"None taken."

"So, Rafa, is it? That's a pretty name. I've actually never met anyone named Rafa before."

"It's Puerto Rican. I was named after my grandmother; she died a month before I was born."

"I'm sorry," he says, obligatorily.

"It's okay–I didn't know her. But, thank you." I feel my shoulders relax. This is the most comfortable I've felt around anybody I've met in Minnesota, possibly anywhere. "I've never met anyone named Ash before, either."

"It's short for Ashley." He looks up at me playfully, holding his hands in the air in mock secession. "Go ahead, laugh if you must, but I warn you, it was my great-grandfather's name, and he was a *very* important dentist."

A laugh erupts from my stomach, the pressure of which hurts my head a little. "You must have gotten some heat for that one in middle school, huh?"

"You don't know the *half* of it."

He is still grinning, and it's contagious.

"Where do you live?" I ask, wanting to keep the conversation going.

"Not far. I come for walks here sometimes. It calms my nerves." He pauses, taking a closer look at me. "You're not from Esko, are you?"

He asks out of genuine interest, not with the intention of leading into his first pickup line, as Greyson had.

"Nope. I just moved from Boston. Well, Cambridge, but I usually just say Boston so people know where I mean. We've only been here a couple of weeks and I've either been in school or in the new house."

I can't bring myself to call it "home." Not without Dad. Not without Ollie. I secretly wonder if anywhere will ever feel like home again.

"We?" He presses.

"Mom and I. Oh, and Benny of course."

"Of course."

He chuckles, and I try to return a smile but my face falls. It just seems to final. Mom and I here, Dad in Boston. I don't like thinking about it, let alone talking about it.

"You don't like it here, do you?"

I think for a moment. It's not exactly that I don't like *here*. Sure, it's not the most exciting place I've ever been, but it's no really the *where* that's the problem.

"It's not quite that. My parents– they're separated, probably going to get divorced."

I come close to telling him about Ollie and talking about Ollie is not something we do in my family. I hold it in, but it felt so natural, almost coming out.

"I'm sorry," says Ash, one side of his mouth turning toward the ground.

"Thanks."

"I kind of get it," He offers. "the loss of it, I mean."

"Your parents divorced too?"

"Something like that." He doesn't offer anything more; it must be too painful to talk about. That I can understand.

"Well, I'm sorry too."

"Thanks, Rafa."

Our eyes lock for just a moment, and some invisible force holds mine there for a beat longer than normal.

"It'll get better," he says, so assuredly that I almost believe him. Then adds with a chuckle, "I mean, it didn't for me, but it will for you."

"Gee, that's encouraging," I reply with an air of sarcasm.

"I mean it." I can tell that he does.

"High school has never been my strong suit. I'm a little shy so it's hard to meet people, and the one girl I tried to talk to hates me for no reason at all. I mean, maybe she doesn't *hate* me–how can you hate someone you don't even know? – but she sure acts like she does."

I don't know why I'm sharing all of this with him, but the words are flowing out of me now without restraint.

"Well, I'm sure that says more about her than it does you. High school was never my strong suit either. Plus, the whole small-town vibe, it's so clique-y."

I nod, trying to think of something to say but all words have escaped me.

"Hey, I don't mean to be rude, but you don't look so good."

"I know, I–"

"Are you bleeding?"

He takes a step toward me and reaches out as if to touch my forehead but pulls back at the last moment. My skin tingles at the anticipation of his touch, and I feel a pleasant warmth in the pit of my stomach.

I touch the spot he almost did and find something warm and viscous. *Crap.* I *am* bleeding. I try to formulate words but don't get further than opening my mouth, leaving it unhinged like some sort of village idiot. The world starts to spin, and it's taking every ounce of concentration I possess to keep the sky and the ground where they're supposed to be.

"Rafa, where do you live? Tell me where you live."

I can hear the urgency in his voice and see the concern in his blue eyes, but his face is so lovely. I feel my mouth curl into a smile and sink into his warmth as my body resists the temptation to sink back to the ground.

"Where do you live?" He asks again.

"I—over there…" I point feebly in the direction of the house, feeling the weight of the day crash down around me. My temples are pulsing and I am overwhelmingly tired, like I might fall asleep any second.

"I don't—I don't feel so good." I drop to my knees, trying to hold onto consciousness. I can sense Ash coming toward me, repeating my name, reaching out to catch me, but then…

Darkness.

Chapter 11

For the second time in a week, I wake up to the hum of harsh fluorescent lights and the steady drip of an IV. Except this time, when I open my eyes Mom is already at my side and she does not look happy.

"Rafaela Amelia Torres, *por que hiciste eso*?! What were you thinking?"

Oh God, not Spanish. Spanish *and* my middle name. Over the years, she's conditioned me to fear my father's native tongue by uttering it only when I'm in some supreme form of trouble.

"Mom, my head," I moan, trying to sound pathetic, which isn't difficult.

"Oh no. Don't you give me that *mija*. If you're well enough to go prancing around the yard, you are well enough to talk to me.*"

I imagine a hundred other places I'd rather be, and even school comes to mind. I try to look at her but there are splotchy lights blocking my field of view, as if I looked into the sun without sunglasses.

"I'm sorry, Benny had to go out, and he got loose, and—"

"Don't even try to blame this on *the dog,* Rafa." She scolds "He was hooked up to his cable when I got back, you were all the way on the other end of the yard. Even if you *were* going to walk him out to his run, why would you then go traipsing around? Not to mention, you haven't been out in the yard *once* since we arrived, and you choose *today?*"

"I'm not *blaming* him exactly, he got loose. He ran after a deer. There was—the woods. And, I don't know."

I trail off mid-thought, confused. My mind is suddenly blank. I don't remember the sequence of events, but I'm pretty sure I didn't hook Benny to his cable. In fact, I don't remember coming back from the woods at all.

"How did I get here?" I ask. Mom's expression is warming from glacial freeze to Boston winter, but it isn't enough to make me feel comfortable. I can see a bit clearer now, but there are still bright lights blocking part of her face.

"You called me. When I answered, nobody was on the other end, so I rushed home from work. You were unconscious in the yard when I got there, blood oozing from your stitches, a staple missing, the whole nine. We're still waiting for the CT scan to make sure there's no further damage to your brain, but don't worry, my guess is your head is so thick you'll be in the clear."

I want to chuckle, but I'm not sure if that was a genuine jovial offering or one of those "mid-scold jokes" where if you laugh, it turns into a trap. A *"Is this funny to you?"* situation, which I'd like to avoid if at all possible. I'm about to ask her more when my phone buzzes from the bedside table, which is funny because I don't remember having it on me. In fact, I am almost positive that I didn't have it with me when I lost consciousness. I reach for the device, but my splinted arm serves as a handicap.

"Can you hand that to me?" I ask, indicating toward my phone.

"You're not allowed. No screens."

"Well can you check and see if it's Dad?"

"I already talked to him. I told him you might be able to call him tomorrow."

I draw my arm back into my chest and roll my eyes.

"Sorry for not wanting him to worry." I reply with a bowl of sarcasm and an eye-roll-cherry on top.

"Worry? *Worry?* Rafaela, what about me? Did you even *think* about how I would worry? Do you know what it did to me, to pull in the driveway and see you in a heap in the backyard? Do you know what it felt like to think I'd lost you? You could have *died*!"

I feel a twinge of guilt eat a hole through the attitude I'd given her a moment ago. She's right–she doesn't deserve this.

"I'm sorry Mom. I'm sorry." I plead, sincerely. "It was stupid, I know. I don't know what I was thinking. I wasn't using my head."

Her eyes soften as her anger fades. "You are the most confusing person, Rafaela Torres. So safe, so cautious, so reckless."

"I'm sorry, I really am." I don't know what else to say, and my brain is racing, searching for answers so I just keep repeating the apology.

"You must have called me right before you passed out. Thank God that call went through, otherwise you might still be alone."

Alone? That doesn't feel quite right. As soon as she utters the word, a trickle of remembrance comes back to me, seeping into my brain like memory runoff.

"I wasn't alone."

She looks at me, quizzically.

"I wasn't, that's the thing."

The image of a tall, sandy-haired boy comes into my mind. Why hadn't she said anything about Ash? Had he left me there?

"Benny doesn't count." She replies, indignant.

"No, it was–there was someone else. I swear there was."

"Who?"

"There was a boy."

"A boy? I think you're losing it. There was no one else there– it's not as if we have neighbors. Besides, if somebody had been there, wouldn't they have called an ambulance or something?"

A valid question. Mom looks uneasily to the right, and I notice that we're no longer alone. An older, bespectacled man in a white coat with the name 'Dr. Raj Sepir' embroidered on his pocket steps forward.

"How are you feeling, Ms. Torres?" he asks, holding a stethoscope up to my sternum.

"My head hurts a little." I reply truthfully, hoping he'll be more sympathetic than Mom. "And there are bright splotches in my field of vision."

Mom chimes in under her breath, but not so low that I can't make out what she's saying. "She thinks she was off in the woods with a boy, but she was passed out in the yard all alone."

"Sneaking off with a boyfriend?" He asks, cocking an eyebrow. My cheeks flush with embarrassment–I've never had a boyfriend in my life.

"What? No. That's not even remotely a possibility." I say, still pink.

"She hasn't even really been at school long enough to make any friends." Mom adds.

Dr. Sepir nods, as if none of this sounds peculiar to him.

"Well, it's not uncommon with grade three concussions like this to experience memory loss, even jumbled memories and hallucinations," he says to her. Then he turns to me, a stern expression on his aging face.

"You're lucky. You've suffered a traumatic brain injury, but other than some bumps and bruises, you're in pretty decent shape. There are people with the same injury who emerge in much darker shape." He takes a black otoscope out of his pocket and uses it to examine my ears while I bite the inside of my cheek and try not to giggle. I have a nervous laugh that emerges at the most inconvenient of times. "The light visions you're experiencing are not uncommon, nor are they dangerous. They're your brain trying to right itself after the big bang."

I laugh a little as he gazes straight into my eye with a different scope, but thankfully he thinks I'm giggling in response to his cheesy big bang reference.

"Things will probably seem a bit discombobulated for the next couple of days, and you may experience some mild tinnitus, which is a ringing in your ears, but as long as you take care of yourself that will get better on its own. If you find you're missing chunks of time or remembering things that don't quite seem right, it's perfectly normal. But I cannot stress to you enough how important it is for you to *rest.*"

I see him exchange a knowing glance with Mom. "No school for a week, no screens, and no –absolutely no– physical activity of any sort for at least a month. You need to let that brain of yours heal."

I nod in understanding and sink into my pillow.

"Well, that's that, then." Says Mom, as the doctor shuffles out the door. "I'm going home to get some sleep, and I'll be back at 5 a.m. for my shift. I expect you to be here, in this bed, sleeping, when I get back." She gives me an almost forgiving look and kisses me on the forehead.

"Thanks, Mom." I reply, and she's off.

Chapter 12

Even though my head is pounding, foggy, and exhausted, sleep does not come easily. I have a million reasons to be uneasy, but the most troubling one is the series of events–or, lack thereof–this afternoon. The way I see it, there are two explanations, and both are equally unsettling.

The first explanation is that I hallucinated a human being into existence. A very handsome, charismatic, and tangible human being, no less. I can still feel the fear I had when Benny ran out of sight, and the relief when I found him again. I can hear the crunch of the leaves beneath my feet and the shortness of my own breath. I can see Ash's face as he came through the woods—his perfectly messy hair and bronzed skin, and that smile so vivid in my memory—and I can still hear the pleasant invitation of his voice. It doesn't seem possible to have imagined something so undeniably palpable, but the alternative is pretty unlikely too.

The alternative suggests that I did feel and hear and see all the things I remember, but that, when I lost consciousness on the forest floor, bleeding and disoriented, a seventeen year old boy I hardly knew carried me back to the outskirts of my yard and dropped me there without so much as bothering to call an ambulance or wait until he knew I was safe. That seems improbable for someone who, minutes earlier, had rescued a dog and taken the time to walk him all the way back to his owner. None of it makes any sense.

I consider the situation from every angle, walking circles in my brain that end where they begin. One thing's for sure—if I *did* dream Ash into existence, I did a thorough job of it.

I'm starting to feel drowsy when my door opens with an interrupting creak. I'd been on high alert, ready to close my eyes the second a nurse came by. I roll over and pretend to be asleep. Someone slips into my room and stands over me as I feign slumber, breathing in and out with slow, controlled breaths. I wait for the scratching sounds of a nurse jotting down my vitals on a clipboard. Instead, I feel the shadow hover over me, patiently, until I become too curious to keep my eyes shut.

It's...*him.*

I try to make words, but I'm once again speechless in his presence.

"Hey, Rafa," Ash greets me, his mouth a thin line of sympathy. He's wearing the same outfit he was in the woods, but somehow looks even more beautiful. "Hope this isn't creepy," he adds, smiling sheepishly. "I had to make sure you were okay."

I blush. *Had to,* not *wanted to.* A need, not a whim.

"I knew it." I say, fighting the urge to reach out and touch him, further proof that he is not an apparition. Sure, it's strange that he figured out where I was and snuck into my room at midnight, but I'm not actively processing any of that.

"Knew what?" He asks, but I ignore him as my disbelief steps aside, its place filling with a small pool of hurt.

"You...you left me out there," I gasp. "I mean, I know we'd just met, but I needed help, and you're obviously strong enough to carry me and capable of calling an ambulance." I eye his exposed forearm muscles, half admiring, half accusing.

"Who does that?" I continue. "You rescued my *dog* for God's sake, but you couldn't take me to the hospital or at least wait to make sure someone found me? My *head* was bleeding!"

He lets me finish airing my grievances before jumping in. I feel almost foolish because, despite my fuming, his expression hasn't dropped one bit.

"Are you finished?" he asks, in an annoyingly charming tone.

"One more thing," I add. "My mother is *furious* with me. Do you have any idea what it's like to have Cordelia Torres angry with you?"

"Not in the slightest."

"Well, it's not great, let me tell you."

"Anything else?" he asks.

"Probably. But my head is starting to hurt again," I say, trying to cross my arms but failing because of the splint.

"Can I speak?"

He's mocking me, trying to be playful. I purse my lips in rejection. He doesn't know me like that and I'm not about to let him get away with thinking he does.

"That's not *exactly* what happened," Begins Ash.

"Well, are you calling my mother a liar?" I ask. "Because Cordelia Torres is a lot of things, but she is *not* a liar."

"I would never dream of calling your mother a liar." He speaks smoothly, unbothered by the precipitation of the small tropical storm I've created in the room. "I think there's been a misunderstanding. Will you let me explain? Please?"

His expression is insistent, and I'm trying not to waver in my stance, but I'm insanely curious.

"It's not like I can go anywhere," I say, glancing at the IV drip.

"You did pass out in the woods," he begins "that part is true."

I nod. Tell me something I don't know.

"I panicked. I didn't know where you lived. You were nice enough to point me in the direction before you went down for your nap, but we were in the woods. So I searched for your phone –I assumed you have a phone– but couldn't find one."

A wave of anxiety floats through my chest at the thought of him searching me. I'm unnerved, but oddly okay with the thought of it. I picture him reaching into my pockets and flush, then snap back to reality.

"That's right," I say. "I left it in the yard."

He nods and continues.

"Anyway, I wrapped Benny's leash around my wrist. I picked you up, put you over my shoulder, and carried you back in the direction you'd told me you lived as fast as I could. Which, mind you, was no easy task," Ash continues.

I raise an eyebrow at him.

"No, no!" He repeals, "Not because you were heavy or anything; because Benny was being difficult. Running in all directions, panting and barking. I could barely keep my balance, and I was *not* going to chase that dog down again. He's faster than he looks."

I half smile, pleased that Benny gave him a hard time.

"I carried you all the way back. I hooked Benny up to the cable in the yard so I could take care of you. I was worried–really worried. You were breathing okay, your heart was beating beautifully, but you wouldn't wake up."

I try to imagine where on my body he felt my pulse—my wrist, my chest, my neck— and I don't hate the conclusions I come to. My animosity is becoming hard to maintain.

"But if you were so concerned, why did you leave me on the ground?" I demand.

"I tried to get into the house, but the doors were locked." That much was true– I'd locked the doors when I'd left because ever since I watched *Saw* in seventh grade, I've been paranoid that someone will break in and hide in one of my closets. "So I noticed a phone, which I assumed was yours, on the ground next to a really ugly sweater."

"Hey!" I interject. "That's my favorite sweatshirt! I was just coming around to you, too."

"Sorry, sorry." He laughs. "Just trying to get a rise out of you. It's a fine sweater. Anyway, I went to your call history and dialed your mom. She answered the phone, but you have such poor reception at your house, she couldn't hear me. I heard her on the other end, and after saying hello a couple of times she said she'd 'be right there.' She must have just sensed something was wrong."

His story is checking out so far, but there is still an element I don't understand.

"So, what, you just dropped me and ran? Why didn't you wait with me until she got there if you were so concerned?"

"First of all, I didn't *drop* you. I wouldn't have." He says, "I laid you on the ground as gently as I could—it was hardly a drop —but then I thought to myself, *hmm, if her mother shows up and sees a strange boy with her unconscious daughter, who'd made a mysterious phone call earlier...* Well, she might just get the wrong idea."

It's a good point, and I can't argue it. Especially since Mom always carries pepper spray in her purse.

"So I waited until I saw a car come around the cul-de-sac, and then I hid in the woods and watched until she had you safely in the backseat."

I look at him incredulously. There doesn't seem to be any dishonesty in his eyes, and though it is a slightly farfetched story, I believe him. It melds perfectly with what I already knew for sure and what Mom told me. I lay silent for a minute, letting the patchwork play-by-play sew itself into my own recollection.

"Well?" asks Ash, his eyes boring into mine. I come back to the present and flush at the locking of our eyes.

"Well...thank you," I say. "And I'm sorry."

"For what?"

"For making such a high-maintenance introduction. And for being so angry a moment ago."

"It's okay." He smirks. "I love high-maintenance introductions."

I blush a little and goosebumps pop up on my arms, but they aren't from the cold.

"And I would probably be angry too, if someone saved my life while I was unconscious. It's a very impolite thing to do without permission."

"*Very.*"

I can't help but break into a grin, and secretly I'm glad that Ash's story checks out. He's a believable hallucination, if that's what he is.

Ash proceeds to tell me that he stressed about how he would ever find me, but in the end it wasn't all that difficult because I'm the only *Rafaela* in Esko. He called both hospitals in the area and pretended to be a family member asking for his dear cousin's whereabouts as he was *very* concerned. A web of warmth spreads through me, dissipating through my bloodstream.

"That's pretty clever of you," I say, after hearing his story. It *was* clever, and I'm surprised anyone would take that much interest in me. Especially considering that, when we met, I was covered in dirt and hadn't showered in days. But maybe it's protocol in Esko to check up on any girls you meet in the woods who pass out, and whom you have to carry half a mile through those woods to safety.

"But one more thing—how did you get in after visiting hours? I know there's no way the nurse let you just walk in. They're super strict here."

"Easy." Ash replies. "Well, more luck than ease. When I got to your hall, I waited outside the door until the nurse stepped away from the nurse's station, which fortunately didn't take too long. Betty over there steps out every hour for a smoke break. I never understand why nurses, of all people, smoke cigarettes. But anyway, as soon as she stepped out, I slipped in and found the door with your name on it."

I roll my eyes at him, but he can see that I'm pleased.

We're an hour into our conversation before I realize that Ash is doing more than just checking to see if I'm okay, and though my head is pounding again, I'm grateful to have his company. We mostly talk about me–the move, my parents' split (though my head hurts too much from the concussion to go into much detail), and the accident. I've had a whirlwind of a few weeks, and until now I have not talked about them with anybody. I usually avoid talking about myself—I always assume my life will bore people— but Ash is doing a good job of making me feel otherwise.

It's different with him. It's easy. I'm no longer stumbling over my words, and the more I speak with him, the more comfortable I feel, which is rare for me. He asks questions eagerly, genuinely interested in my life, and I find I have a lot to say. I'm about to ask him about his story when the motion lights come on in the hall, signaling a nurse on rounds and closing in.

"Crap," he says. "So, since I kind of snuck in here I'm going to hide, and you just act like you're alone. Got it?" I nod, and he slips into the dark space between the open bathroom door and the wall.

A young nurse with ebony skin and long, tight braids peeks in, noticing I'm awake.

"You alright?"

"Um, yeah, fine," I say, trying to sound groggy, as if she woke me up. "Just trying to get some sleep."

"I'm sorry, hun. Thought I heard voices. I thought maybe you were calling for someone."

I feign confusion, which probably looks convincing seeing as there are bumps and bruises and staples all over my face. I mumble a bewildered "no."

"Alright, then. Push the red button if you need me, you hear?"

"Mmhmm."

As soon as she's gone, Ash emerges from his hiding place.

"You are very stealthy," I say, stifling a laugh.

"And you are *incredibly* convincing," he replies. "Remind me never to be on the wrong end of one of your schemes."

"I'm always up for a good heist," I say.

We resume our conversation, but this time closer, and in hushed tones. He doesn't want to be discovered by the night crew, and I don't want him to be either. Talking to him is the most fun I've had in a long time. Since before the separation and moving to Minnesota. Since before everything.

"So, I got the impression you don't love Esko. The school, I mean. How come?"

"Truthfully? It's hard to be the new girl. Nobody is in any hurry to let you into their circle, and the ones who are, well, they're almost *too* eager. Like there's an ulterior motive. The girl I tried to talk to–the one who seems to dislike me–she's so cold. I don't know why she hates me, but she wants nothing to do with me. *Nothing.* She won't even respond when I talk to her. And then I met this other girl who sort of marked her territory all over me."

"As in, *peed* on you?"

"Essentially. I think her peeing on me would have been less intimidating, honestly. She told me to stay away from this guy–this guy I wouldn't have a chance with even if I wanted to, which, by the way, I don't."

"Is that because you have a boyfriend?"

"Oh no, I definitely don't." As soon as I said it, I wish I hadn't said it quite so quickly. I don't need to let everyone know that significant others just aren't a thing that happen to me.

"What I mean is, I don't have a boyfriend, but that has nothing to do with me not being into Greyson."

The conversation that had been going along so smoothly hits a sizeable speedbump. Ash turns somber and seems to fade behind a façade of flesh and bone.

"Ash?"

"You don't mean Greyson Kohl, do you?" His face contorts into an uncomfortable, yet unreadable expression. Is it anger? Is it sadness? Jealousy?

"He's the only Greyson I know."

"Yeah, me too. Unfortunately."

"Why do you say that?" I ask, my interest piqued any time Ash gives me a nugget of information about himself.

"I used to," he says, his voice heavy. He seems to go somewhere far off, somewhere I cannot follow without invitation. I'm not sure if I should dig, but I can't help myself. Besides, I just told him all about Taylor and Ingrid. It's only fair.

"What does that mean?" I ask.

"He's just…" He pauses, searching for the right way to say what he wants to say. "He's not a good guy."

I think Ash is going to say more, but he doesn't, so I try my luck and press a little harder.

"What does *that* mean?"

He studies me, and for a moment I think he's going to try to change the subject or tell me it's time for him to go, but he doesn't.

"It's a long story. Greyson Kohl is one of those entitled, rich kids who charms all the teachers but treats everyone around him like dirt. Less than dirt." His tone sharpens, and the color drains from his shadowed face. "I could tell you he's an asshole, or a prick, but there isn't an insult strong enough for him."

"Jeez, what did he ever do to you?"

As soon as the words are out of my mouth, I know I've made a mistake. I was trying to be playful, but I completely invalidated him, albeit inadvertently.

"Truthfully, I don't know if he ever did anything to me. I just have this permeating bad feeling about him, and I don't think I'm wrong."

"I'm not doubting you, I only meant that Greyson is the only person who's been halfway decent to me, even if it is for the wrong reasons."

"Did he try something with you?" Ash demands, furious. I flinch and freeze, waiting to hear footsteps but none come. We're safe for now.

"No, nothing like that! He flirted a little–maybe–but nothing like that. I swear."

I reach out to put my hand on his shoulder, but he moves out of reach, still fuming.

"I swear to God, if he–"

"Ash, it was nothing, I mean it. It was just a little harmless flirting, and honestly I think it was mostly to make Taylor jealous."

I watch his chest rise and fall as he exhales some of his indignation, his mouth pursed shut, as if he's afraid to let anything else escape it.

"Are you okay?"

Ash looks at me, his eyes locking onto mine again. The same flutter returns to my chest, and after a moment his expression softens and he returns to the Ash I know–light, playful, and steady.

"I'm sorry." He says. "I'm sorry I got so upset. I just– I know how horrible he can be, and the thought of him messing with you… I'm sorry, it's late. I must be a little tired."

"It's okay." I reply, half shaken, and a little flattered that just the idea of Greyson messing with me caused Ash to feel protective. I don't *need* anyone to protect me, but it's nice to think that someone other than my parents would if it ever came down to that. "It's really okay. I appreciate you telling me, if I'm being honest."

"That guy is just bad news. He's bad news disguised in Abercrombie cologne and a trust fund. Be careful with him?"

"I will." I promise, warm with appreciation for his concern.

I think back to the way Greyson insulted Ingrid for no reason, and the way he tried to make me think Taylor is crazy. I'm about to change the subject and ask Ash more about himself when my phone vibrates on the bedside table.

"It's my mom," I say, reading the text in disbelief of how late–or rather, early–it's gotten. "She's going to be here soon. I have to at least pretend to be asleep."

He nods and when he gets up from his seat, I'm acutely aware of how much I don't want him to leave.

"Wait–can I give you my number?" I ask, the words jumping into the air like fledglings before I can stop them. I picture them trying to fly, too confident for their own good. I picture them falling, like Artic Geese chicks plunging to the base of a cliff.

"That is, so we can stay in touch. Since you aren't in school anymore." I add, trying to water down some of my own eagerness.

"I would love that. I want to talk with you again, Rafa. I do. But–"

I hold my breath, waiting for him to drop the bomb. Maybe he doesn't want to stay in touch. Maybe he really was just being nice, making sure I was okay. Maybe he has a significant other, and it wouldn't be appropriate to continue talking to me like this.

–"But I don't have a phone."

I exhale a sigh of relief. Sure, it's unusual for a seventeen-year-old not to have a phone these days, but if that's his reason for not taking my number, I can live with that.

"How about I come find you after school someday next week?" he suggests. I've already mentioned that I'll be on bedrest for the forthcoming week.

"Okay," I say. "My first day back is next Thursday."

I try to maintain a casual air, but inside my heart jumps into my throat, blocking my airways.

"Well, until then, Rafa." He holds out his hand as if to shake mine. "I think I'm over my cold," he adds.

I take his hand in mine and something like a shock of electricity tingles where we touch, surging up my arm and through my body like a current. It's warm and smooth, like soft friction capable of starting a fire with enough time. His skin is so intangibly alive that the thought of him being a hallucination or false memory seems silly, laughable even. I want to hold on, but it's almost too inviting. I pull away, afraid of the feeling a simple touch is stirring up inside of me.

"Bye Ash," I say.

"Goodnight, Rafaela."

The way he says my name, three syllables I've been familiar with all my life, is unlike anything the coils of my ears have ever been touched by.

Chapter 13

The next week sort of bleeds together like a piece of abstract art even a modern art expert would have trouble interpreting. I didn't feel like I was struggling when I got home, I *thought* I was doing okay, but looking back I only have snippets of memories, and nothing quite chronological.

I remember Mom helping me into bed–I spent *a lot* of time in bed–and unplugging my TV, just in case I was tempted. She let me keep my journal and phone for comfort, but I wasn't really supposed to use them. At first, I thought a week without screens or writing or leaving the house was going to be painful at best, but it turns out when you have a TBI you spend so much time sleeping, you don't even notice the things you can't do. Dr. Sepir said sleep is optimum healing time for the brain, and if that's the case I should be back to normal in no time.

Aside from sleeping, I remember talking to Dad on the phone quite a bit. Mom said he called every day that week, but to me it felt like one long conversation that spanned days and didn't make much sense. I remember he was worried about me and told me he loved me about a thousand times and was sorry he couldn't come be with me. He couldn't get off work, as all of his company's projects had to be completed before the snow came so they were in a crunch. Anything else we talked about was jumbled or lost all together. At one point I guess I told him about my upcoming basketball game, which is hilarious because I've never played basketball in my life.

By the time Tuesday rolled around, I was feeling more myself. I had more energy, wasn't sleeping quite as much, and had an appetite again. By Wednesday, the pervasive tiredness has faded, and I become consumed by a cloud of boredom and too much time to think. For the first time, my mind begins to wander to Ash.

I will probably never see him again. That's what I've resigned myself to thinking, because what teenager does not have a phone? It's absurd. Ash probably does have a phone but didn't want to exchange numbers. I'd been too forward. He thought I was weird. I'd talked about my problems too much. He was just being a good Samaritan. Anxiety sends a million and nine *what-ifs* through my head like envelopes on a conveyor belt in a mail-sorting room, but in the end all of the questions remain unanswered.

I've been in bed so long with nothing to do, that the notion of pushing Ash out of my thoughts is near impossible. My only distraction is Mom. She took the whole week off from work and spends all of her time checking on me–whether I need more pillows or food or something from the store–and by Wednesday evening I'm looking forward to going back to school. When Thursday morning rolls around, I actually think she's is going to try to help me get dressed.

"Wear something comfortable. Sweats or something."

"I've been in sweats so long my skin is starting to graft to them," I retort. My attire and hygiene habits of the last couple weeks are making me feel a little disgusting in general.

I throw on a pair of black leggings with a burgundy sweater. Cute and comfortable seems like the right move. I wear a black beanie in an attempt to hide the staples in my forehead, but there's nothing I can do about the ugly stitches on my jawline. I haven't glanced at a mirror in a while and boy, do I look rough.

There are dark, cavernous circles beneath my eyes, which are normally bright green, not listless and grey. The staples and stitches are a problem, but what's even more noticeable is the swelling that has surrounded them. I look like I was in a car wreck or an MMA fight or worse. I'm not one for wearing much makeup other than the occasional hint of mascara, but I borrow Mom's concealer in a desperate attempt to improve my condition. However, being that her skin tone doesn't match mine, it only worsens my appearance. It's like trying to mask an unpleasant smell with something even more unpleasant–like covering up stinky garbage with hard-boiled eggs.

The amount of time I spend gingerly dabbing on makeup and then removing it with just as much care makes me late for school. Mom drops me off at 8:45 and won't let me out of the car until I promise to check in with her at lunch time.

"So, I will pick you up at 2:30 sharp," she says as I gather my things.

"I have practice until 4:30."

"Oh no you don't, my dear. Did you not hear the doctor? Did you not listen to anything I have been saying? Three more weeks. You can get back to it in three more weeks. Maybe."

"Mom, I have to at least show up at practice. There's no reason I can't sit and cheer on the team. I made the cut, if I disappear for four weeks nobody will even remember me. Besides, I need to be at practice so I can run when I'm cleared. I *promise* I won't so much as lay a toe on the track."

"Or the trail," she clarifies.

"I *promise*," I say, holding up my hands so she can see that no fingers have been crossed.

"Alright then, 4:30. Call me if you feel lightheaded or nauseous."

I'm guessing she doesn't mean the ordinary nausea I feel from being at school, but I keep that to myself.

Mom waits in the car by the curb until I make it through the doors, as if expecting me to pass out on my way up the steps. I guess I can't really blame her.

It's halfway through second period by the time I get to school, which means I'll be heading to Art after my obligatory stop at the main office. Art is my favorite class, mainly because the teacher allows us to listen to music as we work and it's usually pretty independent. There are a few other juniors in the class, but it's mostly composed of seniors. Nobody paid much attention to me the first week other than Mr. Garby, who made obligatory comments like "nice job" and "keep up the good work" each time he circulated the room, and I doubted today would be any different.

I could not have been more wrong.

Everybody suddenly knows who I am. When I sign in at the office, both the counselor and the principal address me by name and ask how I'm feeling, though neither of them have ever acknowledged me before. The hallways are empty, but when I open to door to room 136 every single student, seniors included, stop their charcoal drawings to ogle me.

I can feel everybody's eyes on me, or, more specifically, my bruised face. Many of them ask how I'm doing, if it hurts, and how it really happened. There's a rumor flying through the building that Taylor shoved me from behind to get back at me for trying to steal her boyfriend, and an even worse rumor that Greyson and I had been making out off the trail and got a little too feisty. I assure everyone that neither are the case, that Taylor has always been pretty decent to me, that I have never so much as thought about canoodling with Greyson, and that I really want to focus on my charcoal drawing since Art is one of the only classes I'm allowed to fully participate in (apart from being out of track, I'm also out of reading, writing, and anything involving a computer screen). It takes Mr. Garby ten minutes to get the class to stop either interrogating me or whispering about the real cause of my bruises in hushed voices behind my back.

As the day goes on, I learn just how quickly rumors spread in a small town. "Wildfire" would be an understatement. One story suggests that the whole "track accident" was a cover, and that my dad is an alcoholic and pushed me down the stairs in his drunken stupor. This rumor is particularly painful, being that I haven't even seen my father in weeks. I end up spending most of fourth period convincing two very concerned seniors that nobody is hurting me and that no, I do not need to speak to a therapist or a crisis line.

By lunchtime the day has become overwhelming. I wish I could hide my face from the world, or, better yet, disappear completely. It's one thing to come in with a busted-up face and have everyone stare at that for hours, but to see people sneaking glances at you all day, then turning to whisper to their friends is disconcerting. Even when people aren't being obvious about it, I can still feel their burning eyes all over me. I want to call Mom to come pick me up, but I know if I do that, she'll fuss over me more than ever when I get home. I want to be somewhere where I can blend in with the backdrop, like I'd done so successfully for most of my life. I scan the cafeteria, looking for a place to hide. I consider going to the library, but that might make it seem like I'm hiding something, sparking a new round of twisted rumors.

I spy an unoccupied table near the back of the cafeteria and decide to go for it, quickly claiming the spot and pulling out my lunch of hummus, baby carrots, and pita chips. I am only halfway through my first bite before I'm discovered.

"Rafa, you're back!"

It's Greyson. He slides onto the bench next to me, not bothering to ask if I want company. Today of all days I want nothing less than to be seen with him. As he settles in, Ash's cryptic warning about Greyson echoes between my ears.

"Yep," I say, continuing to eat, hoping he'll make like Harry Potter and disapparate.

"Well, how are you?" he asks, shoving half a triangular slice of pizza into his mouth. "You look kinda horrible."

"Gee, thanks," I say sarcastically, through a mouthful of red pepper hummus. Maybe the garlic will drive him away.

"No, I just mean, wow, that was a rough fall. You were out *cold*. I was worried about you."

"Yeah, I got the get-well card from the team. Thanks for signing it," I say, still chewing. Apparently, he isn't a vampire, because the garlic doesn't seem to be working.

"Well, coach organized that. I think he was worried his ass might be on the line for sending us out there when the ground was frozen over. But I mean, *I* was worried about you. I missed you at practice."

"Look, Greyson, I appreciate you wanting to be friends and all, but I really don't want to have Taylor on my bad side. So maybe we should keep some distance until you sort things out with her." I don't need Taylor's judging eye homing in on me with everything else going on.

"Whoa, wait, *what?*" he says, seemingly stupefied. "There is nothing, *nothing* going on between me and Taylor. She's like, obsessed with me or something. It's too much." His eyes linger on me, and I feel my stomach squirm. "Besides, I'm into someone else."

I swallow hard. It must be part of some freaky see-who-can-get-the-new-girl-first competition. As far as I'm concerned, we've never had more than a surface-level conversation, and it can't be my looks given the unfortunate circumstance of my face.

"I appreciate that," I say, trying to keep my tone as platonic as possible without being cold, "but I really don't want to stir up any trouble here."

I'm being as politely obvious as I can, but Greyson can't take a hint. He grins coyly, as if he thinks that what I said is a joke.

"Oh, okay, I see what this is. You're playing *hard to get.*" He inches closer to me so that our thighs are touching, and I get a wave of anxiety that feels nothing like the one I got when Ash touched me for the first time.

"No, Greyson, I'm not," I say, twisting away, but he only slides closer. He puts his arm around me and gets so close that I can smell his breath. Cheese, sauce, and remnants of this morning's coffee.

"Greyson," I warn, but he thinks I'm playing a game with him.

I keep trying to wiggle away, but he has me trapped between his massive, muscular thighs, and the wall. Even though I'm surrounded by a hundred people I feel unsafe and extremely alone.

"Greyson, please."

"Don't *worry* about Taylor," he whispers, moving closer still. "Honestly, it's a non-issue."

He's not getting it. Not because he's incapable or daft, but because he's not listening to what I'm saying. I struggle to breathe, I'm drowning in a sea of blue and yellow with no life guard in sight. Just when I can no longer keep my head above water, a tray slams down opposite Greyson and me. The tray belongs to the girl with icy blue hair, the one who despises me for no reason I can decipher—Ingrid.

Nobody speaks, but Ingrid, in all of her five-foot-one glory, gives Greyson the coldest glare I've ever witnessed. They stare each other down like a gladiator and a lion in a cage—I'm not sure which is which—and somehow, miraculously, it works. He meets her gaze with a look that's pensive, and maybe even a little...threatened? After a few moments of stand-off, he wipes his hands on a saucy napkin and stands up.

"Whatever. Catch you later, Rafa," is all Greyson says before departing. I exhale a huge sigh of relief and feel my heart rate slow and return to normal. I can breathe again.

"Oh my God," I say, my hands clammy with sweat. I rub them on my leggings to dry them off. "That was– that was incredible. Thank you so much. I owe you. Big time."

Ingrid says nothing but sits down across from me and starts devouring her sandwich. It would be awkward had she not acted with such intention. She nods her head as if to signal "you're welcome" and continues to eat, only now she's actually looking at me. She has striking pale blue eyes that match her hair. She gives me half a smile that looks almost warm against her cool complexion and another nod but doesn't say anything. Even against the dull roar of the cafeteria, the silence between us is profound and each crunch of carrot between my teeth is practically a seismic boom, but I much prefer it to the sound of Greyson's voice.

After the tension dissipates and we've broken the ice with our unspoken exchange, I'm dying to ask what the deal is between her and Greyson. Unfortunately, there's no nod or head tilt that can answer my questions, so we eat the remainder of our lunches in silence.

Chapter 14

After lunch, I'm forced to confront the thoughts I've been trying to push aside for two days—I'm wary of how much they excite me. I carry my belongings up to the library where I'll be spending sixth period (Ms. Hodge told me there was no point attending Programming if I can't look at a computer screen) and Ash's words crash through the floodgates of my brain, no longer able to be contained: *"I'll come find you after school."*

There are only two opportunities for him to do that: today and tomorrow. I've been safeguarding my ego by telling myself that he isn't coming at all, but the queasy feeling in my stomach definitely isn't from the chickpeas in my hummus.

As seventh period blends into eighth, the last of the day, my suppressed thoughts are unleashed like a Trojan Horse and my anxiety starts to boil. I'm more than a little bewildered by how strong my desire is to see him again, but I chalk it up to Ash being the only decent person I've found to talk to in this little town. Even so, I catch myself several times daydreaming about his face; his sandy brown hair, his azure eyes, his forearms, the ones that carried me to safety. Between the near-constant ringing in my left ear—tinnitus is no joke—and Ash taking up all the space in my head, it's pretty hard to pay attention to anything—even if I *am* exempt from reading, anything computer-related, and taking notes.

I feign attentiveness through Biology as I watch the seconds tick by. Will he come? And how will he find me, even if he does? Esko is a small school, but the courtyard floods with hundreds of students and parents and teachers after the final bell. I'm halfway through determining the best vantage point for searching through the schoolyard bustle, and imagining what Ash will be wearing, when Mrs. Kelley's shrill voice pierces through my thought bubble.

"Hu-what?" I say, startled by reality.

"What is the probability of a yellow soybean plant growing from a cross pollination of two green soybean plants when one carries the recessive yellow gene?"

"Miss Kelley, you know she has a concussion, right?" a helpful boy named Carl chimes in.

"I'm not asking her to do rocket science. Rafa?"

I don't have the slightest idea, nor do I care. Why the curriculum planners think this type of information will ever be practical to anyone but soybean farmers, I have no idea. I wonder if soybean farmers even care whether their plants end up yellow or green. I highly doubt it.

"Um...twenty five percent?" Total shot in the dark, but I know the answers to these sorts of questions usually present in intervals of twenty-five.

"Yes!" screams Mrs. Kelley, overenthusiastically. "Now, if Rafa can conjure up the answer after suffering a head injury, I think the rest of you can manage to take some notes or at least try to stay awake."

Phew. I don't know much about soybeans, but I do remember Punnett Squares from eighth grade Life Science. Luckily, my unanticipated correct answer gets Mrs. Kelley to leave me alone for the rest of class, which is growing agonizingly longer by the minute. I swear, an entire field of purple polka-dotted soybeans could sprout in the time it's taking to get through this last period.

When the bell finally rings, I jump to my feet and see stars. I sternly remind myself that I'm *not* going to see him –no need to jinx anything– and make my way to the courtyard. If Ash is there, I'll see him. If he isn't, no big deal.

I find an open bench and pretend to flip through Cosmo. I look for him as little as I can help, trying to convince myself that I'm indifferent, but I still find myself scanning each face that walks by. With each passing minute I disparage a bit more, yet a tiny sliver of hope somehow remains. At one point I think I see him through the crowd, but when crane my neck to get a closer look my view is obstructed by someone.

"Hey."

"Oh, Taylor, hi." I try to look around her without being rude.

"So, I feel pretty bad about what happened to you," she says, "I'm really sorry about your fall."

"Thanks Taylor," I reply, taken aback by her sincerity. "I appreciate it."

"No, I mean, *I'm* sorry."

"You don't have to be sorry, Taylor. It was an accident."

"I know," she says, looking distraught. She doesn't move from her position in front of me, still blocking my view of the courtyard. She starts to speak but then hesitates, as if she isn't sure how to form the words she wants to say.

"What?" I ask, a little impatient without meaning to be.

"It's just...well...I'll deny this if you ever mention it to anyone, but I was jealous of you and Greyson and I kind of...wished that you would go away. I feel sort of cosmically responsible."

My mouth drops. *Taylor* jealous of *me?* I'm more shocked by her envy than upset about her confession. Either way, I just want her to move along. I'll be able to mull over the implications of this later, when I'm not searching for a boy that may or may not be coming to visit me.

"Taylor, there *is* no *me and Greyson.* We aren't even friends."

"I believe you now, but I thought you and he were—"

"No. definitely not."

"I'm just sorry." She says again.

"Honestly, it's okay. I appreciate your apology, but you shouldn't feel responsible. I don't think the universe works that way."

She bites her lip, nervously. "You don't?"

"No. I mean, I don't think so. Even if you do believe in karma, if you wished ill upon me, why would the universe *hurt* me to get back at you? That'd be a pretty screwed up way to teach a lesson."

I don't even know what I'm saying, but she buys it.

"What about—what about if you don't just wish something bad, but you've actually *done* it?"

"Well, you *haven't* done anything. Not to me," I say, not sure if we're still having the same conversation.

"Maybe not. But…well, I'm not perfect."

"Nobody is." I say.

"I know that but…" She pauses again. "Let's just say I'm less perfect that most."

We're definitely not having the same conversation anymore, but I'm so distracted by the prospect of finding Ash that I don't care to bite.

"Whatever it is, I wouldn't worry about it. As far as I'm concerned, you and I are good. Okay?"

"Yeah…okay," Taylor replies slowly, pensively. She's still biting her lip. "Maybe I'm overthinking."

"You are."

She looks at me with a concerned expression and I feel a twinge of guilt for being crass, so I add, "Really, there's nothing to be sorry for. I swear."

"Thanks, Rafa." I nod, and she adds "Maybe we could eat lunch together sometime?"

"You don't have to do that." I say. I appreciate the gesture, but we both know its charity.

"Well, if you change your mind."

She gives me a little wave and walks off, hips oscillating with each step. Honestly, why someone who looks like she does would be envious of me is completely beyond comprehension, but I appreciate her apology even if it was unnecessary. I scan the courtyard and find the person I thought was Ash, but it's just one of the soccer players. I keep my eyes peeled but by 2:40 I accept that he isn't coming. I gather my things and head to practice, feeling foolish for being so clandestinely hopeful.

Chapter 15

Ash doesn't show on Friday, either.

I do everything I can to keep my mind off of him, but my thoughts keep drifting back to the boy I met in the woods. When Mom pulls up after practice, I hop in the passenger seat, eager for a distraction.

"How was school?" Mom asks, in her usual energetic tone.

"My head hurts, and my ears are still ringing, but other than that, okay."

"Did you take the codeine?"

Doctor Sepir had given me four doses of codeine, but horror stories about young people who accidentally become addicted to opioids loomed over me every time I so much as thought about taking one.

"No, I've been trying to hold off. But I took some Advil after lunch."

"Probably for the best."

I nod.

"You tired, kiddo?"

I'd been so distracted by the prospect of seeing Ash that I hadn't realized how wiped out I was from the day until she asked. I rest my head on the window and close my eyes when the zoom of blurred trees gets too trippy. When the car plugs to a stop in our driveway, I mutter to Mom that I need some rest and am likely going to sleep through dinner.

Luckily, Mom keeps a hefty stash of analgesics in her bathroom, so I nurse my headache with the highest acceptable dose of Advil. I drown the pills with a swig of Gatorade and shuffle to my room to lie down. I plop onto my new duvet, which is detailed with cornflower blue elephants on an ivory backdrop. I pull my iPhone from my back pocket, half hoping to see a message from Ash explaining his absence. Something like, "Hey! I just got a phone and found your Insta page, wanted to say hi :)" or "Hope this doesn't seem creepy, but I stumbled on your Snapchat." But I know the hope is futile. To my disappointment, not only do I not have a message from Ash, I don't have any messages at all.

Typical.

Chapter 16

On Saturday morning I wake to the sound of rain hammering against my bedroom window. Lake Superior borders Duluth—twenty miles to the north of Esko—and the clouds swallow up as much of the great lake as they can and regurgitate it all over us at least once a week.

The pounding in my head promptly reminds me that I am overdue for a painkiller. I feel like I drank a liter of vodka last night when in reality I spent the night staring at the wall and listening to *Gilmore Girls,* which is the only way Dr. Sepir is allowing me to "watch" TV. I reach for my phone to check the time, and it pings as I pick it up with a text from Mom:

> There's herbal tea in the cupboard above the stove. I'll be home in the morning. Do NOT leave the house. Text me if you need *anything.* xo.

How she's worried that I'll injure myself further is beyond me; all I do is lay in bed. I slept half the day away, but that still leaves me hours and hours to figure out what to do with myself without leaving the house, and there's only so much Netflix a girl can listen to.

After listening to two more episodes of my show and staring at my periwinkle walls until all of my thoughts are purple, I decide to brave a trip to the kitchen. The house is ancient and stone and not well insulated, and on top of that, Mom insists on keeping the heat at 65 even though we–apparently–have enough money to afford this monster house. I would turn it up while she's gone, except that she set the heat to a schedule on the thermostat which can only be changed with a code that I'm not privy to yet. So, I put on two pairs of leggings and the thickest socks I own and make my way downstairs to the pantry to hunt for something to eat.

Benny wags his tail enthusiastically from his bed in front of the fireplace, willing me with his big copper eyes to light a fire. Mom might be able to prevent me from cranking the heat up to 75 degrees while she's gone, but she can't stop me from lighting a fire. She probably wouldn't want me to so much as use the fire starter, as she's been treating me like a ten-year-old since my second accident. But I can feel leg hair prickling through my pants and Benny is practically shivering (at least, that's what my story will be) so I decide, *the hell with it*. I love my mom, but I can't allow her to treat me like a child *all* of the time.

I scoop a dollop of wood chips out of the sack below the mantle and light them up. The tiny flames grow into violent, scarlet wisps that quickly consume all of the kindling and leave behind a pile of black charred bits. I'm going to need more than wood chips to get a fire rumbling, but to my dismay, the wood hoop next to the fireplace is empty.

I peer through the opaque downpour at the tarp-covered wood pile out back. It's only twenty yards from the house. No rocks, no ice, no dangerous obstacles, and my head feels at least okay. I'm not supposed to get my stitches wet, but I can wear a hat.

I slip on a pair of old, black Wellingtons and throw on Dad's giant yellow raincoat from a hundred years ago that somehow escaped to Minnesota with us. I've found a few of Dad's things around since being on house arrest and can't help but wonder if they came here by accident or if Mom is holding onto little parts of him. She would never admit that she missed him out loud, but a few days ago I caught her sleeping in one of his old t-shirts. For the first couple of weeks, I'd only thought about how the separation and move affected me. I never stopped to think how it might be affecting Mom, even though she was the one who had so adamantly pushed Dad away after everything that happened last year.

I open the kitchen door and beckon for Benny to follow, but he takes one sniff of the air and looks at me as if to say *no way, José.* I can't blame him; the rain is wildly unappealing. It doesn't even fall in poetic drops, but a thick, dense sheet of icy cold that permeates every corner of Esko. Even through all of my layers and Dad's enormous coat, I'm still somehow getting wet. I make a mad dash for the wood pile, the old canvas bag we use to transport the logs already soaked through. About halfway there I receive what I can only imagine is a telepathic reminder from Mom to be careful, so I slow down to appease my conscience.

I lift up the tarp that rests atop the pile of logs and start filling the sack. A crack of thunder booms above me as I realize in vain that by the time I get back to the house the wood will be too wet to burn. I struggle to hold the weight of the bag with my good arm.

"Need some help with that?" A voice breaks through the thunder, its pleasantry juxtaposing the torrent of the storm around me. I drop my sack and nearly jump out of my skin. One nimble hand catches me as I stumble in surprise, and another catches the bag.

"Sorry," he says, "did I startle you?"

It's Ash.

"What gave you the first clue?" I respond stubbornly. I'm desperately trying to sound hurt about him ghosting me, but inside I'm euphoric.

"Let me help you with that." he says, his voice growing in decibel against the wind.

"I'm fine," I shout back over the rain, disregarding his offer and reaching for another log. I pull it out of the pile but it falls out of my hand, and I have to admit that I'm glad he catches it because if he didn't, it definitely would have landed on my toes and I cannot afford to break one of those too. He has impressive reflexes; I'll give him that.

Ash holds the rescued log out to me as a peace offering, and I open the sack for him to put it in. He offers to carry the loaded bag and I let him only because the sprain is making it difficult to shoulder the burden of four sizeable logs with one arm. Not to mention I haven't really moved my body or eaten properly in days, so I'm nowhere near tip-top shape.

I nod a curt "thank you" to him, begrudging the fact that I need help, and we trudge together through the swamp that used to be my backyard. As we approach the glass door, I see Benny standing in the window, wagging his tail maniacally. Eager to get out of the rain, I run up the steps and into the kitchen, completely disregarding my soaking wet shoes.

"Thank you," I yell over the torrent, as Ash hands me the bag.

"Anytime."

I take off Dad's massive raincoat and shake out my hair, gingerly checking to see that all of my stitches and staples are still intact. Then, I give myself a mental pat on the back for doing something useful for the first time in weeks. I'm about to go unload the firewood when I realize Ash is still standing just outside the open door, his hair hanging over his forehead like a soft, honey colored mop. I think about the ramifications of inviting in a boy I barely know, but I'm not about to make him walk home through the woods in a lightning storm.

I motion him in.

"You sure?" he asks, looking from me to the house. "You don't have to, I'll be okay."

"Don't be ridiculous," I say, beckoning him in again. "You'll be swimming if you stay out there much longer–you don't want to drown."

"You can say that again," he says, shaking out his hair and rubbing the rain off of his face with a sopping wet sleeve.

"Don't you have a raincoat?" I ask, noticing he's wearing the same outfit from the other night at the hospital. It seems to be either his favorite, or the only thing he owns. I shut the door behind us and we both drip little puddles onto the tile floor.

"It wasn't raining when I left the house, but I guess I should have known. This *is* Esko, after all."

I dig out two towels from under the kitchen sink and throw one to Ash, who catches it easily. I dab the cloth on my face gently, as a bolt of lightning cracks loudly, startling me. I jump, and we both laugh nervously. Whether it's because of the thunder, or being in each other's presence again, I cannot say.

"You're going to have to stay until the storm passes," I say, taking the wet towel from him and handing him a fresh one. "You can't walk back through the woods in weather like this."

"But what about your mom?"

"She's on a double and working overnight." Is it wise to tell him I'm alone for the entirety of the night?

"Well, I don't mind staying if you don't mind having me."

"I don't."

I decide not to ask about the ghosting because I don't want to appear presumptuous. It's not like he owed me anything.

"But you need a change of clothes."

"I don't suppose you have a brother, do you?" he asks, looking from his tall, lanky body to my smaller one.

"I–I..." I stammer, unable to finish the sentence. Not knowing whether to say, "I do" or "I did" or "I don't, anymore." I've never had to answer this question before.

"I'm only joking," he says. "You know, because I don't think I'd fit into your clothes."

"Oh–right. Yeah." I say, looking at my soggy socks. How could he have known? It's not like I talk about it. It's not like *anyone* talks about it.

"Rafa? You okay?"

I slap on a smile and change the subject, not wanting to get into it.

"Yeah, of course. Let me run upstairs quick and see if I can find you something to wear."

I leave him in the kitchen with Benny and run up the cold steps, trying to swallow the thick knot that's formed in my throat, but I can't get it down. The separation was painful, but it was nothing, *is* nothing compared to losing Ollie. I can still feel the way my hands ached when I realized I'd never be able to touch him again. I stared at them for hours and struggled to understand how a mere day before I was holding his beautiful head and then just like that, I would never touch him again. I can still see Mom and Dad collapsing into each other in the waiting room, forgetting anything else existed but their son who used to be so vibrant and alive but suddenly, wasn't.

I swallow the knot in my throat again, this time forcing it down. I dig through the boxes of clothes that sit unpacked in one of the extra bedrooms. I rifle through a box of t-shirts and find exactly what I'm looking for– an old *Space Camp* t-shirt I got from the gift shop in Toronto, after spending a weekend there for a Science Club field trip in 7th grade. I was adamant about getting a shirt even though they were sold out of smalls and mediums, so I'd been forced to buy a large that could've fit three of me at the time. It's nerdy, but it's the only shirt I own that has a prayer of fitting him. As for pants, I grab a pair of baggy grey sweatpants from my bottom drawer that will have to do.

I call to him from the top of the staircase and toss the clothes down.

"Sorry," I say, "this is the best I could do."

"This'll work!" He says. "Thanks."

I quickly change into a dry pair of leggings, an oversized sweater, and fresh socks. I shake out my hair one more time, and miraculously it doesn't look half bad. The dampness has given it a few more waves, which lay over my forehead, disguising some of the hardware in my face. I give myself an encouraging smile in the mirror and head back downstairs.

As I turn the corner at the bottom of the stairs, I catch a glimpse of Ash pulling the t-shirt over his long torso, momentarily exposed. I flush and look away, but not before noticing how toned he is underneath his clothes. I don't have any experience with the male body, but the way his waist narrows at the hips makes it hard not to sneak a second glance. When I do, I catch sight of an enormous purple bruise on his ribcage, so dark it's almost black. It looks like he's been bludgeoned by something, and just the sight of it is enough to make me cringe in phantom pain. I'm tempted to ask how he got it, but it isn't any of my business, so I avert my eyes and pretend I didn't see.

I give him what I think is long enough to situate himself and then meet his gaze. His eyes rest on my hair, and for a moment I think I catch him admiring. He looks away, as I had. He puts his hands in the pockets of my sweats and pretends to model them.

"What do you think?"

"They look…short," I say. The elastic cuffs only reach midway down his calf. "But other than that, I'd say you do them justice."

"I hear cropped is in this season."

"You're right. I am so *not* fashion forward."

"Thank you for acknowledging that I am." he replies jovially.

There's a pause, and the rain pounding on the windows is the only thing that isn't still. The air between us is quiet, the tension in the room as thick as the downpour outside. We both feel it and try to break the silence at the same time which results in a jumble of syllables neither of us can understand. I pause and let him speak first.

"I'm really sorry, Rafa," he says, his voice heavy.

"What for?" He doesn't need to know I spent all of Thursday and Friday with an anxious stomach wondering whether or not I'd see him.

"For saying I'd come and not following through."

"Oh. Right."

I don't know if I should forgive him because I don't know if there's anything to forgive. It's not like he's my boyfriend, or even my *friend,* really.

"Well, what happened?" I ask, trying not to sound too invested.

"I just–it's hard for me to go back there. To Esko High. I saw the building and some of the people and I–I don't know. I froze. I couldn't do it."

Jeez. I know high school can be rough–I'm not exactly a fan– but I didn't know it could be *that* rough.

"You must have really hated it there."

I realize then that I don't know anything about his time at Esko High.

"I didn't always. But there were some bad people there, Rafa."

I think about Greyson and how he made me feel the other day in the cafeteria, trapped and overpowered, and I shiver.

"What do you mean?" I press. "Who? And what did they do to make you hate it so much?"

"I don't want to talk about it," he replies. "I do everything I can to bury high school and all the other things in my past I want to un-know but they won't be buried. They keep rising up out of a grave to haunt me."

I can see pain in his eyes. The way he's talking makes it seem like he was bullied, but I can't imagine someone who looks like him and carries himself like he does being the target of teen harassment. I want to know more but it doesn't feel right to pry, so I say nothing.

"Anyway, enough talk about sad things. How 'bout I get a fire going and you make yourself a cup of tea. I mean, if you're into tea. Not that you can't start a fire by yourself. Or that I'm telling you what to do, that is. I just think…" He looks at me and I smile wryly, enjoying every second of him trying to get out of the little hole he's dug for himself. "You know, why don't I just start a fire–

because I'm cold, not because you aren't capable of doing it yourself– and you drink whatever you'd like. Or don't."

I stifle a laugh, which turns into a snort, and then he laughs, too. I show him where the matches are and boil myself some water on the stove and make a cup of Earl Grey with honey and cashew milk. I walk back to the living room with my mug, and I'm impressed by how effortlessly he gets a fire rolling. I can feel the stone of the hearth warming beneath my feet, and Benny has already settled himself right in front of the fireplace and fallen asleep.

"Impressive," I say, thinking about the pathetic pile of flaming wood chips that had burned out on me earlier. Someone obviously paid attention in Eagle Scouts.

"Thanks. I've always had a knack for it."

"Starting fires in other people's houses?" I ask.

"Ve-ry fun-ny," he says, exaggerating each syllable. I offer to make him some tea or cocoa.

"I think I've had enough liquid for one day," he declines, politely.

He stands up and stretches his arms toward the ceiling, and I'm forced to avert my gaze again when the t-shirt I let him borrow rides up, exposing his taut torso. A shiver of something like excitement runs down my spine but I push the feeling away, not wanting to address it, or even knowing how. He yawns and notices the little clay sculpture on the mantel. He picks up the three-legged blob and rolls it gently between his fingers, pensive.

"You never told me what a talented...um...*artist* you are, Rafa."

I roll my eyes and look up at him in playful annoyance. "That isn't *mine*. It was left here by the previous owners"

"Well in that case, you should hold onto it. It could be a collector's item someday," he says, handing it back to me.

"Hey, I like it," I retort, putting my splinted arm on my hip in defiance. "It makes me feel less alone; I can't really explain it. I know it's stupid, but it makes me feel like there was love here once, not just rain and darkness and...death."

He smiles at me again, but it's the kind of expression that one makes to mask sadness. "It doesn't sound stupid," he says. I'm sure he knows about the fate of the family who inhabited this house before I did. It only took a day for rumors about my accident to go flying around the school; I can only imagine what a death would be like, caught in Esko's rumor mill. I go on, unleashing thoughts I usually keep caged beneath my skull.

"Sometimes I wonder if it belonged to the boy that died. If he made it in Kindergarten, and if his mother told him it was beautiful even if she had no idea what it was supposed to be. I wonder how old he was when he realized it wasn't the masterpiece, he thought it was when he was little, but that his mom displayed the white blob of clay proudly anyway. I wonder if that made him feel loved. I wonder if his mother held it and cried after he died, and if she left it behind by accident, or because she couldn't bear to take it from its resting place after so many years."

I trail off, feeling abruptly self-conscious, like maybe I said too much. Like those are the kinds of thoughts you're supposed to keep to yourself.

Ash nods, thoughtfully. "I think that's kind of beautiful."

I pause, half-thinking he's kidding but he isn't. I wonder if anyone has ever associated something that came out of my mouth with the word *beautiful*. I usually struggle to turn my thoughts into coherent sentences, let alone anything remotely graceful.

"Thanks," I say, my body warming from the fire, and maybe just a bit from something else. He puts the sculpture back on the mantel and adjusts it this way and that, as if having it positioned just-so will change the ambiance of the sparsely furnished room. He sits down across from me in the emerald green armchair Mom and I picked up at a thrift store a couple of weeks ago. For a few minutes we soak up each other's silence, and I'm a half-empty cup starting to feel full for the first time in years.

"Did you know him?" I ask. "The boy who lived here."

"Not really. I mean, I knew *of* him, but I didn't know him well."

"He died in my pool." I blurt

"Rafa, you don't have a pool. You have a giant puddle of mud."

He indicates to the filled-in pool, which is overflowing with brown water.

I roll my eyes again.

"You know what I *mean*. It's kind of...morbid, isn't it?"

"Yeah," he agrees. "Just a little."

We bunker into the comfortable silence again. Usually I stress myself out over what to say next in conversations or wonder if I'm talking too much or not enough. Then, if there ever *is* a silence, it usually feels uncomfortable, like I should be filling it. But with Ash the silence is peaceful, thoughtful. It's warm.

"Anyway, enough about me," I say, testing my tea, which is still scalding. "Where are you from?"

"Oh, you know," he looks around. "Nowhere special. Here."

"So you've been in Esko your whole life?"

"More or less. We used to move around a lot when I was little, but once I got to middle school, I begged my parents to let us stay in one place. I wanted to have some semblance of a normal life. You know?"

"I do know," I agree, thinking about my own situation. "What do your parents do?"

"They're doctors," he says.

"Really? Do you think they know my mom? She's a nurse at St. Marcy's."

"Oh, they don't live here anymore. After I finished school, they went back to their vagabond ways and started traveling for work again."

"So you live alone, then?" I know he's only two years older than I am, but the fact that he lives on his own makes him seem so much more...mature. And so out of my league.

"Sort of. I mean, it's just me. I wish–I wish I appreciated my parents a little more growing up, ya know?" His expression drops. "I think they knew I loved them but...I just wish I'd spent more time with them."

"Ash, I'm sure they know you love them," I say, and then think about how I've been treating my own mother lately. "I think all teenagers can be a little distant, but I think our parents know we love them." I say this partially because I believe it, and partially because I hope Mom knows. I make a mental note to let her know how much I appreciate her later.

"Yeah, you're probably right," he replies, only half here.

"Besides, you could always call them and tell them how you feel."

"Right," he says, coming back to the present. "I just–uh– I don't want to bother them, you know?"

My mind now wanders to Dad, and how I've been pretending I'm doing better than I actually am when we talk.

"Trust me, I do."

"How's your head feeling?" Ash asks, moving closer to the fire. He sits on the hearth next to Benny and pats him on the back, which rises and falls steadily with each slumbering breath.

I truthfully haven't thought about my head at all in at least an hour, but I took three Advil earlier so that may have something to do with it.

"Right now, I feel better than I've felt in weeks."

"Yeah," he replies, "me too."

We lock eyes for a moment, until I feel so full of something I have to look away. He –all of him– is so overwhelming, I have to wonder if he really *is* a delusion. Or if I'm dreaming. I dig my fingernail into my arm until I feel the pain, just to check.

"Hey, about what I said earlier, the brother comment. I should have known with your family being split up that that might be painful for you. If you want to talk..."

I debate whether or not I should tell him the truth. I don't like to open up about Ollie, but something about Ash makes me feel safe and understood. Ollie died eight months ago, and I haven't talked about it with anyone, not even the shrinks my parents made me see, but somehow this guy I hardly know is making me want to lay down all of my heavy inhibitions and walk weightlessly into him.

"It's a long story," I say, and he looks at me with trusting eyes.

"I'm not going anywhere."

Chapter 17

I reveal everything without even meaning to. I tell Ash about the headaches that began sometime after Ollie's seventh birthday, and how, after complaining for weeks on end, we realized they weren't from too much computer time as Mom had theorized. I tell him about the migraine medication and diet change that didn't work, and how depressed Ollie got when he found out he couldn't eat hot dogs or bologna anymore, and how innocent it was that he thought *that* was the worst part of his life; cutting out hot dogs. I tell him about how the headaches got so bad that Ollie started missing school, and Mom had to take off work to get second and third and fourth opinions. I tell him about his first of many MRIs, where the doctors let me sit in the room with him covered in a lead smock and helmet. I tell him about how we knew something was wrong by the way the doctors kept telling us *we don't want to jump to any conclusions before we have enough information,* and how I, then fifteen, couldn't understand how sterile and practiced their voices seemed, as if it was no big deal to uncover the seeds of a family tragedy.

I tell him about how the doctors called my whole family into an office together and had us sit down, and how we held each other's hands while they delivered the news. How Ollie didn't fully comprehend why Dad and Mom were fighting back tears, because, as he said, "kids get sick all the time, guys. Just last week Jeremy was throwing up in Art class and now he's fine." (Again, with the innocence. He was beautiful like that.) I tell Ash how I lived in denial for the next year, as Ollie underwent surgery after surgery, chemotherapy, and countless bouts of unsuccessful radiation. I recount how I spent weeks on end scouring the internet for *malignant skull base tumor* recovery stories, but how there weren't many of them to be found. I tell him how sweet and hopeful Ollie always remained, partially because he could not possibly understand the extent of his illness at such a young age, but partially because he was a perfect creature sent down to us from whatever heaven exists.

Finally, I tell him about Ollie's last surgery. How we spent the night before in the hospital with him, eating strawberry sorbet and birthday cake (though it was nobody's birthday) and celebrating. We always celebrated the night before a surgery because Dad believed in good juju, and that positive thinking could somehow combat malignant brain tumors. The night was full of foreboding, but it was also full of joy. I tell him how I think it was the last time I ever saw my parents in love, and how I like to remember them that way. I tell him about the photos from that night, how Ollie and I took pictures together with every ridiculous filter we could find, and how I still can't bring myself to look at them, even though I know they're buried somewhere in my phone's memory. I tell him about how Dad knocked our heads together and kissed us both, saying that Ollie needed his rest, but we would continue the celebration when he came out of surgery the next day.

I take a breath, prepping for the emotional dive I'm about to take into the Mariana trench of family trauma. I hold the breath, count to five in my head, and let it out, one useful coping mechanism I took from my time in therapy last year. I'm about to tell Ash the one thing I've never told anyone, the painful wound in my life that's still blistering raw.

"You don't have to keep going." He says.

"No, I want to."

I want to, and I need to. I've never needed anything more than to have someone hear me right now, and I'm so glad it's him.

"We had all these treats picked out for him for after his surgery. We always did. The three of us would practically raid the gift shop so that when he woke up, he'd be surrounded by happy things and people who loved him more than anything. We'd fill his room with balloons and flowers and new stuffed animals, pictures, little games to play and sketchbooks and all of that. The surgeries were long, and painful, you know? And he was only a kid. It wasn't easy. After you have your skull drilled into there's a long recovery and a lot of long nights in the hospital. We always wanted to make sure he didn't feel alone from the second he woke up."

"So what did you get for him that time?" Ash asks.

"It doesn't matter, we threw it all away."

"But why?" He asks again.

"Because that time, Ollie didn't wake up."

Chapter 18

By the time I finish recounting Ollie's death, there are silent tears rolling down my cheeks and I feel like I've been hit in the chest by a bus. I wipe my eyes with the cuff of my sweatshirt, preparing for the wave of shame that usually comes after being vulnerable, but it never arrives. I don't know when Ash moved onto the couch but he's sitting next to me now, his hand on my shoulder, letting me cry. He doesn't say anything, probably knowing there's nothing to say, and in that moment, I like him even more. Most people would try to tell me that it's "okay," or that he's "in a better place now," but none of that ever makes me feel any better because none of it can bring Ollie back.

We sit in silence for a few minutes and I rest my head on his shoulder. It's firm, but I welcome it. I've lain my head on so many pillows recently that softness is starting to suffocate me. Ash doesn't feel like pillows or pain meds. Ash feels *real*. He's not a band-aid, he's a staple, holding my skin together when it's being pulled apart.

I press my face gently into his chest and he puts an arm around me, cautiously at first, but I lean into him with silent consent hoping he'll hold me a little tighter and he does. I haven't been held by anyone in so long, I didn't know how much I'd been craving human touch. I can feel his breath on my hair as we sit in a bubble of warmth that wraps me up like a weighted blanket. Heavy, but safe. He doesn't heal my wounds, but he is a balm that softens the ache, and even though I know this moment can't last forever, I'd gladly stay nestled under his arm for all eternity.

He pushes a lock of wavy hair behind my ear and whispers "I know it's not okay now, and that maybe it won't be for a long, long time, but things will be okay someday. I promise." And I swear to God, I have never wanted to believe someone so much in my entire life. I close my eyes and sink into him a little further, absorbing his presence like a sponge. Or, maybe it's he who is absorbing me. I drift off into the first sleep I've had in years that isn't polluted with fear or anxiety, drunk off of painkillers and everything that is Ash.

When I wake up, I've lost half the night and Ash is gone.

Chapter 19

I sit up, disoriented.

It takes me much longer to come-to than it should. I definitely overdid things yesterday, and I'm paying for it now. I'm not used to living in a body that gets exhausted from basic conversation or walking across a yard and it's as unsettling as it is frustrating. I've never been drunk before, but the relentless pounding in my head must be what waking up hungover feels like. Each time I move my neck, a canon-fire erupts from my temples and I'm forced to lie back down.

I close my eyes for a minute, waiting for the tension to subside. I open them slowly once I'm able to and survey my surroundings– the living room. The fire Ash kindled earlier has been put out, and my half-empty mug of tea is sitting cold on the coffee table. I'm covered in a blanket that I'm pretty sure wasn't on me before I fell asleep. Benny is curled up by my toes, somehow sensing that Mom won't be home to scold him for being on the furniture anytime soon. The sky is black as pitch, and the only light in the room is the time on my iPhone which reads 1 A.M.

One a.m.?

I try to replay the events of the last twelve hours in my head but they're fuzzy, scratched up, and dizzying. Did Ash tell me he was leaving, or say goodbye? Did he cover me with the blanket, or did I do it myself and forget?

I can't tell if I'm more upset that my memory is cloudy or that Ash left without a trace. Once again, I'm left not knowing when–or if–I'll see him again. Maybe I'm reading too much into things, but it felt like there was something between us, at least enough for him to have the decency to say goodbye before taking off.

Benny adjusts his position at my feet, and I ask him "what happened here tonight, boy?" But he just snorts a little and falls back to sleep, leaving me alone with my troubling thoughts.

Chapter 20

Monday morning is so typical, it's almost as if Ash never even happened. I know my schedule and my way around the school buildings now, and I no longer have to ask for directions or follow people blindly, hoping we're going to the same place. I've also figured out which classes I need to arrive early to, so I'm not forced to sit in the front. Though I can't say I feel like I belong here with any conviction, I can say that I'm finally starting to blend in. I walk from class to class determinedly with earbuds in– instrumental music only, for now. Doctor's orders. I'm a little fish amongst a shoal of a hundred others, trying desperately to avoid drowning. Or being eaten by a shark.

I am only allowed to attend three classes a day and gym is completely out of the question, so when I'm not in class I'm either in the student lounge (a privilege usually granted only to seniors) or the nurse's office. My concussion is a perfect excuse to skip being spit on all period by Mr. Finch, but I do go to Art and Spanish in the morning and I'll go to Biology in the afternoon.

By the time I get to lunch, I'm pretty sure some people are still whispering about my battered face behind my back, but I don't care. I sit down in the same empty booth I claimed last week and immediately spread my lunch and the rest of my belongings out around me. I try to shake the ringing out of my left ear, but it doesn't budge. The tinnitus has been bothering me almost every day, but at least music drowns it out. I pop my earbuds in and open up my copy of *The Great Gatsby*. I'm not really reading, just pretending for effect, hoping it will act as a social repellant. I'm determined not to make eye contact with a soul. After last week, I don't want to deal with any unwelcome guests.

I "read" in peace for a couple of minutes and munch on crackers and carrots, but soon enough my bubble is pierced by a pile of textbooks landing with a *thud* right across from me. I flinch, my body filling with dread. I know he's going to talk to me, and when he does, I'll feel like an animal caught in a trap. Or in his sharp, perfect teeth. Like I'm the little fish and he's the shark coming after me. My mind immediately starts searching for an escape route, but I don't have to search for long because when I look up, I see that it isn't Greyson after all, it's Ingrid.

Her hair is now dyed a pale lavender hue but is still styled in a curtain over one of her eyes. I exhale an audible sigh of relief and she smiles at me, with restraint, out of the corner of her lips. But it's a smile nonetheless, so I'll take it. I notice she's wearing cat ears, and has a little black nose drawn overtop of her own.

"Why are you a cat?" I ask, "Not that I don't like it– you pull it off."

She holds up her smartwatch and points to the date. Right. It's Halloween. I'm so out of it these days. I scan the cafeteria and notice quite a few people are in costume–some in full character, some with a bit of makeup, and some wearing animal onesies, unabashedly using Halloween as an excuse to come to school in pajamas. Ingrid sits down, takes a tin bento box out of the messenger bag that's slung across her shoulder, and begins to eat a peanut butter sandwich and some Oreos. She offers me a cookie and I take it, never one to turn down free chocolate.

"Thanks. My mom is such a health nut we *never* have stuff like this in the house."

Ingrid laughs a little, and through it I can almost imagine what her voice might sound like. She offers me another, then opens up a manga book and starts reading it from back to front, intensely and without blinking. I leave one earbud out in case she feels like talking and resume my lunch.

Ingrid turns the pages intently, and I can tell she's completely lost in whatever world she's reading about. I envy her concentration–lately all I can think about is Ash and his disappearing acts. It's impossible to imagine–even with all of my anxious second guessing–that what I felt the other night wasn't real. I almost ask Ingrid if she knew Ash, but I don't want to break her focus and I don't think she'd be able to answer me anyway.

When the bell rings, the two of us exit the cafeteria together and join the bustling crowd of juniors heading in various directions. I soon feel the tickle of hot breath on the back of my neck, and I turn my head with a start. I know it's Greyson before I even turned around– no one else would get so close.

"Hey Rafa."

"Hello, Greyson," I reply curtly, quickly turning back around to indicate that I'm not in the mood.

"Hey Ingrid," he continues. "I like your costume."

I almost think he's being genuine, and it almost makes me soften. But when she turns around to glare at him through her cat eyes, he asks what she's supposed to be: a freak, or a psycho.

A surge of anger pumps through my veins like thick, hot molasses. I feel protective of Ingrid, though she doesn't seem to need protection. Ingrid keeps walking as if she didn't hear him, but my hands ball into fists, the skin of my hands stretching over my knuckle bones. I knew I didn't like Greyson, but right now I hate him.

"*Screw you, Greyson.*"

I say it without even thinking. I'm usually not confrontational and hearing myself tell him off both scares and excites me.

"Well, look who's talking to me again," he says, snickering and elbowing his friend in the ribs. "Teo, I think she's *flirting* with me."

Ingrid must be able to feel the rage radiating from my skin, because she puts a hand on me, gripping my forearm as if to say *he's not worth it.* And he isn't. We keep walking and look straight ahead, trying our best to ignore Greyson and Teo still chuckling behind us like chimpanzees. I wouldn't be surprised if they started eating fleas out of each other's hair or throwing poop.

Ingrid is still holding onto me as we turn upstairs to go to Bio Lab, and through her grip I feel an unspoken bond forming between us. She rescued me from Greyson in the cafeteria, and in return, I defended her honor. It's more than having a common enemy, it's an alliance, an understanding, and a mutual appreciation. We walk into Lab and sit next to each other in the back of the room and my chest flutters with something like relief mixed with joy, knowing in my heart that Ingrid and I just became friends.

*   *   *

By the time Mom picks me up from school I am completely exhausted. Not only does my head hurt, but I actually feel physically tired from walking. I drag my feet all the way to the car and the passenger door weighs a hundred pounds. It swings open after a strong tug and I pause, trying to catch my breath before sitting down in order to avoid suspicion. Of course, Mom notices anyway. If she were a Marvel character, her superpower would be detecting whenever someone around her isn't in pristine health.

"Oh boy, that doesn't look good," she says, shifting the car into drive. "You only went to three classes, right?"

"Yes, Mom."

"And no screen time? No reading?"

"Yes, Mom. I mean, no, none of that. Only used my phone for music of the instrumental variety."

"And what about–"

"Mom, my head. Please." I make my voice sound pitiful in the hopes that she'll have mercy and cut short her relentless line of questioning. It works, because she reaches over to feel my forehead, and keeps driving without any more questions.

We pull into the cracked driveway, and as soon as the car is in park I'm out of my seat, eager to get upstairs and into bed. But as I shut the door and walk toward the house, I feel suddenly faint, as if all the blood in my body rushed either to my head or from it. There are sparks in my line of vision, which is quickly narrowing from the edges in. I look around but can no longer tell which way is up, and I'm swept into a black hole of vertigo.

I hit the pavement, but somehow manage to catch myself on all fours and remain conscious. After a second, my vision returns, the sparks disappear, and I'm breathing slow, even breaths. I'm getting better at this.

"Oh-kay," Mom says, matter-of-factly running over to me. She crouches down beside me and feels my forehead again.

"Are you going to pass out?"

"I don't think so," I say.

"Do you feel nauseous?"

I pause for a moment, trying to figure out what my stomach feels like and give her a thumbs up to show I'm not going to hurl all over her white Crocs.

"Good enough for me. Let's get you upstairs."

She grips my shoulders and pulls me to my feet as if I'm a rag doll, then guides me inside even though I insist that I'm fine.

"Mom, really, I just got up too fast, it happens to everyone."

"People get up too fast all the time, *mija*. They don't *usually* pass out. You're headed right back to the doctor if it happens again."

"Sheesh, Mom, *please*! I'm already out of track for the rest of eternity. Next they'll be telling me I'm not allowed to *walk*."

"Well, maybe you shouldn't be out of bed at all," Mom shoots back. That wasn't the response I was looking for.

"Okay, I'll go lie down, just please don't call the doctor."

Benny jumps on me as we walk into the house. He licks my ankles affectionately, but I don't have the wherewithal to bend down and return the love. All I can think about is crawling into bed. I walk in a straight line with my index finger glued to my nose, proving to Mom I can escort myself upstairs. She kisses me, then sets a kettle of water on the stove for tea. I head up the cold staircase, taking one step at a time, trying not to lose my footing.

"And Rafa?" she calls up after me. "Don't worry about school tomorrow; I'll call the office and let them know you have to take a few more days."

Under normal circumstances I would've taken full advantage of an opportunity to skip school, but right now the thought of not being able to go causes my heartrate to quicken. I finally made a friend–one who doesn't disappear on me– and I don't want to risk losing that. What if Greyson harasses her again? I don't want her to have to face him alone.

"Mo-om," I whine, "can't we just see how I'm feeling tomorrow?"

"Absolutely out of the question," she replies matter-of-factly.

Ugh. I know I'm being unreasonable, but it's taken me so long to find any sort of real comfort here in Esko. I don't want to jeopardize a potential friendship over a dizzy spell. I storm the rest of my way up the steps and fall onto my queen-size bed, face first into my pillow. I guess I fall right to sleep, because I don't remember anything after that.

Chapter 21

I open my eyes and for the first time in weeks, my senses are crystal clear. No heaviness in my head, no ringing in my ears, no lights floating near the ceiling. I feel each breath as it passes through my nose, into my lungs, and travels out again. The sky is so bright that I can make out everything around me even though it must be nearing midnight. The moonlight is trickling through my window like a waterfall, full and incandescent. I see a mug of green tea on my nightstand that I vaguely remember Mom bringing up earlier as I hovered between sleep and consciousness. It's cold now, undrinkable.

I plant both of my feet firmly on the ground and it's surprisingly warm. Usually the old wood floors are cold and clammy at this hour, but not tonight. In fact, my whole body feels pleasantly warm, as if I just stepped out of a sauna. I slip on my moccasins, walk over to the bay window, and sit down on the padded window seat. I look at the brilliant moon against the star-dotted sky, which is indigo blue and endless. I hover in a trance – for how long, I cannot say– and only snap out of it when I hear someone calling out to me.

"Rafa!"

I look down. It's unbelievable, but it's…Ash. He's in my yard wearing only a t-shirt, though it can't be more than thirty-five or forty degrees. I check the time on my phone, and it's exactly midnight. I watch the time turn to twelve-oh-one and the date rolls from October 31 to November 1. I realize I completely missed handing out candy to trick-or-treaters, but that's okay. It's not like many of them would've made it to the creepy stone house at the end of the street.

"What are you doing?" I whisper, the air so clear that the sound of my voice carries for miles. He motions for me to join him on the lawn, and despite the strange nature of this situation there's no question in my mind that I'm going to accept his invitation. I slip my silky grey robe on overtop my white cotton sleep shorts and camisole, and briefly consider putting on a pair of sweatpants before deciding against it–I have nice legs.

I tiptoe down the stairs and through the kitchen where Benny is dreaming of squirrels. His back legs are twitching, and his muzzle is pulled over his teeth in a snarl. It isn't difficult to creep by without waking him.

"You make a terrible watchdog, Benny.

I ease open the latched glass door, not risking the front door as it's heavy and it creaks. I carefully shut it behind me and slink out into the night.

Ash is waiting for me in the yard. He holds out his arms and when I close the space between us, he embraces me. I run into him without thinking, it's almost instinctual. Even against the crisp November air, his hug is warm and comforting, like a mug of hot chocolate on a cold winter night, and though I'm not wearing a jacket, there isn't a single goosebump on my silver skin.

I still don't know what we are, if anything, but it doesn't seem to matter. All the hours I spent wondering why he keeps disappearing, or whether or not he actually cares seem silly and fruitless now. Of course he cares. He doesn't need to say it for me to know. We let go of one another after an embrace that lasts longer than anything I've ever shared with just a friend.

"Hi Rafa," he says, beaming brightly as the moon.

"Hello, Ash," I say, outshining the stars.

He surveys my face, which is plastered with uncontainable elation, and I watch as his eyes drift down my body to my bare legs. Opting not to put on sweatpants was *definitely* the right choice.

"I'm sorry I disappeared on you the other night. I know I keep doing that."

"Yeah, you kind of do," I say, not demanding an explanation but hoping for one all the same.

"I don't know how to explain it."

A wild idea crosses through my head and it pours out of my mouth before I can stop it.

"You don't have a girlfriend or something, do you?"

I visualize a tall, beautiful pre-med student, and my stomach twists unpleasantly.

"What? No! It's nothing like that."

"Good," I blurt. Again, before I can stop myself.

"So... you'd be upset if I had a girlfriend?" he asks, raising an eyebrow.

"Not if she made you happy."

His eyebrow returns to its resting place, and I detect a hint of disappointment.

"But yeah, maybe a little," I confess.

A wry curl tugs at the corners of his lips as he reaches for my hand, and I don't pull away. Electricity courses through my every synapse as his fingers weave effortlessly through mine, two vibrant threads that have been longing to be intertwined. I've never held hands with someone before but even so, I'm not nervous.

"I want to show you something," he says, seeking my approval. I nod.

"Show me anything."

We take off into the night. I know I'm not supposed to be running, but a pleasant wind is whipping through my wavy hair and I feel like I'm floating through the trees, levitating above the ground. We disappear into the forest and the scenery zips by, faster and faster until we're practically flying. We're heading in the direction of where I assume he lives, the same direction he came from when he found me that day in the woods. We come to a clearing in the evergreens where the silvery light from the night sky illuminates the sleeping greenery, and the only sounds are bats flitting through the sky and our breath, hot and steady against the cold, silent air.

We stop and stand, our fingers still woven through one another's like wool through a loom. I'm perspiring after darting through the trees, so I let my silk robe fall to the ground and the moonlight soaks into my exposed shoulders. Ash turns to me again, his cobalt eyes absorbing and reflecting the entire Milky Way. He slowly reaches up and touches my cheek so delicately that I tremble with anticipation. I'm not quite sure what's happening, but my body seems to be. My hips turn toward him and I take a step closer, leaving barely a foot between us. He takes a step and closes the gap even more. Ash is so close now that I can smell his breath—sweet peppermint. I feel a hunger growing in my belly, one I've never felt before. It's a hunger for more of him.

"Rafa."

I think he's going to kiss me. I *want* him to kiss me, like I've never wanted anything before. But, unlike when he took my hand, I'm nervous, and I reach up to scratch my head absentmindedly. When I touch my forehead, I am shocked to find soft, smooth skin— as fresh and new as a baby's.

"My stitches! They're—gone."

Ash nods his head; I'm telling him something he already knows. He pulls away and studies me, as if deciding whether or not to trust me. I touch his hand to tell him that he can, and he squeezes it, believing me.

His hands travel to the base of his shirt and he lifts it up, slowly, purposefully, exposing his torso. I have such a strong urge to touch him that I have to cement my arms to my sides to keep from acting on it. He points to the smooth, flawless skin of his stomach.

"There's a bruise here," he says. The place he points to is devoid of injury, but I remember the wound from the day of the rainstorm. I wonder if he knows I saw. I get the feeling he does.

"Or at least, there's supposed to be," he continues, "but sometimes it's just, gone. Like suddenly everything is healed, and nothing hurts."

I touch the pink skin of my forehead. Ash meets my fingertips and traces his thumb down the silhouette of my face, pausing where the stitches should be.

"Your arm," he asks. "Does it hurt?"

I bend my splinted arm gingerly to test it, and it follows my movements easily. I rip off the splint and roll my wrist around, feeling no pain.

"I don't understand."

"Neither do I." He says. "It's like…when I'm with you, my bruise is healed"

"And my accident never happened."

I touch his skin and get that feeling you have right before you wake up on Sunday morning, when you're only half-conscious and all the pains and problems of Monday are far away. His skin is foreign to my touch, otherworldly, yet I feel like I'm sinking into the comfort of something I've always known.

"What are you thinking?" He asks.

"Sometimes I wonder if–if this is a dream."

"Well then I'm dreaming all the time."

"And I want to be," I say. He takes my hand. "Rafa?"

I cling to each syllable, wishing he would say my whole name just so I can hear his voice for a little while longer. Ash looks like he's about to say more but appears to lose his train of thought before he can verbalize it. He opens his mouth again to speak, but nothing comes out.

He reaches for his throat and looks at me, fear invading his eyes.

"What is it?" I ask.

His hands fumble at his windpipe and he starts gagging desperately, grotesquely for air.

"What is it? Are you having a reaction to something? Choking?" But there's nothing to choke on, and no symptoms of an allergy. He's just drowning in the dark air that surrounds us.

"Ash!" I throw my arms around his torso which, just minutes ago was smooth as porcelain. I attempt to give him the Heimlich Maneuver, though I hardly know the form. I place my fist under his ribcage as he sputters and gags, and when I bring my other arm around and squeeze, he buckles forward in pain and I see a flash of swollen, black and blue skin above his waistline and my sprained arm starts to burn again, worse than ever before.

Ash is now down on the ground, frantically trying to get air. I kneel down beside him, begging him to breathe. I touch his arm to comfort him, and it's unnaturally cold, as though I'm touching a corpse. As I'm fruitlessly trying to help him, a sharp pain ricochets through my head, bouncing from the base of my skull to my forehead. I reach up to hold my own head and discover a hot, wet trickle–my own blood. I bring my hand down to study the blood and find a loose staple, and a steady stream of thick, red liquid trickling down my cheek.

He looks at me in horror, still clutching his throat. Then, for no reason I can explain, a sudden wave of calm washes over him and he's okay. Ash touches my cheek again, then pulls me in and kisses my forehead. His lips are icy but they soothe the white hot wound on my temple, like aloe to a sunburn. Electric sparks permeate from where his lips meet my skin. I close my eyes and soak up as much of him as I can, as much as I'm allowed. I angle my chin up toward him, wanting more, my body taking over once again. But I feel him slipping away, as if he's fading into the background, dissolving like watercolors while I remain acrylic. Then, just as our lips are about to meet, the sparks disappear, and so does he.

Chapter 22

I wake up cold and disoriented. The sky is overcast, but I can tell that the sun is mid-morning high in the sky behind the veneer of clouds. The mug of tea still sits abandoned on my bedside table. My mouth is completely parched so I suck my cheeks, trying to collect enough moisture to swallow. My throat feels windburned and hoarse, so I take a sip of the cold tea and gag. I lie back down, and a fragment of a memory awakens somewhere in my consciousness—a strange dream that's lingering just beyond focus.

I shake my head, trying to lose the brain fog, and the memory becomes clearer, like tessellated shapes sliding back to their original form. Ash comes into view, followed by a path through the forest, a moonlit clearing, and— but it can't be. I reach up and graze my head with my fingertips, and sure enough, my injuries are not miraculously healed as my dream suggested. However, I count only three staples. Crusted blood has congealed around where the fourth used to be. I rifle through my sheets, toss my pillow onto the floor, and search under the bed, but I don't find the missing staple anywhere–conflicting evidence. I wonder…?

"No." I say aloud, putting my foot down. It was nothing but a dream. A vivid dream, but no more real than the monster I used to fear lived under my bed, waiting for an opportunity to eat my toes. But I touch my forehead again and swear I can feel where Ash's lips collided with my skin, but there's no mark, no physical remnant of his touch, so even a feeling like this can't be trusted. I can't help but wonder if I'm starting to lose my sense of what is real and what is not.

I sit on the edge of my bed and try to piece together the dream, the vision, whatever it was. Not that I really believe in dream lore, but at this point I'm desperate for answers and willing to accept the improbable. I walk to my window and look at the yard, on the off chance that something could give me insight into Ash's whereabouts or existence in general. The lawn looks like it always does in the late morning, the grass still crisp and dewy from the morning's melted frost. No answers there.

I look to my phone and remember watching the date roll from October to November, the glowing numbers still bright in my memory. I scroll idly through my contacts, hoping Ash's name will magically appear. This would be so much easier if I could text him; but even if I could, what would I say? *Hey Ash, can you tell me if last night was a dream or not?* Right. That wouldn't make me seem insane or anything. It's one thing to question reality, it's a whole other thing to admit it you're questioning it to someone other than a psychiatrist.

My left ear is ringing too loudly to think, so I decide to go downstairs for a bite to eat. I'm opening up my closet to pull out an oversized, rust-colored cardigan to bury myself in, when I notice something peculiar. The hanger that usually holds my silk robe is empty. I'd been given that robe as a birthday gift from Mom when I turned sixteen, but always felt like it was too sexy for me. I've never worn it, not once. There isn't even a chance I've left it hanging in the bathroom or thrown it in the wash.

The rush of adrenaline that shoots through me when I notice the naked hanger is electrifying and I suddenly don't care if I'm losing it. Maybe last night *did* happen. I can't put much stock into not remembering the journey home; I've lost a lot of time over the past couple of weeks and there's no easy way to reclaim what a brain injury takes away.

I throw on a pair of worn jeans and thick, wool socks, and head to the bathroom to wash up. I gently rub away the dried blood on my face with warm water, brush my teeth, and run a comb through my unwashed hair. It rakes through my curls, and as it does, the brush dredges up a single pine needle that flutters to the ground. My heart jumps through my chest and into the air. How *else* would that have gotten there?

I gulp down some water from the sink and toss two Advil in my mouth to combat the headache, which has been worsened by all of my frantic movement. Once downstairs, I inspect the sliding glass door in the kitchen. It's unlocked. Mom *never* leaves the door unlocked. The only explanation I can come up with is that when I snuck back in last night (if that *is* what happened) I was either so out of it or so focused on not making a sound, that I didn't remember to lock the door behind me. I glance at Benny, who's looking at me as if I have three heads. He cocks his ears but regurgitates no answers.

I give him a good scratch and pick up a folded piece of paper with my name on it near the coffee maker. It's a note from Mom, penned in her scribbly handwriting.

> Rafa,
>
> Working late (again.) –
>
> There's $$ on the fridge for you to get takeout (save me some!) Don't leave this house. Benny will tell me if you do! Call if you need anything, I'll have my cell on me all day.
>
> XOX, Mom

I secretly love that she still leaves notes even though she could easily text me at any time. I fold the slip of paper and slide the cautionary memo into the pocket of my leggings. Despite loving her to death, I can't heed Mom this time. There are things I need to figure out, and I won't be able to heal in peace until I do.

I grab my reusable water bottle and a protein bar from the cupboard, then, remembering how thin I looked in the mirror this morning, take two more. The water bottle, the snacks, a sweatshirt, and a box of Band-Aids get stuffed into a nylon backpack. As I pack, I find myself looking over at Benny, debating. If I take him with me, I'll undoubtedly feel safer. On the other hand, my arm is still sprained, and I'm not sure I could hold onto him if he decided to chase after something and I don't need a repeat of that.

"Sorry, Benny," I say, bending down and kissing him on the forehead. "Next time. Promise."

He whines his disapproval as I slip out the unlatched door and I feel a twinge of guilt, not only because of Benny, but because of the note burning a hole through my conscience. I know that what I'm doing is illogical. I *know* it's risky–I could get caught or hurt, or worse–but I have to go. So, I push my conscience out of the way and depart, heading into the woods. As much as my mind has failed me lately, I somehow remember the path Ash led me down last night with impeccable clarity.

We'd entered the forest where the dusk sun meets the horizon, so I know I'm heading west. I have a pretty good sense of direction as it is, but I'm not worried about getting lost since I have the map on my phone handy for directions. I double check my coat, making sure my iPhone is tucked into a zipped pocket, and it is. Though this may not be the wisest thing I've ever done, at least I've taken precautions. I estimate that Ash and I traversed about a mile before we reached the clearing, and somehow, I can feel in my gut that I'm right even though I'm going off intuition. I take each step carefully, mindful not to trip over any rocks or roots in my path, and forage on.

The forest is undeniably beautiful. As much as I complained about the endless expanse of evergreen trees when we first arrived, they're growing on me. As I walk, I think about Ollie, and wonder if he would have liked it here. He used to love to go to the park–to climb trees, to run in the grass and explore every nook and cranny. If only he could see this place. Then I think about Dad and how worried he would be if he knew what I was up to, and how much he's lost already. The guilt begins to creep up on me again, so I quickly turn my attention toward the journey and the sounds of the dense Minnesotan jungle.

I come to a spruce tree with a trunk so wide it could be as old as time. It towers over me; on a clear day it would block out the sun almost entirely. For a moment I think I've lost my way, but the breeze picks up and I get a whiff of mint on my tongue and somehow, I can sense that the clearing is straight ahead. I walk another fifty yards past the mighty spruce and, sure enough, a patch of stark light in the shady wood comes into view. I walk toward the light and emerge into the clearing from my dream. But then, how could it have been a dream? How could I be standing here, in the thick of it, if what I'd seen was merely a concoction of my unconscious mind? But then again, that's the nature of hallucinations. They make it impossible to tell dream from reality.

I wander into the clearing, unsure of what to do next. Unsure of how to prove anything. I guess I'd hoped something would reveal itself to me, a sign that would *prove* last night was more than a dream, but nothing does. My feet plow pathways through the tall grass, which is fresh and green and has somehow survived the thick frosts that have begun to kill off most of the flora in this part of the world. June bugs hum in the trees of the clearing, which are also very much alive– and not just the evergreens. It's almost too flawless to believe.

In a moment of suspicion and clarity, I reach up to touch my forehead and find that, once again, the stitches and staples have been replaced by brand new skin. Though I have no way of explaining this phenomenon, I'm neither surprised nor troubled by it. The sparkling pond beckons to me from afar so I make my way over to it and look down into its depths, locking eyes with my own reflection.

I've grown paler over the last couple of weeks. My green eyes are weighed down by heavy dark circles that drape beneath them in curtains of fatigue, even though God knows I've been sleeping enough. I poke my cheeks and the reflection girl pokes hers too, prompting some color to return. The bruises on my face have miraculously faded from the awful black and blue splotches of this morning and the stitches along my jaw have disappeared as well. Dissolved into thin air. *Just like last night.* The peaceful aura of this place engulfs me like a hot, cleansing shower, and the worries that I'm still holding onto begin to drift away like little helium balloons.

I wait by the pool for several minutes, which meld into an hour. I sit on a downed tree by the edge looking for something, anything tangible to confirm my suspicions. Every time I hear a stick snap in the woods or a rustling of leaves, my heart jumps, hoping that it's him. I see a doe and her fawn, a bunch of bullfrogs, and a bird of prey diving for an unlucky field mouse, but no Ash.

After what feels like hours, I take one last look at my reflection, and face the reality that maybe it was all a dream. A sweet, delicious, terrifying dream, but a dream all the same. Or worse, maybe the doctor was right; maybe I *am* delusional and the reason this feels so real to me isn't because it is, but because the TBI has altered my state of reality. I wonder if when people take hallucinogens, or when schizophrenics have psychotic episodes, their delusions feel as real as Ash did to me.

When the shadows start to get longer and the sun begins its journey down, I know I can't stay any longer. I feel a twinge of guilt over my decision to go home, as if I'm giving up on Ash. As I get back onto my feet, my movements spook a dozen little frogs lurking in the grass, causing them to dart anxiously into the pool. I squint my eyes, studying the rippling water, and am joined a second later by a new reflection in the pool. This one is tall and thin, with sandy brown hair and eyes that shine the most intense dark blue I've ever seen. I look up, trying but failing to catch my breath, and meet the eyes of the reflection's owner.

Chapter 23

It's him.

Ash is standing at the water's edge, looking at me in awe as if *I'm* the one who materialized out of thin air. His hands are in his pockets and slipped under his arm I see a shiny, silvery cloth.

"I *knew* it!" I exclaim at the sight of my robe in his possession.

His mouth curls upward, his cheeks warm against the cool tones of the wood, but his eyes conceal something heavy, something I cannot place. We walk toward one another, and without thinking I throw myself into his arms. He hugs me, and I can feel the muscles in his arms as he squeezes my rib cage, his hands resting for a moment on the small of my back. I shiver. He's comforting and smells like peppermint and the trees, and I can't believe I ever despised the smell of evergreens. We let go, and though he looks glad to see me, a hidden expression remains in his eyes.

"Can we talk?" Ash asks, and I nod. He motions for me to sit next to him on the downed tree I'd been perched on all afternoon. We sit close enough that our thighs brush one another, sending a tingle through me. I wait for him to start, but he doesn't, and I can't stand the suspense of not knowing what he's going to say so I blurt something out before I'm even sure of how to articulate it.

"Just tell me. Last night—was it real?"

He fiddles with a long blade of timothy grass, twirling it between two fingers absentmindedly.

"It was real to me."

He hands me my robe and pulls another pine needle out of my tangled hair. He motions to toss it onto the soft earth, but I stop him and claim it as a souvenir, sliding it into my pocket. Any tangible proof of him—no matter how small—is valuable.

"It was real to you?" I ask, unsure of what he means.

"Yeah." He replies, as if that's all I need to know.

"Ash, I don't know what that means. I don't know what *any* of this means. One minute you're here, and the next you're—

"Gone?"

"Yes."

"I don't mean to, I promise you, Rafa. I don't think I can even begin to explain it, because I don't yet understand it myself."

"Understand what, though?"

He's even being cryptic *about* being cryptic, and I'm as lost as ever.

"It's confusing, okay?" He's getting frustrated. Maybe not with me, but definitely with the situation. "It's like, I'm here one minute, and the next–"

"You're gone."

"Exactly."

He says it like I've caught onto something, but whatever he thinks I've caught onto is still eluding me. He searches my face, finding my confusion and softens. He takes my hand to reassure me and rubs it between his thumb and forefinger. Such a small act, but my body responds as if I've been swept up into a hurricane. A tidal wave of emotion spills into and out of me, and I feel as though I might spontaneously combust.

"I'm sorry, know I'm being unclear, I swear I'm trying." He says.

"I know you're trying," I reply softly, threading my fingers through his.

"I want to explain everything, but I'm afraid you'll think I'm—"

"Crazy?" I cut him off, this time completing his thought. We're getting good at that.

"Yeah."

"You want the truth? The only sanity I'm doubting is my own. I have been for weeks. Since—since the accident."

"It isn't you, Rafa. You're completely sane."

"Yeah but see, that's exactly what one of my own delusions would say to me." I say, only half-joking.

He laughs halfheartedly and tears begin well in his eyes. I'm taken aback by his emotion, his vulnerability. He stands up and paces, and I follow, afraid that if he vanishes this time he won't ever come back, and that I won't get the answers I need.

"I know it's hard, but you have to try," I say, pain throbbing below my sternum. "One minute you're disappearing for days without a trace, and the next, you're showing up Romeo-and-Juliet style, below my window in the middle of the night. Where do you go when you're gone?"

"I want to tell you, but I don't know the words."

"Well then maybe you should invest in a dictionary." I say, sharper than I intend to. "They come in handy sometimes."

"Maybe *you* should invest in a search engine. Or say, an old yearbook." He snaps back, and it stings like a swarm of yellow jackets.

"Maybe this was a bad idea," he says after a moment or two of silence. He's pulling back, and even though he's right in front of me I can feel myself losing him again.

"What do you mean?"

"This. You. Me. Coming here."

"Don't say that," I beg quietly, my own tears beginning to well.

"I'm afraid I'm going to hurt you."

"I have an idea." I begin. "Why don't you let *me* decide what's good for me and what's not." I take his hand once again and hold it tightly.

"You're something else, Rafa. You know that?"

I don't tell him that I don't know where my confidence has been coming from these days. Even now, disheveled, in the middle of the woods, I can feel it filling me. This is all new to me, but it feels good. It feels *good*.

"Alright. But I'm warning you, you are genuinely going to think I've lost my marbles." He continues.

I snort. He's worried about *me* thinking he's out of his mind, when I woke up this morning not knowing whether he was a real boy or a fever dream.

"I'm sorry," I say. "I'm not laughing at you, I swear. It's just that, well, Dr. Sepir and Mom are convinced that I sort of...made you up."

"So they think I'm an imaginary friend?"

"Not quite. They think I'm suffering from post-traumatic brain injury delusions. I mean, you *did* appear right after my accident, and I *have* been seeing things, but only flashes of lights and stars, not attractive seventeen-year-olds."

"So—you think I'm attractive?"

"Well…" I stammer, tripping over my own tongue like a surprise speed bump.

We share a moment, and his uncertainty transforms to clarity.

"You know, you're one of the best things that's happened to me, Rafa. You're the only one I have–the only break in the merciless boredom of this existence. You can't possibly know what you mean to me."

I disagree, silently. Since losing Ollie, Ash has been the only light in all of my darkness. I think I have an idea of how much true human connection can mean to someone that's lost.

I reach up and touch his hair, unable to resist the urge to be as close to him as I possibly can. I want to get rid of all the space between us, to exist in a vacuum with him and only him.

"There must be other good things in your life. Things you enjoy, family, friends?"

"I feel like I'm losing everyone."

His voice sounds desperate, like he's trying to hold onto something. I step closer to him, our bodies almost touching and our lips inches apart.

"You're not losing me," I whisper, and I mean it with every fiber of my being. "You're not going to."

"Yes, I am. I can already feel it, the tugging. We probably only have minutes, if we're lucky."

"Ash..." I begin, but he cuts me off, removing something from his pocket. I see a glimmer of turquoise, and he presses something into my palm and closes my fingers around it. I open my hand carefully, as if whatever it is might fly away into the atmosphere. It's a delicate bracelet, beaded and blue. The tiny glass beads are a shade of blue green, almost the color of his eyes.

"I want you to have this."

I stammer a thank you, and he slips it onto my wrist. I can feel a heart beating, but we're so close now that I'm not sure if it's his or my own about to burst through my chest. I can taste peppermint in the air, dancing between his mouth and mine.

"Ash—"

"Find a yearbook."

"Ash, you have to expla—"

"Promise me, Rafa. Promise you'll figure it out?"

I promise. I promise like I've never promised before. I want to say more, to ask a thousand and one questions, but somehow, I know our seconds are precious and I just want to be here with him. Ash cradles my cheek with a hand that's beginning to feel dangerously like home, and I close my eyes in anticipation. I can feel our lips, only centimeters apart, about to intersect like two celestial bodies in the night. Every nerve ending in my body is on edge, every ounce of adrenaline ignited and racing through my veins. I can feel him on every inch of my skin, buzzing, and it's too glorious for words; something I know I'll never be able to write about.

Our lips are so close now I can taste his breath, and I swallow the air between us. For a moment, we are suspended in time, on the precipice of something I've been yearning for; a part of him I've never had. I'm as eager to get to the next moment as I am to freeze time and stay suspended in this one.

I'm not going to get what I want though, because soon I feel the familiar weight of his absence engulf the space he'd just occupied, and I know he's gone before I even open my eyes.

*   *   *

This time, I remember everything. I know exactly where I am and there is no doubt, *no question,* in my mind about what just happened, except that I have no idea what the hell just happened.

I'm flooded with shock and sour disappointment in the universe. To dangle such a precious, perfect moment in front of me and then whisk it away without so much as a goodbye is so unfair, it's almost criminal. Even so, whether it's fair or not is irrelevant–sitting here feeling sorry for myself will accomplish absolutely nothing.

I look around the clearing that minutes ago held Ash in its grassy hands and decide the only thing to do is throw all previously accepted rules of reality out the window. Whatever laws of physics Newton thought he discovered do not apply here. I am one hundred percent sure that a fully-grown human being disappeared into thin air right before my (albeit, closed) eyes, and as far as I know there is no formula that can explain that to me.

I also now know definitively that I am not losing my mind. I finger the intricate details of the turquoise bracelet tied snugly around my wrist, proof that Ash is not, and never was, a delusion. That he *can't* be. Last time I checked, hallucinations don't give gifts. They can't touch or be touched, and they certainty can't –almost, I hope anyway– kiss me.

I'm going to figure out what's happening here, even if I have to come back to this clearing and wait for him a hundred times more.

Chapter 24

It's five o'clock when I get back to the house. I let Benny out then send a text to Mom, telling her I'm feeling good and have been resting in bed all day. Lying doesn't normally come easily for me, but I find I'm getting better at it by the day, which I don't love. I still feel a pang of guilt in my gut, but she replies with "Good! Love you honey" and doesn't question me.

I take the laptop Mom and I share from the mahogany desk in the study and set up camp in the living room. She'd kill me if she knew I was using a screen, but I know how to clear the history and cookies from the browser, so she'll never have to know. *Another lie.* I make a nest of pillows and blankets on the floor and grab a notebook and pen to write down my hypotheses and theories, though I have no idea what those entail yet. I pour myself a giant glass of water, order a veggie pizza from the Italian restaurant downtown, and get to work.

The first thing I Google, just to rule it out, is *hallucinations caused by concussions.* I click on a few of the most legitimate looking search results and, though I do find a few accounts of post-TBI hallucinations, most of them are auditory, and the ones that aren't usually involve very strange, nonsensical things, like giant talking house plants. I click on a link titled "*can concussions cause hallucinations?*" and read a few anecdotes of people who started living in their own worlds after experiencing a TBI, but almost all of them didn't know or even think they were having delusions. Most of them were reported by family members to have been conducting full length conversations with no one, or outright talking to themselves. As far as I know, I haven't exhibited any of the strange behaviors that the people in these stories did. I click on link after link but find nothing akin to imagining an attractive seventeen-year-old who keeps dissolving into thin air.

By the time the pizza arrives I've read almost everything I can on hallucinations and delusions caused by traumatic brain injuries, and I'm convinced that I'm not suffering from either. I consult my notebook, in which I've jotted down both plausible and not-so-plausible hypotheses and draw a thick black line through "*I could be experiencing an ongoing hallucination.*" I devour a slice of pizza, and then another, tossing the crusts to Benny and contemplating my remaining ideas, which include things as believable as *I have schizophrenia* and *Pain meds overdose,* as well as items like *Something supernatural (?)* and *Ash went through a particle accelerator and is able to come and go with such speed that he's invisible to the human eye.*

After two more hours of deep investigation, I rule out both *Schizophrenia* and *Pain meds overdose.* The latter was kind of a stretch, but a few times over the past couple of weeks, when my head was really bothering me, I did take three Advil instead of the recommended two. As for schizophrenia, there's no history of it in my family, and, on top of that, most schizophrenics don't *know* or even suspect they're schizophrenic before being diagnosed, and I'm very aware of my "delusion." Growing desperate, I google *Particle Accelerator Accidents*, getting no further than the first article before groaning at my own ridiculousness and flopping onto my pile of blankets. Benny jumps up and starts licking my face, covering it in slobber. I'm lying there in defeat as he continues to lick me, when, all of a sudden, something Ash said clicks in my brain.

Maybe you should invest in a search engine. Or an old yearbook.

I sit back up, fresh curiosity blooming. I don't have a yearbook, so I open up a new window and type *Esko High, MN* into the search bar. Within seconds, ten thousand results pop up, but nothing looks conspicuous. I see the Esko Census Bureau Data for 2017, a few football headlines (I get a bad taste in the back of my mouth when I see that most of them feature none other than Greyson Kohl), and a few Facebook menus for restaurants that offer deals to Esko High students if they present their student IDs. I'm about to get discouraged all over again, when something about three quarters of the way down the page catches my eye. The headline reads "Esko High Mourns Tragic Accident and Honors Student at Vigil." I click on the link, wondering if this could be the same story Taylor had told me, and am taken to a newspaper article from the *Esko Evening Times*.

There's a black and white picture of a group of students gathered on the track holding paper lanterns in their hands. Some of them are crying, some look shocked, and some have their heads hung so low I can't make out their faces. I notice Greyson in the front row wearing his blue and yellow letterman jacket, and he's holding hands with a blonde girl who looks like Taylor. Greyson appears to be crying. It's hard to believe someone like him can even produce tears. I spy a small girl in the corner of the picture who looks familiar but unfamiliar at the same time. She's short in stature and has shoulder length black hair. I zoom in to get a better look and realize it's Ingrid, just with different hair. Unlike the rest of the students she isn't crying or standing in disbelief; her brows are furrowed and her lips are pursed into a thin line of anger. I scan all of the faces, wondering if I'll recognize anyone else but after several minutes of squinting at the computer screen, I can't find anyone that looks like Ash. I start to think it's yet another dead end, but then I start to read:

> Esko High students gather at a vigil for deceased classmate Ashley Gable. Gable passed away unexpectedly on Saturday at his home, after a tragic accident.

Ashley…Gable? I think back to a conversation with Taylor on my very first day at Esko High. What had she said? *"the kid–Gable–got really drunk and wandered outside alone, fell in his own pool, and drowned.* Even through my concussion, I remember the words like she spoke them yesterday. I thought that "Gable" was the dead boy's first name, I never even considered that it could be his last. My bottom jaw comes unhinged and sweat begins to pool on my skin. I can hardly believe what I'm reading, but I read on.

The Vigil was organized by Esko High's own Greyson Kohl who, together with girlfriend Taylor Lewis, fundraised for the lanterns and paid to have a new sidewalk square poured at the top of the school hill in Gable's memory. The student body gathered together tonight to remember Gable and mourn together as a community. Gable is survived by his parents, Charles and Lenora Gable, who both currently practice medicine at St. Marcy's. Mr. and Mrs. Gable ask that in lieu of flowers, you send donations in honor of Ashley "Ash" Gable to Doctors without Borders, which you can access at doctorswithoutborders.org.

I read the article again, then again, then again. I feel dizzy, but for once it's not from my head injury. My mind races trying to piece it all together, and everything starts to make so much sense and absolutely no sense at all, simultaneously. I can't bring myself to say the word *dead* aloud or even in my head. He can't be dead. He can't be.

I suddenly remember something else and jump to my feet so quickly that the blood rushes to my head like a building seismic boom. *Not. Now.* I grunt under my breath and bend over, touching my toes until the dizziness evaporates and I can right myself again. As soon as I'm stable, I rush to the fireplace, snatching the little three-legged sculpture off of the mantel. I hold it in my palms like an injured bird, daring myself to look at it, being too afraid to at the same time. Eventually I work up the courage to do what I need to, and, with shaky hands, flip the clay animal sculpture over.

I knew what I was going to find, but it knocks the wind out of me all the same. On the bottom of the sculpture, clear as my memory was before the accident, are the initials *A.G.*

Ashley Gable.

Ash.

My Ash.

I sink into the couch, stifling a pounding knot in my throat as I cradle the porcelain creature between my hands. The story I made up about it–the one I'd told Ash that had made him smile–it all feels so real now. Again, I think of a mother clutching it, wondering where her baby went. I think of her baby; the boy who keeps finding me, somehow, beyond all reason, beyond any explanation, beyond anything and everything I've ever known to be true. The boy who ignites things in me I've never felt before. The boy who used to live–here. In my house. This little sculpture, it *had* belonged to the boy who died. The boy–I've just realized–I'm falling in love with.

*   *   *

The rest of the night is a daze. I have the wherewithal to get rid of my search history on the laptop, but not much else. Once I clean up the living room and let Benny out one last time before bed, I walk upstairs in a trance. I go through the motions of washing up and brushing my teeth, but don't really feel any of it. When I spit, I realize I must've brushed too hard because there's blood in the sink. Blood. Does Ash even have that anymore? A hundred more questions blossom under my skull. Do I have sufficient evidence that Ash is not a hallucination? And if he isn't, is he a ghost?

I can't fathom Ash being anything but alive. When he laughs it echoes in my ears, and when he touches me my whole body responds, right down to my bones. I go through at least four of the seven stages of grief all at once. I cry, I deny, I try to brush it off as impossible, but most of all, I long for him. To reach out and prove again and again that he's real. To comfort him. The sadness I've seen in his eyes makes sense now, and I want nothing more than to ease some of that pain.

Soon enough, though, the longing steps aside and fear sinks in. *What if I never see him again?* I wouldn't believe I could live with that, if I hadn't already made it through the last year without Ollie. Ollie. The thought of him sparks even more questions. Where did Ollie go when *he* died? Is Ollie a ghost, too? Worse yet, can I see Ash because *I'm* dead*?*

"No*,"* I say aloud, and Benny looks at me like I'm crazy for the second time today. I pinch myself and feel it. I pinch myself again and again until my arm is covered in fingernail marks. I stupidly rip out the stitches that have reappeared in my jaw one by one, just to see the new skin, just to *prove* to myself that I am still here. That my body still feels pain and can recover from it. The skin is pink and raw and a little oozy, but close to being healed. There's a ridge in my skin that didn't used to be there, and sigh with relief. Dead skin doesn't scar.

Finally, when I can't take it anymore, I collapse on my bed and cry silently, feeling the tears slowly soak my pillow. Benny crawls under the covers to comfort me, but even he cannot begin to fix this. My head hurts, my tinnitus is back, and I'm more exhausted than I've ever been, but I can't sleep. I toss and turn all night, slipping in and out of dreams about Ash, which always end in him dying and me waking up in a panic. And despite how desperately I yearn for it, good sleep never finds me.

Chapter 25

I live in bed for the next couple of days—I'm not even sure how many. Though I'm more anxious and distraught than ever, it's my physical health that ends up keeping me bedridden. I've been staying up all hours of the night hoping to hear Ash calling to me again from below my window, but night after night it's just coy dogs and wind. Every single minute of every single day I keep hoping he will appear, but he never does.

The sleep deprivation combined with the extended computer time I had the other night has my brain feeling fried, and I don't just mean exhausted. I mean it feels like I've been through electroshock therapy. I guess I look pretty bad too, because Mom takes the day off from work to stay home and take care of me. The ringing in my ears is unbearable, and I can hardly speak in coherent sentences without wearing myself out. I complain of headaches night and day and Mom somehow convinces me to take the codeine, which sends me into a deep, medicated sleep for the rest of the week and most of the weekend.

When I come out of it on Sunday morning, I feel a bit better. My migraine is finally gone, I can hear clearly, and the only lights I see are the two that are screwed into my ceiling fan. When Mom comes up to bring me vegetable soup around lunchtime, she tells me I'm looking halfway decent for the first time in almost a month. I don't have the energy to be offended, so I thank her and ask her to bring me three pieces of toast, too.

"An appetite? This is a nice surprise." She smiles and I smile back, doing my best to hide the turmoil within, even if my physical body is feeling better.

"I'm ravenous," I say, and it's the truth. I've spent so much time sleeping over the past few days that I haven't eaten more than a few bites here and there. Mom tells me I must have lost ten pounds, but I couldn't care less. All I want is for my brain to be back in working order, and to see Ash again—and not necessarily in that order. I'm determined to make both things happen as quickly as possible. Mom touches my chin and tells me she'll be right back with my toast, but I stop her before she goes.

"Hey, Mom?"

She halts in the doorway, turns to look at me, and I put on the sweetest face I can muster because I know this is going to be a big ask.

"Do you think I could go to school tomorrow?"

She raises an eyebrow and it shoots like a mountain into the sky of her forehead.

"*Please?*"

"I'll tell you what, how about I take you in around eleven? You can do half a day and see how things go. But you can only go to two classes and you absolutely cannot have—"

"Any screens—I know Mom." And I do. Staring at the computer all night really did a number on me, and I don't intend to make that mistake again if I can help it.

"Thank you!" I jump up from my reclined position and give her a giant hug, nearly knocking her off of her feet.

"Well I guess you *are* feeling better!" she says cheerfully, kissing my forehead. "Now don't screw it up. Get back in bed before I change my mind."

I blow her kisses from my bed.

"Yeah, yeah." She says, rolling her eyes through a smile. Mom leaves to go put some bread in the toaster and I lay down on my back, staring up at the ceiling. So much is swirling around inside of me, but all I can think about is learning more about Ash. I only hope that going back to school will lead me in the right direction.

Chapter 26

I make it to school in time for lunch the next day, but I'm much too strung out to eat. I sign in at the front desk, handing the secretary a note stating I'm still medically excused from Gym, Programming, and two other periods a day and head straight to the cafeteria. I see Ingrid sitting in our usual spot and I go over to join her. She's reading a graphic novel today, but when I plop down across from her, she looks up at me and gives a little wave. I'm not sure, but I think in Ingrid-speak that means *I'm glad you're back*. My first order of business is to figure out a way to communicate with her.

"Hey," I say, returning the wave, hoping she'll say something back and make things simpler. I have no such luck, though, and before Ingrid can dive back into her book I ask, "Can we talk?"

She slides a bookmark into her novel and puts it down, nodding her head up and down. She might not be able to speak, but as long as I stick to questions with "yes" or "no" answers, there's no reason we can't communicate.

"I'm sorry I've been out," I say, and she shakes her hand as if to say *no big deal.* "I was afraid Greyson might be giving you a hard time. And I wanted to be here. I've just been dealing with–some stuff."

She points to my head and gives me a look that says, "*Obviously.*"

"Right," I say, "not just that, though. Anyway, I wanted to ask you a question."

Ingrid clasps her hands in front of her like a diligent student, which to me says *ask away.*

"Do you–did you, I mean, by any chance know the family who used to live in my house?"

She nods her head. At first, I think she's nodding "yes," but it finishes looking like a "no."

"Did you know the boy in the family? He went to school here, would've been a year above us in school?"

She nods her head, more resolutely this time. *Yes.*

Okay, now we're getting somewhere. I consider where I want to take this conversation. It's not as if I can say "*Well, I've been seeing him, and I was wondering if you could tell me a little more about him and the manner in which he died. Also, if you can think of any reason why he may not have fully passed over, that would be great, too.*" I would sound like a raving lunatic.

"Was he…nice?"

That was a lame question, but she nods her head. *Yes.*

"Okay, how do I say this. I know this probably seems weird being that I didn't know him," I stumble over the words, almost saying 'when he was alive' but have the sense to stop myself before I do. "I saw this article and I just got to thinking about the house and the family that lived there before we did–general curiosity I guess."

I'm trying to sound nonchalant, but I'm rambling hard and I know it. Ingrid reaches out to touch my hand and I let her. Her touch has a calming sensation, and I get a wave of appreciation for her. Ingrid may not communicate in the same way most people do, but she is incredibly perceptive.

"Thanks," I say, earnestly. "It's weird knowing I'm sleeping in the same house where Ash died." I bite my tongue, realizing I shouldn't have said his name so callously, as if I knew him.

She cocks a curious brow.

"I read the *Evening Times* article online."

She nods her head and bites her left cheek, as if chewing at some hidden pain.

"I'm sorry," I say. "If this is too much to talk about–"

She shakes her head quickly, indicating that it isn't. She wants to talk.

"I guess what I want to know is, do you know *how* he died? I mean, I know they say he drowned, and the filled-in pool in my backyard is evidence enough that something went awry, but how does an athletic, seventeen-year-old with *doctors* for parents drown in his own pool? I don't get it."

She looks as if she can see right through me, and I have the ridiculous notion that she knows why I'm asking her all of this even though that's impossible. Ingrid rips a corner of scrap paper out of a binder, scribbles something on it, then passes it across the table to me. However, just as I'm about to take the note, it's intercepted by an uninvited hand.

"Passing love notes, now?" Greyson asks, looking from Ingrid's face, which is shooting him daggers, to mine. He seems to come out of nowhere, but not in a good way like Ash does. Ash is an unexpected summer shower; Greyson, a storm.

"Rafa, if you were into girls all this time, you could have just told me, and I would've backed off."

I roll my eyes. I am less intimidated when I'm not alone with him.

"Get *over* yourself, Greyson. Can I have that back, please?" I hold out my palm expectantly and he holds the note into the air, raising his eyebrows if to say *come and get it*. After reading about how he organized the vigil for Ash and paid for the memorial I was starting to think he had a heart underneath all of that ego, but now I'm second guessing.

"You know, anything *she* has to say isn't going to be good," he whispers to me, throwing a nod in Ingrid's direction as if she isn't there. He then points to his head and makes little circles in the air with his index finger. "Cuckoo, that one."

"Greyson," I say, sternly, his offensive antics not worth a response. "The note, *please.*"

He looks from me to Ingrid and back again, clearly getting the hint that I'm not going to side with him in whatever came between them. He places the note into my palm, and before he can even let go, I snatch it.

"*Thank you*," I say, squinting my eyes in mock politeness.

He looks at Ingrid one more time, then says "Later, Rafa," and lopes back to Teo and the rest of the football team. I don't know what kind of insect repellent Ingrid uses on him, but whatever it is, I want some.

"You're like garlic to a vampire when it comes to him." I say in awe, but when I study Ingrid, I realize now isn't the time for jokes. Her tough, tree bark exterior dissolved as soon as Greyson walked away. She suddenly looks small, smaller than usual, and uncertain. Her eyes are dilated in the brassy cafeteria light, her hands are gripping the booth so tightly that her knuckles are losing their color, and she's shaking uncontrollably.

"What's the matter?" I ask. "What is it?"

Ingrid doesn't respond, but turns her attention to the note, using it as an effective distraction from my question. She silently urges me to open the note, and I obey.

> Can't talk like this. not safe. add me on snap and we can talk there: Ingrid_shh

I absorb her words, and nod my head indicating I'll add her. Then, she slides another bit of paper across the table.

Are you sure you want to know the truth?

My heart sinks right into my toes because I know whatever it is, it isn't going to be good. I nod my head again. Even though it's bound to hurt, I don't think I've ever wanted to know the truth about something so badly before in my life.

Chapter 27

When I get home from school, I race upstairs to my room. I tell Mom I'm exhausted from school and that I need a nap, and she doesn't question it. For once, this concussion is coming in handy.

I close the door and turn off the bedroom lights to make the ruse convincing, settling into my bed and pulling the covers up to my neck. My body teems with anticipation as I open Snapchat on my phone and fiddle with it for a minute. It's been so long since I've used it that I need to reacquaint. Ollie and I used to play around with it when he was stuck in the hospital for treatments. He would send me selfies with goofy filters, and I would send them right back. I have a bunch of screenshots saved in the archives of my phone (Ollie with reindeer ears, Ollie's head with Benny's face, Ollie's eyes sitting atop his head like an alien) that are still too painful to flip through.

I type "Ingrid_shh" into the search-for-friends bar. Up pops an avatar with pale skin, large, almond shaped eyes, and a pastel pink pixie cut–definitely Ingrid. I wonder if she dyed her hair again or if her Bitmoji can't keep up. I tap "add," and wait for a response.

While I'm waiting, a few suggestions pop up under "people I may know." One of them is thick-skulled, with a dark brown crew cut, and a blue and yellow jacket. His icon is pumping a fist in the air and I recognize who it is right away—the resemblance to Greyson is uncanny. I see Taylor too, as well as the pimply boy in my History class and a few other kids I recognize. I hover over Greyson's name and block him, just to be safe. Seeing his face, cartoon or not, doesn't bring me any joy, and there's no need for him to take up more space in my life than is absolutely necessary.

While I'm waiting for Ingrid to answer, I change into my pajamas. I wiggle out of my leggings and pull my sweatshirt over my head, catching a peek at myself in the mirror. I stop and study myself, really noticing me for the first time in a long time.

I'm more slender than usual; I have lost weight. Though I don't have much going on in the chest region, I do have a butt. I don't carry much fat on my body—Mom would tell me to *enjoy my metabolism while it lasts*. I study myself for a while because, truthfully, I've never done it, and secretly I wonder if Ash thinks I'm attractive. I never put much stock in what other people thought of me – aesthetically, anyway– but now I find myself wondering what he sees when he sees me.

I inspect my nearly naked body from every angle, deciding I'm almost pretty, and I can settle for that. I feel a draft sweep against the backs of my legs and get the sudden feeling that someone is watching me. I whip around, quickly scanning the room. Despite how ridiculous it is, I open my closet and look under the bed double checking that I'm alone. I think for a moment it might be—but it's nothing.

A few minutes later Ingrid sends me a wave. I wave back. As much as I'm focused on finding out everything I can about Ash, it's also fun to have a real friend. I type out a message and tap the little blue arrow to send it off into handheld cyberspace.

> **Me:** I know this might make me sound like a loser, but I'm really glad we're friends.

> **Ingrid:** Not a loser. I'm glad to have a friend too:)

I send a smiling emoji back.

> **Ingrid:** So what do you want to know?

My insides flutter a little. I want to know *everything*, but I don't want to be so eager that my ulterior motives leak through in the subtext.

> **Me:** Why isn't it safe to talk in school?

A thought bubble pops up. I'm grateful she responds so quickly we can talk at an almost normal conversational pace. I'm also grateful that now I can talk to her, period.

> **Ingrid:** People

Hmm. Cryptic, but leading.

> **Me:** What people?

Ingrid: Well, Greyson, for one. And his girlfriend.

Me: Taylor?

Ingrid: Yeah.

Me: I don't think they're together.

Ingrid: Who can keep up with those two?

Me: I think Greyson is stringing her along.

Ingrid: Of course he is. That's what he does.

Although I can't entirely decode her tone in digital form, she seems to know more than she's letting on. I decide to leave it, not wanting to be brazenly nosy.

Me: You seem to really hate him.

Ingrid: I do.

Me: He seems afraid of you. It's impressive actually. I'm kinda envious

Ingrid: Don't be. and he should be

Me: ...?

Ingrid: I know some things about him. Let's just say it would kill his football career if anything came out. He's a bad guy. Your instincts are right about him.

My instincts? I've never thought of myself as someone who has good instincts, or instincts at all for that matter, but now that I think of it, maybe I do. I knew Greyson was bad news from the first class we had together, and Ingrid was the first Esko High student I gravitated towards even though I knew absolutely nothing about her. It makes me wonder if my instincts might be right about Ash. That there's so much more to the story. I'm about to ask what Greyson did that was so bad, but Ingrid shoots me another message before I can type the words.

> **Ingrid:** So why the curiosity about Ash earlier?
>
> **Me:** I live in his house, idk, I just want to know more about what happened here.
>
> **Ingrid:** Seeing ghosts? :P

I nearly choke on my own saliva and stifle a cough. I type "you could say that" and hope she doesn't take me seriously.

> **Ingrid:** Ash was one of the good ones. Unlike Greyson. He always stuck up for the underdog, ya know? Never let kids feel hurt or excluded or picked on.
>
> **Me, smiling:** That doesn't surprise me.
>
> **Ingrid:** You talk like you know him.

Shoot. I need to be more careful of the words that slip out of my mouth. Or, in this case, through my fingers.

> **Me:** I just read a lot about him. I have had a lot of time on my hands
>
> **Me:** You guys were friends?

Ingrid: You could say that.

My heart catches. Were they something more? Does it matter? Why is there a jealous green lump forming in my stomach? I don't want to ask, but I can't help myself.

Me: Were you guys...involved?

Ingrid: Oh, no not like that. I consider him to be one of the greatest friends I ever had, but we weren't really friends while he was alive.

My throat catches again. *While he was alive?*

Ingrid: Not until the end, I mean. He did something for me. Something most people, even good people, wouldn't have done. I don't think.

Me: What did he do?

My curiosity is inflating, I'm a balloon ready to burst.

Ingrid: I don't like to talk about it, I'm sorry. Maybe someday, but not right now, okay?

The balloon stops blowing up but does not pop. Even though I'm dying to know more, I have to respect her boundaries.

Me: So Ash...drowned?

Ingrid: Yeah

Me: How?

Ingrid: How anyone drowns I suppose.

Me: I know, but I mean what were the circumstances? Did he hit his head or something? Were his parents not home? I read through the obituary but there were no details. It just seems strange.

Ingrid: Idk

Me: You must know more than I do!

Ingrid: It just happened, okay? People drown all the time, just leave it alone.

I pull back, set my phone down for a minute, and then reread the conversation. What did I say to make her snap at me? Did I ask too many questions? Have I been selfish? I feel a pang of guilt, though I'm not sure what for.

Me: I'm sorry, I didn't mean to pry.

Me: We don't have to talk about this anymore.

Me: Ingrid?

She doesn't answer. I seem to be developing a talent for making people disappear.

Chapter 28

I close the door behind me and slip out into the night like a wraith.

This time it's much colder and I have to wear layers, even if they make me look bulky and shapeless. I have to take a flashlight with me too, because, unlike the last time I snuck out, the moon and stars are hidden behind a blanket of clouds and the air is thick, dark black.

Now that the cuts and bruises on my face are healing and my arm doesn't hurt so much, I'm not as worried about being alone outside in the dark. Though technically I haven't been cleared and declared concussion free, the past few days my mind has felt clear as it ever has. No tinnitus, no sparkly lights in my vision. Sure, I still have headaches, but that's to be expected.

I don't use my flashlight until I'm well into the woods. If Mom woke up to go to the bathroom and happened to glance out the window, a moving light in the backyard would definitely arise suspicion. I walk down the path, which is familiar to me now, and surprise myself with my own daring. I'm not afraid of the dark or the hoots of hunting owls, and my neck doesn't prickle when I hear a coyote howling in the distance. The old Rafa would've had an anxiety attack as soon as she entered these woods, but this Rafa is courageous. Courageous or just plain stupid, it's difficult to say. All I know is I can't think of anything except the possibility of seeing Ash again, and if he isn't coming to me then I have to go to him.

I pass the giant spruce tree in the middle of the path and jump behind it when I hear the thumps and snorts of something close by, but when three bobbing white tails vanish into the night, I realize all I'd done was spook a few sleeping deer. I continue walking at a brisk pace and finally arrive at the clearing, which is illuminated despite the sky being coated with clouds. As I walk into the center, I close my eyes, willing him to appear, praying to whoever is listening that he will be here when I open them again. My breath is like smoke in the cold air, draping me in a cloak of silver, and I allow myself to submerge completely into the night.

Like magic, when my eyelids drift upwards, there he is on the other side of the clearing. I used to imagine that his house was through the woods, and that this was somewhere he came to think, but now I know differently. He wasn't lying when he said that he lived past the evergreens– I just didn't realize it was the same house that I now call home.

"Hey, Rafaela."

He calls to me softly, using my full name. My heart does somersaults below my ribcage.

I run to him, unable to hold back. And why should I? I never know how much time I'll have with him. My body collides with his and I'm sent spiraling back to the realm of disbelief. His chest is as solid as a stone wall, his skin soft as velvet. How can someone that's dead feel so– human?

Ash hugs me and I cling to him, breathing him in, soaking up his scent–sweet peppermint and pine, always. I reach up and touch his face and he touches me back with warm hands. Too warm to be bloodless. Too warm to be unalive. I slip my thumb under his jawbone, into the soft flesh of his neck, and feel the steady thump, thump, thump of a pulse coursing through his arteries.

"What are you doing?" he asks, smiling at me. I thought I was being stealthy, but not stealthy.

"It can't be," I stammer. "You can't be…"

He looks at me expectantly, like Benny sometimes does when I'm eating. But, unlike Benny, Ash isn't looking for food, he's looking for me to say something I'm not sure I can.

"You can't be…" I trail off again, the words escaping me. My hand is still on his cheek, which is rough with an even stubble. Strange, I remember it as being smooth. I make a mental note to google if hair still grows after you die.

"Dead?"

He finishes the sentence for me, and I look at him with heavy eyes.

"Dead," I confirm.

He shifts his hands to my hips where his fingers find a little strip of skin between my night shirt and sweats. I feel a warm ache spread through my body, like honey swirling through hot tea. My hips gravitate towards his in response, as if we're opposite poles of two magnets; as if the magnets are deep in our bellies.

"I'm sorry, Rafa," he says. "I tried to tell you, but you had to find out for yourself. There are some things I'm just not allowed to say."

My head is spinning and my heart is tripping and I can't decide if I want to ask him the thousands of questions I'm holding back or just kiss him, but before I can choose Ash takes my hand and leads me to a fallen tree where we sit close enough to feel each other's breath. He looks incredibly sad, and hopeless.

"So you found a search engine, I take it?"

I nod my head, trying to figure out what to say. What do you say to someone who died almost a year ago?

"Are you a dream?" I ask, still not entirely convinced that I'm not making him up, that he isn't a sweet delusion of my subconscious.

"Sometimes I feel like I am. Like I'm stuck in someone else's dream and can't get them to wake up. Sometimes I scream and shout and pound my fists on anything within reach until my knuckles bleed, but I feel no pain. It sounds like a dream, doesn't it? Or a nightmare. But no, I'm not a dream. I'm real. Or, as real as you can be when you're half dead."

"So, are you a ghost?" I feel stupid for even asking, but this is new territory for me.

"I'm not sure–that's what I've been trying to figure out. I always imagined ghosts to be more, I don't know, transparent? Floaty? But I can't float and I'm as solid as you are. Sometimes, anyway."

"Where do you go when you're gone?"

My chin is trembling now, threatening to quake my face and unleash a barrage of tears so I keep asking questions to distract myself. Ash takes my hand and weaves his fingers through mine. They feel sturdy, soft and alive.

"I don't know," he says. "That's the confusing part. And d'you want to know something even crazier?"

I nod.

"I lost eleven months of my life. Or, is it death? Whatever, you know what I mean. I remember absolutely nothing from the day I died until..." he trails off.

"Until what?" I ask.

"Until I found your dog. Until I found *you.*"

I squeeze his hand tightly, daring the universe to try and take him from me this time.

"I woke up in the woods. At first I thought I was in the hospital, but then I realized I was standing, and the bright lights were the sky, and I was surrounded by trees. I tried to piece together how I got there. I remembered the party, and the pool, and I remembered the pain."

I squeeze tighter.

"The pain in my lungs. I started to panic, but realized I was breathing and absolutely nothing hurt. In fact, my body felt good. So clean. So healthy. I thought maybe I was dead. Thought maybe I was in heaven. I have to admit I was a little disappointed, because I'd always imagined my heaven to be by the ocean. I became convinced that I was dead, had decided that was the only option, but then I saw your dog. I thought it strange that a leashed dog would be running around in the afterlife. And he looked so real. So I called to him, and he came to me, and he felt so solid. *Really* solid. What do you feed him, by the way?"

I laugh, trying to soak up everything he's saying, but I can feel it all trickling out of me like water through cupped hands. I'm hearing him, but I'm feeling him too. And the words he's saying do not align with his solid hand holding mine.

"He came right over to me, wagging his tail. And I thought to myself, well, if this is heaven, at least I have a dog. But then I thought, why would God or Allah or Elvis or whoever is up there send me *someone else's* dog? Because I had a dog, too, when I was little. So where was *my* dog? And then I thought I might be going mad, but I took hold of the dog's leash and he started dragging me through the woods. He dragged me right past the giant spruce and I realized where I was. I *wasn't* dead; I was home! So I thought I must have fallen asleep in the woods or something. That's what I told myself, anyway. That it was all a dream. And then I found you, and you told me where you lived, and I half thought to tell you *you* were bonkers and that you couldn't live in that house because *I* lived in that house...but I didn't, of course. I went right back to thinking I was dead again. I had this...feeling. I don't know. I didn't think I would even be able to touch you, which is why I told you I was sick with a cold and couldn't shake your hand. But I wanted to touch you, feel you, be close to another person. Not in a creepy way, or anything crass—I just hadn't felt human touch in so long."

I rest my other hand on his leg, another bold move the old Rafa would've never attempted. My hand moves up, slowly, cautiously, finding the hem of his shirt, lifting is up just enough, touching the skin where the bruise is, or should be. I pause there, letting my hand tell him that it's going to be okay, concentrating all of my energy on taking away his pain, physical and otherwise.

"I wish I could make the bruises stay away forever for you."

"Nobody can fix that." He says, "But you fix pretty much everything else, just by existing."

I smooth my hand over his skin, letting the shirt fall back down and find his bare arm, every inch of him more alive than the last. I'd imagined what it would feel like to touch him a thousand times, but the reality is so much better than anything my imagination could conjure. He leans in close, angling his body toward mine. In a sort of unspoken ritual, I let him find the skin below my shirt, which prickles with magnetic goosebumps at his touch. He doesn't go any further, but his fingers rest on my bare skin and I don't ever want them to leave.

As if by instinct, I angle into him too. I lower his shirt and let my hand move up his body, from his bruised abdomen to his neck. The skin is soft there, like the new skin under my staples. My breath catches in my throat as his fingers glide over one of my collar bones. It's as if I'm a spool of thread, but I'm not coming undone, I'm being rolled up into him.

Finally, he places his hand on my cheek and turns my face toward his, our lips just inches apart now. The last time this happened, the moment was taken from us, but this time it's different. I can feel it, and I'm not afraid. He leans in slightly and I follow his lead. The air is stolen from my lungs as his lips finally collide with mine, gently but not without intent. His kiss is warm and visceral and my entire body sighs with joy and relief, as if for one moment every little thing in this world makes sense. It's like I'm dying and coming back to life all at once. This– *this* is what oblivion feels like. I press my lips into his again, harder this time. I want to absorb him slowly; I want to make sure he sticks. He wraps his arms around me and this time I think he's the one daring the universe to try and keep us apart.

When we pull apart my cheeks are flushed, and my skin is so hot I can feel it melting the frost around me.

"How's that for human touch?" I ask, breathless.

"Incredible. Perfect, even," he says, smiling. "And I never, ever want to lose it."

"You won't," I say, wanting it to be true.

"But I will," he says, his mood doing a one-eighty. "I'll keep disappearing. Again, and again and again. And you'll get tired of waiting for me, tired of me not being there, tired of me only existing to you."

"No!" I exclaim with desperation. Can't he see how he makes me feel? Can't he tell I would wait for him forever if I had to?

Ash pulls away from me; just a little, but it hurts nonetheless. I've been thrown from life-altering bliss back into uncertainty, and I can't keep up.

"Rafa, I don't know what to do." He chokes up again, just a little, and a knot tugs at my throat begging me to join him but I can't. I can't cry right now. I have to be strong. For him. No matter how much I'm hurting, he must be hurting more.

"Tell me," I say. "Tell me everything. Maybe we can figure this out. Maybe you're in a coma somewhere or something. I saw a movie like that once, where the main character was a ghost, but his body was alive somewhere."

I don't know why, but for a second that idea seems so radically genius I believe it.

"I'm not," he says. "You read the obits. They don't write obituaries for the comatose."

"Well there has to be some explanation," I say desperately. "There has to be something we can do. What if I stay with you? Will that make you stay?"

"I don't think so. It doesn't always work like that. There have been a few times where I've…"

He pauses, looking a little embarrassed.

"Where you've what?"

"Where I've tried to find you, but you can't see me." He looks away. "It's like you're right in front of me, but I'm just a wisp of invisible smoke. Like you're rooted to the present, and I'm timeless, floating around behind this stupid, sticky veil, unable to touch you without floating right through your skin."

I shiver at the thought of him wading through me, like legs into a lake in summertime. Even though it breaks my heart to think of him like that, here but not, it comforts me knowing that he's with me even when I cannot see him. Then I remember.

"Last night!" I exclaim. "You were in my room last night, weren't you? I knew it. I *knew* I felt something."

He nods his head, and I can feel the space between us grow smaller again.

"How did you know? How did you…I couldn't reach you."

"I can't explain it. I just *felt* something. I thought my head was playing tricks on me, but now I know it was you. I'm sure of it."

I think for a second about that moment, and blush.

"Were you watching me *change?*"

His tan cheeks redden a little, a mischievous smile tugging at the corners of his lips

"I looked away," he says, crossing his heart. "I promise."

I'm half relieved, half disappointed. If he *had* looked, would he have liked what he'd seen?

"But I wanted to. You have *no* idea."

The disappointment is replaced by a surge of self-assurance.

"Well, maybe next time you shouldn't look away," I say under my breath. He kisses my forehead in response and puts his arm around me, and for a moment it feels so natural. Like we're just two kids at a drive-in movie, staying out past curfew, the time we spend together worth a good grounding. But then reality flicks me in the back of my head and I know that I have to keep asking questions. I *have* to know.

"What do you remember?" I ask "From before you–"

"Died?"

"Yeah. Sorry, it's still hard for me to say."

"Try being me." He laughs.

"I remember a party. *I* was throwing the party, for God's sake. Everyone was there. Greyson, Taylor, even Ingrid came. I remember her so vividly for some reason, but I can't figure out why. I remember broken images, like pieces of a puzzle I can't quite put together, or jumbled shapes in a kaleidoscope."

"And what else do you remember? Did you get really drunk? Did you drink too much and fall in the pool?"

He looks pensive and ponders that for a long time before answering.

"No," Ash says softly. "No, I wasn't drinking at all. I'm sure of it. My parents were out of town, and I wanted to make sure no one messed up the house or got behind the wheel drunk. I remember now, clearer than when I tried to think on my own. Someone offered me a beer but I didn't drink it."

"Then it just doesn't make sense," I say. "It doesn't make sense for you to drown. I mean, there were lots of people there, right?"

"Yeah," he confirms. "Yeah, I guess so. But nobody would've been outside; it was November. The pool wasn't frozen, but it was still way too cold to be outside. No one was out there, I'm sure of it."

"Then why were you?" I ask, feeling like we're finally getting somewhere.

"I don't know." He's looking more confused by the second. I know what it's like to lose chunks of time, but I only lost little bits here and there. He lost almost *eleven months*.

"Rafa?"

"Yeah?"

"I think something bad happened to me."

I feel a shooting pain through my chest at just the thought of something hurting him.

"I don't know how I know," Ash continues cautiously, "but I think–I think I have to figure out what happened to me. Maybe that's why the universe won't let me pass over. Maybe that's why I'm stuck."

"I can help," I say, biting my lip, praying he won't cross over to a place I cannot follow. "I can help you."

"No," he says. "It isn't your responsibility."

"Don't be so noble. I want to help you."

He shakes his head in despair, but I force him to look at me, daring him to tell me otherwise.

"I think it might not be pretty," he says, still resisting.

"I think I might not care."

I refuse to believe he's dead. I can see him, I can feel him, I can taste him when we kiss. I can smell the peppermint on my skin when we're apart and I wear the bracelet he made for me on my wrist. I don't know what he is, but he isn't dead. And somehow, I'm going to get him back.

"I'm afraid," Ash admits, his shoulders slumping.

"Of what you might find?"

"Yes. And–afraid of losing you."

I place his hand on my heart and put mine on his. Our chests rise and fall together, our hearts beating to the same rhythm.

"You're not going to." I say. We just have to figure out what happened to you. You're here for a reason, can't you feel it?"

I don't know why I think I have any idea what I'm talking about, but once you've been forced to discard all laws of physics, you start to realize that maybe the universe isn't as black and white as it may seem. That maybe, just maybe, some laws are meant to be broken.

"You're not dead. I can feel it."

Ash leans in again and we kiss each other until our bodies and our breath and the sky dissolve like watercolors into the ether of this beautiful night.

Chapter 29

"Rafa. *Rafa!*"

I can feel Mom shaking me awake, but I roll over and push her back out of my cozy bubble of sleep.

"Rafaela, you have to get up. *Now.*"

Mom's voice is deep. *Too* deep. I open my eyes and see a dazzlingly handsome boy, and my mind is rushed with memories of his lips on mine from the night before.

"C'mon, you have to get up," Ash says, shaking me again. He's tense, clearly not in the same place I am upon waking up.

"I like when you say my full name."

"Well I can say it more later, if you're still alive, but I don't know if I'll get the chance because I'm pretty sure your mom is going to *kill* you."

I sit up, suddenly realizing the sun is resting well above the horizon. This can't be right. The sun is up and I'm in the woods. In the woods, or *still* in the woods? *Oh God. Did I fall asleep here?*

"Shit, this is NOT good. This is not good," I say, gathering up my sweatshirt and flashlight off the ground where we must have fallen asleep. "Why didn't you wake me sooner?"

"I tried to," Ash says, "but after you fell asleep, I went beyond the veil again. You couldn't feel me. When I tried to touch you, I went right through you. I've been trying to wake you for hours and just now got through."

I'm too frazzled to process what he's saying. I take his face in my hands.

"I have to go," I say. "Please, *please* come find me tonight."

"I'll try," he says, eyes ridden with guilt. "I tried to wake you; I swear I did."

"I know, it will be okay, I promise," I say, even though I'm not sure it's true. I'm surprised I don't hear helicopters circling overhead. "It will be okay, but right now I have to *go*."

I kiss him and soak up as much of him as I can, pausing there for a moment even though I have no moments to spare. Then, I turn around and run.

I make it to the edge of the wood, still unsure of what angle I'm going to use to get myself out of this mess. I've gotten pretty good at telling little white lies, but I have absolutely no idea how to crawl out of the hole I've dug myself this morning. To make matters worse, I was only half wrong about the helicopters. Mom might not have sent the coast guard out looking for me, but there are two police cars in my driveway with their blue and red lights flashing angrily against the mid-morning air. I feel a rush of adrenaline and my heart is pounding out of my chest. It's going to burst this time, I know it.

I stumble through the front door, somehow swallowing the panic attack that's attempting to explode from my insides. Let Mom be angry with me for running, I'm sure it will pale in comparison to disappearing in the middle of the night. There are two state troopers in grey uniforms blocking the doorway, and I practically run right through them.

I half expect Mom to start yelling as soon as she sees me, but instead she falls into my arms, sobbing. The police officers look from her and then to me.

"I take it this is your daughter?" one of them asks, a white woman with a pinched face that appears to have never felt joy.

"Yes," Mom says, collecting herself. "Yes, thank you so much for your help."

The other officer, a tall, dark-skinned man rolls his eyes at the woman and they share an exasperated sigh. One of them mumbles something about *taxpayer dollars* and *teenagers,* which is brazen of them given they know nothing about my situation.

The woman snaps her notepad shut and tucks it back into her pocket, and the two of them show themselves out the door. Their cars have hardly left the driveway when I can feel Mom's head growing hot, and I know Vesuvius is about to erupt right here in the entryway.

"Where. Were. You."

She says it quietly, like a distance squall, and it terrifies me even more than if she were to yell.

"I...I..." I stammer. I didn't get a chance to invent a lie, so I blurt out the first thing that comes into my head. "I couldn't sleep, so I went for a walk. In the woods."

"You couldn't sleep, so you went for a *walk*?" she asks, her voice starting to rise.

I nod my head furiously, thinking if I nod it hard enough, she will have to believe me.

"Have you ever heard of turning on the TV? Or having a cup of tea? Or, I don't know, READING A BOOK?" Her voice crescendos and white-hot tears burn my eyes. I blink, trying to contain them, not wanting to add shame to my list of current emotions.

"Mom," I squeak. "I'm sorry. I really am. I went for a walk and I...I fell asleep."

"You went for a walk...in the middle of the night...and fell asleep.... outside?!"

I really wish she would stop repeating everything I say. I nod my head, not giving her anything more to work with.

"Haven't you put me through enough, Rafaela Torres? I know this is hard for you to believe, but all of this—the move, this house, losing Ollie, *losing your father*—is hard for me too. You might not believe this either, but I am a human. Not a robot, not an android, but an actual *human being* with *feelings*. Do you know what it's like, going to check on your sick daughter to find that she is *gone?*"

The welling tears have officially begun to spill over.

"I'm not sick, okay?!" I yell, despising her for treating me like an invalid. Despising myself for getting caught.

"YOU HAVE A TRAUMATIC BRAIN INJURY." She's shouting now, and I wish more than anything that I could just disappear, like Ash. *With* Ash.

"I'M FINE!" I yell. I never yell at her, but I feel like an injured wolf trapped in a corner, thrashing around, trying to escape with no real strategy other than to bare my gnashing teeth.

"You most certainly are not fine. Do you understand what a TBI is? Do you understand that people *die* from them!?"

"My head doesn't even hurt anymore!" I fire back. "I feel fine. I just wanted to go for a walk. I feel so *trapped* here. I can't do *anything*. It's no wonder I feel like I have to escape sometimes."

I meant for that last one to burn, and it did. She recoils, and though I'm not proud of hurting her I'm glad she stops scolding me for a second and a half. I take my story in a different direction, hoping to garner sympathy instead of anger.

"I made a friend, okay?" I say, lowering my voice. It's not a complete lie, I *have* made a friend. "I knew you wouldn't let me hang out with...erm...her, and I felt cooped up, and we just went for a walk in the woods. We were just talking. We laid down on a blanket and fell asleep. I know it was wrong, but it was completely harmless."

"You made a friend?" she asks, a slight lift in her tone. I can tell part of her is relieved underneath all the anger and hurt.

"Yeah, I did," I say, and wanting to make it all the more real, I show her the beaded bracelet Ash made me. She doesn't have to know it's from him.

"Her name's Ingrid. She made this for me."

Mom stares at my wrist, incredulously. I finger the turquoise beads delicately, and they catch the sun like prisms in the morning light.

"Rafa, what are you doing?" she asks, now more concerned than angry.

"What do you mean?" I ask. "I just wanted to show you what Ingrid made me."

"Rafa..." she trails off, still looking at me as though I've lost an arm. "There's nothing there but your arm."

I look down at the bracelet, which most definitely is there. I can see it and feel it, rough between my fingers; I haven't taken it off since Ash gave it to me.

"Mom," I say, frustrated. She must be working too much because she's losing it. "Right here, look."

I hold my left wrist right up to her face but she's making a semi-horrified expression, so I take the bracelet off and put it in her hand. I close her fingers around the beads.

"It's just a friendship bracelet, relax."

Mom opens up her hand and drops the bracelet on the floor, then shows me her palm.

"Rafa. There is nothing here. There is no bracelet."

"Well yeah, not anymore because you *dropped* it."

I bend over and pick the bracelet up, putting it back on my wrist. Mom puts her hands on both of my shoulders and squints her eyes, and I wonder if she is peering through my lies.

"What?"

"Your pupils– they're ultra-dilated."

Not this again.

"Can you *not* be a nurse for a second? Can you just be *my mom?*"

I shake her off and nearly lose my balance in the process.

"Sorry Charlie, not this time. Let's go. We're going to see Dr. Sepir."

"*Ugh, Mo-om.* This is so ridiculous. My eyes probably just haven't adjusted to the light."

"I don't want to hear it, get in the car."

"Mom, I'm–."

"You. Car. Now. And don't even think you have a leg to stand on after what you pulled last night.

She grabs her purse and kneads her forehead, waiting for me to move but I stand my ground.

"I'm not going. I'm–I keep telling you–fine."

But even as I say this, I know that she's right. The lights grow brighter and brighter, and my legs begin to wobble as if they're made of thick pudding. She puts an arm around my waist to steady me, and I let her.

"Maybe you're right." I admit, leaning into her apologetically as my ears begin to ring.

"Maybe?" She quips, but suddenly I'm too weak to joke with her. I walk to the car with my hand to my head, fighting a headache threatening to split my skull in half.

"I don't feel so good."

I crawl into the car, and even though the hospital is only a few miles across town, I fall asleep in the backseat.

Chapter 30

I'm in an empty pool, floating on air. The water that isn't beneath me feels cool against my skin, and I'm wearing the pink and white striped bikini I got for a class trip I never went on. The anxiety that had once prevented me from wearing it is nowhere to be found. I flip over onto my stomach and swim through the air to the other end of the pool, where Ash is standing. He's wearing swim trunks. I touch his skin which, despite the lack of water, is wet. He takes my hand and holds it up to his neck where, just like before, I feel a pulse.

His eyes roam my body, my face turning the color of my swimsuit.

"You're beautiful," Ash says, tenderly, his hand drifting to my waist. It fits so perfectly that I have to wonder if we aren't two pieces of a jigsaw puzzle designed by the gods themselves.

"So are you," I say. I blink a few times, trying to clear the fog away, and each time I do the sky gets a little darker, though I'm not sure if there even is a sky. My hands are still on him, but I can't feel him anymore. He's fading.

"Rafa?"

His voice calls to me and I try to hold on, but he's slipping away before my eyes. He's translucent, fading into transparence until he's gone, and I'm knee deep in an empty pool that's filling with water from an unknown source. It isn't pouring in from anywhere, it's just appearing.

I can feel someone creeping up behind me soon after Ash disappears, but I can't turn my head to see who it is. I hope it's him, but I know it isn't, and the water that's inching up my thigh has ice cold hands that claw into me.

The pool gets deeper and wider and I'm treading water now, struggling to stay afloat. A strong hand materializes on the top of my head and it plunges me underwater with such force that I have no way of defending myself. I punch and scratch at the unknown, but nothing seems to faze it—the hand just pushes me further and further under the water. The remaining air in my lungs grows heavy and I use my last exhale to scream Ash's name, to warn him not to come back. My mouth hangs open, suspended, and water floods every crevice of my body, replacing the blood in my veins, filling the cells in my skin until they're near their bursting point.

I'm surrounded by this thing that gives me life, but suddenly it's killing me. I drown and know no more.

Chapter 31

I gasp and my lungs flood with air.

Still feeling the phantom ache of water in my chest, I sit up and force a cough, but nothing comes up. I'm as dry as the Sahara. I open my eyes to find three floating heads staring down at me.

"Honey?"

Mom's face comes into focus, first her crystal blue eyes, and then her rosy cheeks. Her demeanor is warmer now than before–no longer angry, just concerned.

"I'm sorry." I croak. "I'm sorry about last night."

"Oh sweetie, don't think about that right now." She tucks a lock of wavy hair behind my ears with cool fingers and I relish that small, gentle touch. I try to push the remnants of what I now realize was a nightmare out of my head, but a feeling of unease remains. I blink my eyes a few times and the second head comes into focus; I recognize this person.

"How's she doing, Dr. Sepir?" Mom asks, looking from the doctor to the machines I'm hooked up to. I don't pay attention to the answer, because the third figure has just come into focus. It's Ash. Of course it's Ash. Of course he would be here if I were hurt.

I hold out one hand to him and whisper his name, but my mouth is so dry, it doesn't come out. I'm compelled to tell him about the dream, knowing he would be able to alleviate my anxieties, but before I can he puts an index finger over his lips and quietly shushes me, shaking his head back and forth. I have trouble comprehending what he's trying to tell me, and why he's saying no. I'm still dazed from my dream and waking up– again– in the hospital.

"It's okay," I mumble, to which he shakes his head more vigorously and widens his eyes.

"See? She's doing it again." Mom whispers out of the side of her mouth, eyes darting from me to where Ash stands. "This is just like what happened earlier. Remember, I told you about the thing with the bracelet?"

The bracelet! I look at my wrist and sigh with relief–it's still there. I look at Ash once more, finally coming to my senses. He points to my mother and the doctor, leaning closer to whisper into my ear. I'm so distracted by the tickly of his breath on my neck, I almost don't comprehend what he says.

"They can't see me."

"They can't?" I whisper, and he shakes his head again.

"Shh. Be stealthy, like that first night in the hospital."

I remember him hiding behind the door when the nurse came to check on me, though I guess he needn't have hidden because right now he's out in the open and

Dr. Sepir and Mom have no idea. However, their faces turn bleach white looking at me, and they *do* look like they've seen a ghost. I laugh in my head and realize halfway through a chuckle that it's become audible.

Crap. They must have me on morphine again.

"Honey, *who* are you talking to?" Mom asks.

"And what's so funny?" Dr. Sepir asks.

I focus with all of my might and try to repress whatever drugs are messing with my head.

"Nothing. No one, I mean," I say, and smile, trying to look convincing. I wink in Ash's direction and I hear Mom mumble "Oh Lord" under her breath.

"Can I see your bracelet?" Dr. Sepir asks. Finally, someone who isn't blind.

"Of course," I say, and hand it to him. He takes it gently in his hand but, to my dismay, it slips to the floor and he doesn't even notice. Ash reaches for the bracelet, our fingers brushing for just a moment, but long enough for a warm, tingly sensation to course through me.

"Thank you." I say, picking it up myself, and he winks at me.

"Rafa..."

Mom's voice is laced with concern. I wish they would give *her* some morphine.

"You kept saying a word—or a name, maybe—while you were coming to. You kept saying *Ash*. Where did you get that from?"

I shrug, determined not to make myself look any more unstable than I already have. Mom looks at Dr. Sepir and begins to speak as if I'm unable to hear what she's saying.

"The house we live in, it was Ash Gables' house."

Dr. Sepir nods in understanding.

"I knew both of his parents. Beautiful people. Tragic."

I want to tell them Ash is alive, that he's right *here*. I want to scream it at the top of my lungs but when I glance over at him, he continues to motion for me to keep quiet.

"*Act. Normal. Rafa,*" he says with obvious restraint. I struggle to maintain eye contact with Mom—it's difficult not to acknowledge Ash when he is present.

"Rafa," Dr. Sepir asks, "Do you know someone named Ashley Gable?"

I hear Ash's voice, urgent.

"*Say no.*"

It's almost impossible for me to force the next word out because it feels like a betrayal, but I do it anyway.

"No."

"You don't know him?"

I swallow, hard. This next part is even more difficult to get out.

"Ashley Gable is—he's the one who died, isn't he?"

"He is."

"Then, how could I?"

"Rafa, just try to be cooperative here," Mom cuts in.

"Rafaela, I think you are experiencing some of the neuropsychological effects of Traumatic Brain Injury.

Your mother and I—we believe that you're experiencing an ongoing hallucination." Says Dr. Sepir.

I look to Ash and roll my eyes. *This again.*

"I am not hallucinating."

"Show me your bracelet again," the doctor says, but I'm not falling for it this time. I clamp my hand over the wrist I'm wearing it on and try to look innocent.

"Lift up your hand," He asks again, but I don't move a muscle.

"Rafa," Mom warns. I begrudgingly obey, more scared of what she'll do to me than what the doctor will. I lift up my hand to reveal my wrist.

"There is no bracelet on your wrist," Dr. Sepir says gravely, shaking his head. "You are the only one who can see it. Don't you think that's a little odd?"

"Just because you can't see it, doesn't mean it isn't real," I reply, the drugs making me feel as though I've just said something profound. I don't care what people think; Ash is as real as anyone I know, and so is the bracelet he gave me for that matter.

Dr. Sepir nods and looks at Mom for backup.

"I'll tell you what; why don't you get some rest while the doctors and I work out what to do."

Ugh. Not this again.

"Mom, please," I plead. "I just want to go home and rest in my own bed."

"I know you do. But you need to stay here until they figure out what's wrong. I'm worried about you, your Dad's worried too."

I groan, knowing in my gut that she's telling the truth—at least about Dad. Let's just say I didn't inherit the anxiety from Mom's side of the family.

"Is Dad okay? Can I call him?"

"Not right now, but I will. Just try to get some sleep, and we'll talk more in the morning."

I concede, accepting that I'm not going to win this one. She leans in to give me a hug and I hold on for longer than I usually do, needing her to feel that I'm still here and still me.

Dr. Sepir and Mom leave the room, but not before Mom looks back and blows me a kiss. I pretend to catch it on my cheek. She turns off the light and shuts the door almost all of the way, a shimmer of light still visible through the crack. I turn to Ash, finally free to do so without scrutiny.

He walks over to me, slips off his sneakers, and crawls into bed next to me. He places one arm under my neck, and I turn to face him, snuggling into his chest. *Peppermint and pine.* We lay in silence, aware that the sound of my voice talking to "no one" would summon another round of questions from any doctor walking by. I almost fall asleep to the soft rhythm of his breath on my forehead, but then I remember the dream and force myself to stay awake. Ash gives me a concerned look, but I just shake my head, indicating that everything is fine—I don't want to worry him for nothing. Even so, I can't help but feel that maybe the dream wasn't just a dream. That maybe it was something more.

Chapter 32

Since they can't find any concrete reason to hold me hostage, the doctors let me go home the next day with some antidepressants, hoping they will help me with what they're referring to as hallucinations. I promise Mom that I'll take them, but only if she lets me return to school. She reluctantly agrees on the condition that I check in with her at lunch and promise to attend no more than two classes a day. I keep the pills in my desk drawer and don't take a single one.

Since the hospital, Ash has hardly left my side. It's a little comical, really, considering Mom can't see him, so we've been forced to spend most of our time in my room talking in hushed voices, playing card games, streaming movies, and kissing. There's *a lot* of kissing. The other funny thing is that even though no other human seems to be able to see him, Benny definitely can. Whenever Ash walks into the same room as him, Benny barks and bounds over to him playfully. At least I'm not the only one Mom thinks has lost their mind.

Ash doesn't stay with me at night, because we don't want to feel tempted to explore more of each other than we're ready to, but he comes over most mornings for breakfast. Well, to watch me eat breakfast. He also doesn't feel comfortable being on the school grounds because he hasn't figured out why I can see him, or whether anyone else can too, so he offers to walk me home after my first day back instead. Mom is working late, so she agrees to let me walk home with "Ingrid" if I call her as soon as I get into the house.

"Are you *sure* you want to do this?" she asks as I grab my backpack and slip into my shoes.

"Yes. I can't afford to miss any more school. Besides," I add, sensing her concern, "I'll be sitting in the nurse's office for half the day anyway, and you can text me whenever you want."

"You are so like your father," she says, kissing me lightly on the forehead, and despite the state of their relationship, I know it's meant as a compliment. "I'll go start the car."

I wait for her to leave before throwing my arms around Ash and kissing him goodbye. It's deep, long, and blissful, and it makes me wonder if it's possible to fall completely into someone and remain there in warm happiness forever.

"I'll see you after school?" I confirm, only a little apprehensive that he won't be there. He hasn't had any trouble staying with me the past couple of days.

"Nothing could keep me away."

I move toward the door but Ash takes my good hand as I turn and pulls me back to him, our bodies colliding. Even though I've spent the better part of four days with him, I still get a flutter of adrenaline every time we touch.

"Rafa?"

"Yeah?"

He pauses, and I almost think he's going to tell me something I don't want to hear.

"I...I love you."

My heart drops into my gut, and I melt into a puddle on the floor. I didn't know it was possible to feel so much happiness all at once, and if I were to die right here, right now, I wouldn't have one single regret.

*   *   *

I'm giddy with excitement by the time I get to school, and I'm smiling so much that my face is actually starting to hurt. I cannot wrap my head around the idea that the boy I love is in love with me too. Up until this point in time, if someone had asked me what the best day of my life was, I wouldn't have had an answer, but Ash changed that this morning. Now I can say with absolute certainty that the best day of my life is *today*. I feel like I'm walking on air, as if gravity no longer affects me, as if my body is completely, deliciously weightless.

I float through the morning, not minding that I have to spend most of it in the nurse's office listening to middle-schoolers complain about their imaginary ailments. I have to keep pinching myself just to prove that I'm awake, so much so that by the end of third period I've pierced a dozen red fingernail marks into my arm. It's hard for me to remember that I have a job to do; I need to figure out what happened to Ash so I can release him from his cosmic purgatory, and we can finally be together.

All of this probably sounds irrational, mad even, but at this point there are no longer any laws of the universe that I can trust. Maybe Ash cannot be explained by science, but when have formulas, equations and graphs ever been able to explain love? When have white-haired men in lab coats ever been able to quantify souls and consciousness? Never. Not even once. I'm convinced that if Ash and I can figure out what happened to him, we can bring him back to my world. To *our* world. It's more than a theory, I feel it deep in my bones. Within my marrow. I'm going to prove that I'm right–to Mom, to the doctors, and especially to myself.

I decide to use one of my class allowances on English, because we usually just work on Chromebooks the entire time. I'm still not supposed to have any screen time, but I doubt Ms. Roe will pay any attention to the nurse's notes; she's far too busy texting her art school girlfriend, pretending to grade papers behind the pile of novels on her desk.

When I get to class I nod to Taylor, who's been civil with me ever since our uncomfortable interaction in the courtyard. She's sitting in the back of the room next to Greyson and Téo, her body turned toward Greyson while he disregards her completely. I grab a laptop from the cart, my ears tingling at the sound of two boys snickering behind me. I'm dying to turn around, but I don't want them to know that I care, so I just pretend to be immersed in my own world.

Keeping up appearances, I open a tab to Google Classroom and bring up one of the seven hundred assignments I owe. Pulling a journal out of my bag, I open it up to a page where I've taken some notes about the things I know for sure about Ash's death: the time, the place, details from the obituary that don't tell me much other than that he was loved by many. I then open up a new window and start digging again, though I'm not confident that the search engine will have anything new to offer.

I read the obituary again, combing through it for something I might have missed, but nothing jumps out at me. Then I open up the article from the *Evening Times* about the vigil arranged by Greyson and Taylor and re-study the grainy photograph. I go deeper than just looking at the faces this time, I examine the postures, the body language, the masks anyone might be wearing. Some of the students in the picture look numb, and I imagine they're more upset by the reality of the universe and the realization of their own mortality than they are about Ash. Grief inhabits the faces of many–puffy eyes, swollen lips. I locate Ingrid's coarse image, but this time I notice something more.

Ingrid isn't crying, and she looks more sharp than the others, more hardened. She's not looking down or off into the distance, just staring intently, angrily even, to the side. I've only been to a few funerals in my life, but mourners don't usually look the way she does, as if she's a Medusa reincarnate, about to turn an unwelcome invader into stone with hardened eyes. I wonder–I might be reading too much into it, but I can't help but wonder–and draw a line with my finger, tracing Ingrid's line of sight across the photograph right to its certain target.

My stomach drops. How hadn't I seen it before? She isn't gazing down despondently, or into the distance mournfully like the others, she's looking front and center, right at Greyson and Taylor.

As if on cue, Taylor gets up to go to the bathroom. I look over my laptop screen and see that the teacher still has her nose in her lap, her face illuminated by the glow of her phone. If she manages to secure tenure, there are going to be a lot of happy slackers in this building. I seize my opportunity, getting out of my seat and skirting to the back of the room. I quietly steal Taylor's chair and gulp down the bile that has jumped into my throat from being so close to Greyson. It doesn't take long for him to notice me.

"Well, well, well, look who it is," Greyson says, nudging Téo. I secretly wonder if Téo has his own personality, or if his sole purpose in life is to provide a meaty upper arm for Greyson to elbow.

"Hey, Greyson," I say softly, trying to sound as nonchalant as possible. "I know we haven't had a chance to catch up lately and..." I almost can't get the words to form, but I push them out with all of my might. "I just thought I'd see what you were up to." I don't want to sound too eager, but I know I don't have much time.

Greyson eyes Téo as if to say, "I've got this," and Téo turns his focus back to figuring out the spelling of his own last name. Just the two of us now, Greyson leans across the aisle, and I can feel his hand brush uninvitedly against my thigh. He does it casually, as if it's an accident but when he doesn't move it away, I know the move is intentional. A power move. I fight the overpowering impulse to retreat because I need all the ammunition I can get, and the only ammunition I have is the ability to outsmart him. So I allow his heavy hand to rest on my thigh, a place where it should never be allowed to find comfort.

"Where's your girlfriend?" he sniggers. I don't want to say what comes next, but I think it will be my best chance at cracking him, so I say it anyway.

"Oh, Ingrid? You were right about her. *Total* effing weirdo."

A triumphant gleam lights up his face.

"Well, glad you're finally catching on, new girl."

He squeezes my thigh and I nearly lose my lunch. His hand is so big, it reaches three quarters of the way around my leg. I feel a grimace surfacing on my face, so I force a smile and lean in a little closer.

"Actually, I wanted to ask you about something," I say in a whisper. The teacher isn't paying attention to us, but I don't want to push my luck. "I found this article, in my house. In an old stack of newspapers near the fireplace." He doesn't need to know that I've been combing every corner of the internet for information. "You know I live in the Gables' old home, right? Well I found the article about the vigil held here at school, and it said that *you* were the one who put it on. Is that true?"

Greyson and Téo, who's clearly been eavesdropping, exchange a look that I cannot read, but Greyson turns his attention back to me before I can analyze any part of it. I twirl a lock of hair around my index finger, trying to look as appealing as one can in the middle of an eleventh grade English Literature class.

"Yeah, that's right."

He says it casually, but something about his tone doesn't fit the circumstance. It's almost defensive, as if he's afraid of being accused of something.

"Were you guys close?" I shift my body toward his, near enough to smell his aftershave, and bat my lashes a few times for added effect.

"I guess you could say we were close... at the end." He's cryptic about it, just like Ingrid had been a few nights ago. Why can't anyone just be transparent in this town?

"So how did he *die?*" I widen my eyes, trying to seem enthralled by the drama of it all. "I mean, it's *so* horrible. One of your classmates, dead? That never happened to me back in Boston, and there were five hundred kids in my class alone. It's hard to imagine something like that happening here."

He appears to study me but can't see through me the way Ash does. I don't think he can read me at all.

"You want to know the truth?" he says, so close to me now that our faces are almost touching. "Ash put his nose in places where it didn't belong." He scrutinizes me through challenging eyes, wide open and clear as glass, and I get this sick feeling in my stomach that we aren't just talking about Ash anymore.

"Do you believe in karma, Rafa?" He asks, his glare paralyzing me like the sting of a jellyfish. It doesn't matter that I don't have an answer because he doesn't wait for one. His hand remains wrapped around my thigh, which he squeezes it like a hungry boa constrictor, but I don't say anything. I refuse to show him weakness, or even hesitation.

"I don't really see what any of that has to do with his drowning," I say, ignoring his question. "Being that it was an accident and all."

"And I don't see why you care so much," he retorts.

"I haven't had much to do these past few weeks, and when I found the newspaper clipping, I got curious. I am living in his bedroom, after all."

I'm not sure if I'm imagining it, but it looks like he buys what I'm selling.

"Look, as far as I know, Ash drowned because he was wasted out of his mind and swam about as well as the average skipping rock. But there's a part of me that thinks maybe, just maybe, he had it coming. The universe has a way of giving people what they deserve in the end."

I can't take it anymore and pull away from Greyson. I wiggle my leg free of his grip, but I'll feel the imprint of it for hours.

"That's a pretty messed up thing to say, Greyson," I reply, narrowing my green eyes. "Especially for someone who cared enough to plan a vigil."

"Yeah, well, you didn't know Ash," he spits back. "I planned the stupid vigil because it was the right thing to do, and because you can bet it will look good when the football scouts Google my name. But as far as 'friends' go, that fucking freak was never one of them."

I want to punch him right in his strong, symmetrical nose. I want to claw at his eyes and sink my fingernails into them until they bleed. I'm in the midst of wondering how much trouble I would get in if I kneed him right where it counts, but I don't get to finish my thought because Taylor has come back from the bathroom.

"Hey, Rafa," She says, confused, looking between me and Greyson. "What's...going on here?"

I give her a smile, wanting no bad blood between us even if her boyfriend is the spawn of Satan.

Greyson switches his attention to Taylor, turning on the charm.

"Rafa just missed me," he says playfully, and Taylor's eyes narrow with envy.

I want to tell her it wasn't like that, that what he said couldn't be further from the truth, but I can't have Greyson knowing how much I despise him. Not yet, anyway. Not while I can still use him.

"Yeah," I agree, weakly. "I've been out so much, I just wanted to say hi."

I smile at Greyson and break eye contact only once I've asserted what I need to. I head back to my seat a few rows up, and as I walk away, I can already hear Taylor feebly seeking reassurance from Greyson. I feel sorry for her.

"Don't be needy," he says dismissively, and I hear her mention something about "*last night*" and "*not fair, Greyson.*"

Once I'm back to my seat, I can't hear their conversation, but I don't think it would yield much anyway. I chew on the end of my pen and try to declutter my brain, getting ready to take some notes. I'm writing everything down, no matter how small. I can't be sure I can trust my memory right now.

For one, I learned that the vigil was a ploy—just an opportunity for Greyson to advance his own image. It had absolutely nothing to do with mourning Ash or caring about him or trying to do right by a deceased classmate. It was an act of pure selfishness and personal gain. On the surface, this doesn't tell me much about Ash, but it does tell me that Greyson, for whatever reason, hated him so much he has no problem admitting his insincere motives almost a whole year post-mortem. What makes someone want to hold a grudge for *that* long? Too much testosterone and a massive ego, or something more?

I've also learned that Ash was involved in something with Greyson that Greyson wasn't too happy about. I have no idea what it is, but the whole situation likely holds another clue as to what happened to Ash. I sit at my desk, staring at one of my owed assignments, running the conversation I just had through my head until I nearly have it memorized. Something about it sounds familiar, but I can't figure out what it is. I don't have to ponder it for too long before it registers.

Freak.

I've heard him say that before in the same icy tone, the one that wears a mask of repulsion and hatred, trying to hide an undercurrent of fear. Maybe he uses the term often, or maybe he just reserves it for people he hates with a passion. People like Ash.

People like Ingrid.

Chapter 33

Mom asked me not to go to the cafeteria, afraid I would be overstimulated by the fluorescent lights and noise. Clearly, she doesn't realize that my brain will be buzzing in a million different directions no matter where I am. I heed her advice anyway, though, and when the bell rings for sixth period I wait in the hall outside the nurse's office to intercept Ingrid on her way to lunch. After spotting her colorful head bobbing on the outskirts of the hallway, I grab her by the arm and pull her aside. I don't have to ask Ingrid twice if she wants to come eat in the library with me—I'm certain she doesn't want to eat in the cafeteria alone, even if she's still upset about our conversation the other night.

She picks up on my sense of urgency as I practically drag her up the stairs, giving me a look as if to say *what's going on?* I whisper that I will explain soon, focused on getting us to the most remote area of the school as quickly as possible. When we get to the library, I drag her back to the Reference section and pull out a book on John F. Kennedy, so if Mrs. Krakauer comes to spy on us it'll look like we're working diligently. We aren't allowed to come up here and have lunch unless we're doing something "productive," though I'm not sure what could be more productive than getting to the bottom of a mysterious death.

We sit cross-legged on the floor, and Ingrid pulls a bagel and cream cheese out of her bag. I pull out my lunch as well but find I'm too anxious to eat. I'm not sure if I should begin by apologizing to Ingrid or asking her what the deal was the other night or avoid addressing it entirely, but before I can decide she puts down her bagel and writes *I'm sorry* in large letters on a sheet of paper.

I breathe a sigh of relief, happy she decided to take the lead.

"No, don't be. I was pushy and I didn't mean to be. You know what they say about curiosity."

She sketches a stick figure cat and decapitates it with the tip of her pen, ink blood spilling from its throat.

"Exactly." I wait a beat.

"Is it okay if we talk about it a little more?"

She nods her head in a way that makes it difficult to tell whether she's saying "yes" or "no," like she wants to talk about it but isn't sure if she should. I think about how many people tried unsuccessfully to get me to open up about the last year of my life, about Ollie and the split, and completely understand where she's coming from.

"You sure?" I ask, cautiously, and this time she nods her head a bit more definitively in response.

"Okay. I just want to make sure because, honestly, you're my best friend, and I don't want to do anything to risk losing you."

She smiles, then writes, "you won't," and it warms me through and through.

"I'm really sorry about the other night," I start. "I went too far asking questions, but it's important, important in ways I don't even fully understand. You just have to trust me."

She nods, showing that she does. It's strange; she doesn't say a word, but I've learned to read her smirks, gestures, and nods almost to a T.

"I need to know why Greyson hates you."

I don't know what it is, but I can't help but feel there's a connection between Ash and Ingrid, and I think Greyson might be the link.

She looks down at her hands and puts her half-eaten bagel back in its bag. I'm half afraid she's going to shut me out again, but, instead, she pulls a yellow notebook out of her messenger bag and starts scribbling something into it.

Promise not to tell? is what's written on the page that she angles toward me, and I nod my head, crossing my heart with my fingers in affirmation. She pulls the notebook back onto her lap and scrawls something else on it, her hands unsteady. She passes the notebook to me again.

It's ugly..

"I would never judge," I say. "Whatever it is, you can tell me."

She gives me a small, grateful glance, the trust we've established a beacon of light between us. Her writing now is deliberate, yet quick. She passes her words to me as if it were a dish at *The Last Supper*, three words written in light frantic penmanship, as if she almost couldn't get them onto the paper. Upon reading my jaw becomes unhinged and my insides burst into angry flames. I have never wanted to hurt someone so badly in all of my life. As soon as I finish digesting this new information, she shreds the paper with deft hands, as if it might start shouting her truth if it's left alone for too long. I look at Ingrid, and she parts her lips, her mouth hanging open timidly. To my complete surprise, the first thing I've ever heard her speak stumbles out of her mouth. It's just a timid stutter, not even a word, but then she takes a breath and collects herself. When she opens her mouth again, her voice is fresh, clear, and resolute.

"I wish I were lying," she says. I gape, momentarily choking on disbelief before I collect myself. I feel tears flooding my eyes but I blink and swallow them— I have no right to cry if Ingrid isn't crying.

"I wish you were, too."

I scoot over to where she's sitting and put my arms around her instinctively, and she lets me. She rocks in and out, like a weary rowboat on the ocean and I rock with her, following her flow.

"I wish you were too," I say again, finding no other way to respond to what she's just revealed to me. I wish to God she was lying, but in the pit of my heart, I know she isn't.

Chapter 34

We decide to skip seventh period, sneaking out the emergency exit in the library and down the fire escape to the courtyard. If anyone sees us, they don't follow, and we run to the bottom of the school's hill to talk in peace, without risk of being heard by passersby.

We sit on the blood-red court checked with white out-of-bounds lines, and Ingrid's stoicism crumples and she cries into her hands, violent heaves wracking her small body. I want so badly to console her, but I know that no comfort I can offer will take away the scars Greyson left on her, and that talking over someone's grief does more harm than good. I let her lean into me, her lavender head on my shoulder, until her body stills, and her tears stop coming in monsoons. I don't know how much time passes—maybe ten minutes, maybe an hour—but when she sits up her face is red and puffy, a river of eyeliner trickling down the sides of her cheeks like black silt.

"I'm...sorry." Her voice is barely above a whisper. I'm not at all used to hearing Ingrid's voice yet, to the point that my brain is having trouble registering it.

"Why? What on Earth do *you* have to be sorry for?"

"I..." She sniffles. "I don't know. I don't know what else to say. I have to blame myself, because if I didn't, I would feel so...pathetic. Blaming myself is the only way I've gotten through any of this without wanting to just end it all." She trails off, staring at the tops of her kneecaps.

"You mean like...?"

"Yes."

"Well I'm really, *really* glad you didn't," I say, putting my hands on both of her shoulders. "I am so glad you're here."

A taught smile forms on her lips and I grip her tight, bracing her for what I'm about to say.

"Ingrid, we *have* to tell someone. We have to tell the police. He can't just be walking around this school–this town, this *planet* even–when he's capable of something like that."

Panic flashes in her eyes and at first, I assume it's because I suggested legal action, but I'm wrong. A shape glides up behind me and I feel his presence before I hear his voice, sharp metal razors cutting through my silk eardrums.

"Go to the police *about what?*" Greyson asks, lips curled and ready to fight. I face him, standing up and creating a five-foot-six human barrier between Ingrid and him.

"None of your business," I say, trying to sound brave. I can still feel his hand on my leg in the classroom, my small body pressed between his and the wall in the cafeteria. "Get lost, Greyson."

He's fiddling with something in his pocket, and my mind jumps to the worst possible conclusions. What if he has a pocketknife? What if he has *a gun?* I swallow my fear and will my body to take up as much space as it can. He takes another step toward us and I feel Ingrid shudder, a miniature earthquake erupting inside her. I block her instinctively with an arm and he looks from me to her and back again.

"Well that's adorable," he sneers. "First, she's your girlfriend, and now what? You're her guard dog, too? Does the little mute need protection?"

"Leave us alone, Greyson."

"Oh look, she barks."

I plant my feet into the ground and clench my fists, fully prepared to fight him. "I think you've done enough, don't you?"

"You don't know *anything.*" He points to Ingrid. "I've been telling you since day one that she's not to be trusted. Don't you think it's convenient that *now* she decides to talk, after all this time? I don't know what the hell she told you, but if it was the 'truth,' wouldn't she have come forward sooner?"

I glance at Ingrid, her eyes silently pleading. She doesn't want to be here, and all I can think about is getting her out in the safest way possible.

"You know what I do find convenient?" I counter, sneering right back at him. "That every time you don't get your way, someone ends up hurt."

"She's LYING," he yells, rage boiling in his throat. "Think about it, Rafa. Why would I want *her* when I could have Taylor? Or any girl for that matter? Why would I waste my time on a no-good little c–"

"BECAUSE!" I scream, drowning out whatever poison was about to leave his mouth. "Because it's not about popularity, or status, or *any* of that. It's about power with you. It's always about power."

I can tell I'm getting to him now. His olive skin is slightly paler than normal, and both of his hands are balled at his sides. For a second I'm terrified he's going to grab me, but he doesn't. He just points a sharp finger into Ingrid's face and warns in a low, terrifying voice.

"Remember what I told you about keeping your mouth *shut*."

He looks at me once more and spits on the ground next to where I stand before storming off, a cloud of rage settling like dust behind him. As soon as he's gone, I squeeze Ingrid's hands and pull her into me.

"Nothing bad is going to happen," I say. "It's going to be okay; I promise."

Though as I watch him disappear into the woods behind the basketball court, I don't know how I can possibly keep that promise. He's almost a foot taller than I am, and probably weighs twice as much in pure muscle. Even if Ingrid and I were both up against him, we wouldn't stand a chance. He could squash us like bugs.

"Ingrid, we have to go to the police *now*." I plead. "At least make a statement, at least get the story out there."

"N-n-no," she stammers. "No, we can't. I sh-shouldn't have said anything. Please, *please* can we just forget this?"

"No, we can't. We can't let him get away with what he did to you. If we tell the police they'll arrest him, and you won't have to worry about him anymore. You won't have to be afraid. No one will."

"No, Rafa, you don't understand," she says, fighting back tears. "There's no proof. Nobody is going to believe me. I'll just humiliate myself and embarrass my parents."

"Embarrass your parents?"

The words leave my mouth more critically than I intend. I just can't comprehend that anyone's parents would be embarrassed because of something awful that happened to their child.

"They're not like me," she says. "They won't understand it. They're the type of people who think virginity should be reserved for your wedding night and that women shouldn't draw attention to themselves, the way I do with my hair. They'll just say I shouldn't have put myself in the position in the first place."

My mouth hangs open for a moment, because I'm not sure how to respond. Parents victim-blaming their own daughter? It felt like a thing of the distant past.

"Ingrid, that's...mental," I say. "No offense to your parents, but they're living in the dark ages. It's totally backwards, it's ludicrous, it's…"

"I know," Ingrid says, cutting me off. "I know that, I really do. I know, deep down, that what happened wasn't my fault. *I* know that. But they will never see it that way. If there was proof it might be different, but there isn't."

I can't accept it, I refuse to believe that there's no way to make Greyson Kohl pay for what he did.

"What about witnesses?" I ask. "You said it happened at a party, right? There must be someone who saw or heard something. What about Taylor?"

"She's useless. Completely brainwashed. She knows what happened, at least some of it, she heard it through the door. She heard it happening and did nothing because she thought I wanted it. Greyson told her afterward that I begged him to kiss me, to touch me. Told her he felt too *embarrassed* for me not to go along, and that he felt *bad* for me. He convinced her that I somehow manipulated him into doing it and she buys it. Can you believe that? She thinks that I manipulated him into...into...and that I…"

She starts sobbing again and I hug her close to my chest.

"It's okay, you can cry." I say. As much as I want to assume the best in Taylor, she's so enamored with Greyson that I don't doubt what Ingrid is saying. People can convince themselves of anything if they want to badly enough.

"There has to be a way," I start again. "There just has to. Can you think of anyone else who might be able to help? Anyone else who could've seen or heard something?"

She sniffles. "Just one person."

"Okay, that's great! Just tell me who it is and we'll talk to them–I'm sure it won't take much to convince them to come forward. Imagine how many people Greyson has hurt, how many people he could still hurt. We can't be the only ones who want to see him face consequences for his actions."

Ingrid shakes her head from side to side. "It's no use."

"Yes, it is. I'm serious, we can do this. We can fight this together."

"No, we can't."

"Just tell me the name," I insist, confident that I can convince whoever it is to help us.

"Rafa—"

"Ingrid, please," I beg. "Just tell me who."

"He can't help." She says it so hopelessly.

"How can you be so sure? How can you *know*?" I ask.

She pauses, sighing after a beat of silence. "I know. I know because he's dead."

Chapter 25

I run home. I don't care that I'm not supposed to, or that it might hurt my recovery, I run so fast that the ground trembles beneath my sneakers, little earthquakes erupting from my feet. I'm out of breath and near exhaustion well before my house is in sight but I don't stop until I'm home, knowing that to stop would give me too much time to think and I cannot think right now. I cannot think of Greyson and what he did to Ingrid, what he'll do to me now that I've put myself in the middle of it.

Once I step onto my driveway I barrel straight for the doorway, barely stopping to say hi to Benny once I'm inside. I call for Ash, sprinting up the stairs, not even bothering to be careful as I do so. In my room I check the closets, dresser drawers, and underneath my bed. I smell the air, searching for lingering peppermint and pine, and even lift up my sheets. But it's no use; Ash isn't here. And if he isn't here, and he didn't show up after school to walk me home, he must be having trouble getting to me.

I beg the universe to release him from its grasp. "Please, Ash. If you're here, give me a sign."

The cruelest part of this is that he's probably right in front of me–an invisible, soundproof veil between us blocking all forms of communication. I check the time; Mom won't be home for hours. So I do the only thing I can think to do, which is shoulder my backpack and sprint out the back door. If he can't come to me, I'll go to him. To the only place I know I can always find him.

I make it to the clearing in record time, and sure enough he's there within seconds. Ash emerges from the woods behind me and runs to me, kissing my forehead, my cheeks and my nose. I'm frantic, bursting with questions, but even that can't stop me from soaking up a moment of him.

"I'm sorry," he grunts. "I was right there with you the whole time, just beyond the veil. I could see your pretty face and hear your pretty voice but I just…*ugh,* damn this is hard."

He rubs his forehead, knitting the frustration radiating off of his body like heat waves in a desert. I kiss him, trying my best to be a soft rain and cool him down.

"We can't worry about that right now, okay? We have a bigger problem on our hands."

He looks at me dubiously, clearly wondering what could possibly be a bigger problem than bringing someone back from the dead.

"It's Ingrid," I say. "I think–I know–she's in trouble. I don't know what to do." I hold back tears but feel the weight of a knot in my windpipe.

Ash's eyes glaze over for a second, as if he's trying to grasp some far-off memory, but he returns to me with nothing.

"Ingrid told me that you know what happened to her that night. The night you...you..."

"Died?" he asks, filling in the word I still can't bring myself to say.

"Yes."

"I told you, I don't remember anything from that night. I've tried to remember and I just...I just can't. It's right there, too, I know it is, just beyond my reach, but no matter how hard I try it's blurry. Out of focus."

"Well," I think quickly, breathlessly. "You said that you couldn't remember anything when you first woke up here, and then when you met me you remembered the water. What if we go back there, to the pool? Or, what used to be the pool. We could go together, maybe it would trigger something."

"No," he says obstinately. "No, that's not an option."

"Why not?" I demand.

"I'm scared," he blurts out. "Freaking terrified, okay? Have you ever had a nightmare, one where someone was hurting you, and actually *felt* the pain? One where you know you're dreaming but you can't wake up? That's what it will be like if I go back. And at least when you have a nightmare, you get to wake up. I'm stuck in this half-body, this half-existence...there is no waking up for me. I can't. I can't do it."

I search for the right words, taken aback. I guess I'd never considered how hard this must be for him.

"Ash, I know you're scared, but what Greyson did to Ingrid...you might be the only one who knows anything about it other than the two of them. You could help get rid of him for good and uncover what really happened to you in the process."

He looks stressed, pained even. I hope I'm not being selfish–maybe I am–but I don't give up. I take his hand, pleading with my touch.

"I'll be right there with you. I'll hold you the entire time and promise not to let go."

He looks at me for a few moments, taking in everything I've said, and nods, seeing the inevitability of it all. His fingers dance their way along my exposed collarbone, and a familiar warmth runs down my spine.

"You are incredible, you know that?" he says softly.

"I'm alright, I guess."

"You are so much more than alright. You're beautiful and clever and strong and... well, you're everything."

I can feel my cheeks get pink, but I no longer care if he sees me blush. For the first time in my life, vulnerability feels like something beautiful. He takes my hand and our fingers intertwine, our lifelines blending into one.

Chapter 36

We go back to my—our-—house and sit by the remnants of the pool. I'm wearing two sweaters and a jacket, but Ash doesn't seem to notice the cold though he's in nothing but a t-shirt. I check my watch; Mom will be home in an hour, so we have time. If she sees me sitting in the frigid air, talking to myself, it'll be all the confirmation she needs that I've gone completely nuts.

We sit on the concrete edge with our feet in the dirt that fills the pool like a fresh grave. I take Ash's hand and give it a reassuring squeeze, trying to convince him, and myself, that everything will be okay. I feel my knuckles turn white from the pressure of his grip, but it's the good kind. Like a weighted blanket, gluing me to the world even when my head is drowning somewhere in the abyss.

"Well," I say, breaking the silence. "Can you remember anything?"

He closes his azure eyes and breathes slowly and steadily, disappearing into his thoughts. After a few minutes of silence pass, he opens his eyes and re-emerges, defeated.

"Nothing."

I try to think of a solution, and after a moment one comes to me. It's a little crazy, I'll admit, but it might be just crazy enough to work.

"Okay," I begin, "So this might sound a little out there, but after my brother died my parents made me go to therapy. Like, *a lot* of therapy."

"That doesn't sound crazy at all. Healthy, actually."

"No, that's not the crazy part," I say. "I was pretty messed up, so I went to a bunch of different therapists in the first few months, trying to find anything that could help. Turns out not sleeping and constantly ruminating isn't the best way to cope. Anyway, I went to this psychiatrist who made me do this thing where I sort of...relived the trauma of losing Ollie. She made me close my eyes and walk her through everything that happened that day, from the big things to the seemingly insignificant things like the color of the curtains and the way the waiting room smelled before we found out he was gone. At first, I could only remember seeing Ollie's little, helpless figure on the surgery table, but the more she asked me and the more I gave her, the more I remembered."

Ash looks at me, skeptical.

"Of course the point wasn't to get my memory back, it was to heal, but in those sessions my brain was able to conjure up so many things about that day I had never even thought about before."

"But I can't see a therapist," he says. "Well, they can't see *me."*

"I know," I say, biting my lower lip. "That's definitely a problem. But we could try it, just you and me. I can try to walk you through that night. I know I'm not a therapist, but it could be worth a shot. Sometimes we remember more than we think we do."

Ash nods in agreement, a bit hesitantly.

"Okay. Okay, I'll try it. If it will help Ingrid."

"And if you can't remember, it's okay."

It's about four p.m. and the sky is already darkening, but we agree that Ash has the best shot at remembering if we stay by the pool, so we sit across from one another and share a blanket I found on the back porch. I'm not at all qualified to guide someone through their trauma, but I'm all Ash has so I have to wear a few different hats, even if they don't quite fit.

His eyes close, and mine follow soon after. I can feel his body rising and falling to the steady rhythm of his breath, his clammy hands both tense and unwavering as they rest in mine. I think about all those dreams I used to have about falling; from bridges, from fire towers, from hotel balconies. Those dreams where you wake up just before you die. And here Ash is, trying to bring himself back to a night so horrible that most of us couldn't even dream it up. I give him another squeeze of reassurance and we begin.

"Okay. Tell me anything you *do* remember. Oh, and say it like it's happening right now, in the present. Like it's happening *to* you."

He takes a deep breath.

"It's November the twenty first," he says. "It's the beginning of Thanksgiving break and my parents are out of town. Some of the football team caught wind of that and took it upon themselves to throw a party, even though I don't like to drink."

I rub the tops of his hands with my thumbs and think back to my own sessions post-Ollie.

"What about sounds? What do you hear? What can you smell?" I ask, trying to keep my voice even.

"I remember...I remember the smell of the house; you know the one I mean. The smell of whatever wood the walls are made of and the fireplace. And the smell of beer from the keg. I left my bedroom door open because I didn't figure anyone would venture upstairs, and there was a draft in the house like there always is in the wintertime."

"When did the party start?"

"I told people to come at seven, but people didn't really show until seven-thirty. I remember thinking maybe no one would come and I could just read my book and go to bed."

"Go on." I say, and he does.

"The football team came first, with the keg. I remember watching the door, not wanting too many people I didn't know to get in."

"Present-tense." I remind him. "As if it's happening now."

"Right."

He takes a moment to re-orient himself and continues.

"Greyson and Taylor are both there, but he isn't

paying attention to her. He's drinking a lot and preoccupied with his phone. Taylor seems upset."

I think back to my first day at Esko High, remembering something misaligned.

"Taylor wasn't there." I tell him.

"But I remember her." He replies. "Distinctly."

"She told me she wasn't there that night, I just– why would she lie if half the school were there, too?"

"I don't know." Ash says, thoughtfully. "But I know she was there."

I shrug, Taylor's presence isn't important right now anyway.

"Can you remember any other smells?" I ask again. I don't know why this is important, but I remember my therapist really fixating on it.

"Thick cologne. Not mine. The kitchen is cloudy with it. It was...it is his, I think."

"Greyson's?"

"Yes. Yes, it's definitely him. He's wearing a black polo shirt and jeans."

"What about Ingrid?"

"She comes later, around eight. She is more done up than usual. Pretty. Her hair is bleach blonde and long."

I try to picture Ingrid with a normal hair color but can't.

"Once she arrives, Greyson puts his phone down. I remember that because Taylor made a comment about it." Ash fidgets a little but remains steady. "I'm sitting in the living room, making sure nobody breaks anything. I don't know why I let them have the party, I was–am– so paranoid about the whole thing. I think..."

I keep stroking his hands, not knowing what else to do, but instead of getting warmer from the friction they grow icier, less viscous.

"Ash?" I prompt, but he doesn't answer. He can't.

Oh no. It's just like what happened in the clearing. I rub the tops of his hands harder now, trying to feel the blood beneath his skin. He can't leave now, not when we're so close. His eyes suddenly open wide and when they meet mine, I can tell that he's afraid.

"Ash!" I yell, shaking him, willing him to stay even though I know it's no use. I can still feel his hands in mine, but I know that I'm losing him. He's disappearing.

"Rafa" he says, finding the strength to speak. "Come with me."

Before I can process his proposal, I feel myself being pulled practically out of my skin. The whole world jolts as if it's been knocked out of orbit, and I hold onto him tighter than I've ever held onto anything in my life. I try to find purchase on the earth, but the ground is gone, and it feels like I'm stuck in a dream. A falling dream. I close my eyes and cling to him because he's all there is. Just him and blackness, and then only blackness.

Chapter 37

When I open my eyes, I'm on the floor of my house. Only it isn't my house anymore. Structurally, everything is in the right place, but Benny's bed isn't on the hearth and the decor is all wrong, much fancier than Mom's mismatched DIY, *I-found-it-at-a-thrift-store* style. Old-fashioned wallpaper coats the living room like intricate skin, and the windows are hidden by deep maroon curtains drawn all the way shut. I feel like I'm having reverse Deja vu; rather than having the sensation that I've been here before, I can visualize where everything will be in the future.

"Where—where are we?" I ask. Though I already know the answer, I need to hear it from someone else to believe it.

"This is my house." Ash confirms. "*Our* house."

I try to take a deep breath to clear my head but find that I can't inhale. My lungs feel like they've been replaced with a million tiny, popped balloons.

"It's okay," Ash says, meeting my panicked gaze. "You get used to it; the not breathing thing."

"Are we— am I… *dead?*"

I'm definitely disoriented, but not nearly as frightened as anyone who thinks they might be dead should be.

"No."

I swallow my disorientation and trust him. Once I get a grip and stop trying to force air into my lungs when I clearly don't need to, my other senses awaken and I notice that we are far from alone.

We're surrounded by slightly younger versions of teenagers I recognize from school. They look mostly the same, but some have braces, longer or shorter haircuts, or more or less acne. Ash pulls me to my feet, and points to the kitchen. I follow the direction of his index finger and see something that causes me to do a double take, disbelieving what I'm looking at.

It's *Ash,* and unlike the others at the party who look like slightly younger versions of the people I know from school, Ash looks exactly the same, as if he's spent the last year frozen in time. He's wearing the same tapered track pants, the same sneakers, and the same white t-shirt. Even though I've seen it on him a million times, I can't help but notice how perfectly form fitting and sexy it looks on him.

He's sitting on the counter I prepare my meals on, his shoulders slightly hunched, his eyes wandering around the crowded kitchen. I look from the Ash standing next to me to the other Ash—Memory-Ash—so many times that I dizzy myself.

The first Ash, *my* Ash, grips both of my shoulders to calm me.

"How...what is this?" I stammer. Even though after meeting Ash, I had to accept that some of the fundamental rules of reality were bogus, this scenario is wildly beyond my comprehension.

"I told you, when I disappear to you, it's like time and space disappear to me."

"So is this like...time travel?" I ask, trying to remember the H.G. Wells novel I read last summer. I quickly pray that there aren't any cannibalistic humanoids in this version of reality, if you can even call it that.

"Not exactly," he says, "It's more like looking through a window into the past. We're not actually *here.*"

I reach out to grab the counter and steady myself, but my arm goes right through it, as if it's merely a mirage. I stumble, and Ash catches me. At least we can still feel each other; that doesn't seem to change regardless of what reality we're in.

"So. Weird." I watch Memory-Ash for a few minutes. He looks so unsuspecting, so... *seventeen*. So nowhere-near-death. I look at my Ash and he shrugs in response, unfazed.

A few meters away from Memory-Ash, drinking what appears to be his third or fourth beer, I spot Greyson and shiver unconsciously.

"He can't hurt you here," Ash whispers, reading my mind. I don't know how to tell him that it's not me I'm worried about. We walk over to Greyson and Ash puts his whole arm right through his thick, intoxicated skull. "See?"

I nod, putting my own arm through his face just to test it. If only I could do this in real life. Greyson doesn't seem to be any the wiser–he's sitting, drinking beer, and staring at his phone, just like Ash remembered. I peer over his meaty shoulder, taking the opportunity to get any information about this night that I can. He's typing out a message and I can hardly believe the recipient. I can't imagine a world where Ingrid would want to talk to Greyson, but there her name is on the top of his message stream.

> **Greyson:** I've been thinking about you all week. I just want you to be here. When are you coming?

Three little dots pop up on the text screen as Ingrid types a reply.

> **Ingrid:** Why don't you come let me in?

> **Greyson:** Be right there. Btw, I liked the pics.

> **Ingrid:** I thought you might ;)

This can't be Ingrid. Not the Ingrid I know, anyway.

We follow Greyson to the door, and he opens it conspicuously, scanning the room beforehand–probably for Taylor, but she's nowhere to be seen.

It's Ingrid in the doorway alright, but she is almost unrecognizable. She's wearing knee-high black boots, a low-cut, flowy mauve blouse, and sporting platinum blonde locks. A wry, playful smile expands across her face when Greyson meets her at the door, something I've never seen on her before. She doesn't look meek or standoffish or dark like the Ingrid I know. She's not wearing baggy clothes or hiding behind thick eyeliner and long bangs. I've always thought Ingrid was pretty, but tonight she has a radiance to her that I've never seen. She's absolutely stunning.

As Greyson steps aside to let her in, dozens of hungry eyes follow her movements, as if a slab of perfectly seared Kobe beef had just walked in. I look to Ash in disbelief, but he's watching Memory-Ash, whose eyes are following Greyson and Ingrid across the room.

"I can't believe that's Ingrid." I say, but Ash isn't listening to me.

"I remember now," he says under his breath. "Ingrid was new to the school and Greyson was always hitting on her whenever Taylor wasn't around. I remember he would act so soft and charming around her– this must be why Taylor was so pissed off."

Greyson slides Ingrid's jean jacket off of her shoulders and whispers something in her ear. She giggles, and I gag, sickened. I'm immediately reminded of my first week of school, when Greyson was so pleasant and inviting, and cool; when he was the first person to make *me* feel noticed. It's so wrong that guys like him are allowed to walk freely on this Earth. They're nothing but emotional con-artists.

Ash and I watch Greyson and Ingrid chat intimately for a few minutes, and even though I want to look away, I can't, too in awe of what I'm seeing. He's playing her like a fiddle and she's eating it right up. This isn't the closed-off Ingrid I know, but I guess there's a reason she is the way she is. He gets her a drink and she guzzles it, fast. He grazes the small of her back with his fingertips, and she leans into his touch.

I think I'm going to be sick.

I notice Memory-Ash moving toward the door, opening it to a new guest. An enraged Taylor storms in from the cold and starts throwing daggers at Greyson and Ingrid with her eyes but says nothing.

Ash was right, Taylor was there. Which means she deliberately lied to me. But why? She didn't even know me, and I certainly didn't know any of this.

As I ponder this, she chugs a nearby cup of something that definitely isn't water in ten seconds flat and turns to Memory-Ash, probably because he's the closest person to her. She shoots a pointed look at Greyson, coughs loudly, and takes Ash's head between both of her hands. Then she stands on her tiptoes and kisses him right on the lips.

I feel nauseous watching her lips meet his, a thousand punches to my gut at once. To Ash's credit (both of him) he looks as surprised as I do. Memory-Ash disconnects himself from Taylor and gently pushes her back. I feel a wave of ecstasy knowing he had the perfect opportunity to hook up with the most popular girl in school and didn't, and somehow fell in love with me when I was at my worst.

Taylor storms off again, out to the patio overlooking the pool. *The pool.* I hadn't noticed it until now. It's full to the brim with deep turquoise water and illuminated by fluorescent, underwater lights. Ash was right, it isn't cold enough to be frozen. It isn't even covered. Part of me wants to follow Taylor, but I don't get a chance to because when I turn back to the kitchen, Greyson and Ingrid are slipping away, down the dark hallway toward the stairs. I take Ash's hand and pull him along with me, though now he looks like he's going to be sick.

"We have to," I say. "We have to know."

He follows reluctantly and tightens his grip on my hand. I no longer think we're stuck in his dream, or memory; I think we're visitors in his nightmare.

We walk up the stairs behind them, keeping a safe distance though I know it's unnecessary. We follow them to the top where they take a left and they walk into a room–my bedroom. Just the thought of Greyson in my bedroom makes me want to hurl. My brain can hardly process what's happening but there's no time to argue with logic or reason, so I push my bewilderment aside and focus on Ingrid. Greyson leads her farther into the room by the small of her back, and latches the door shut behind him.

"Dammit," I whisper, forgetting that volume isn't an issue since no one can hear me other than Ash.

"It's okay," Ash replies, walking right through the door and pulling me behind him. I brace myself to feel something as we traverse the threshold, but I don't. Only his hand in mine.

"You get used to it," he says, but I don't think I ever could.

Once we're in the room–*my room*–everything happens so quickly. Greyson has his hands on Ingrid's hips, and she's pulling him toward her. She smiles like a girl in love, and he smiles like a lion who's just found an easy kill.

Greyson starts kissing Ingrid and at first, she reciprocates. She kisses him back, placing her hand on the back of his neck, standing on tiptoes to reach more of him, but the dynamic shifts quickly, and not for the better. He starts kissing her too hard, practically forcing his tongue down her throat, and when she tries to pull away, he just presses his body into hers and keeps going. She says his name, which gets partially drowned out by his mouth. She gets away from him for a moment, and he looks like a little boy who's never heard the word "no" before, like he's about to throw a tantrum in the grocery store when he can't have the candy he wants.

"Greyson, wait. You're drunk."

"Shhh," he slurs, placing a finger on her stunned lips. "You're going to like this."

She shakes her head. "Not like this."

He smirks, and stares at her with condescension. "You're joking, right?"

"No, I'm not. It's not supposed to be like this. You're too drunk and I've never…I want this to be special."

He paces back and forth like a feral dog.

"This has to be a joke, right? You know Taylor is here. You know what I'm risking just to be with you."

"I thought she wasn't your girlfriend?"

"That's not the point!" He snaps, still pacing. "Just come here, please. I want you."

Ingrid tries to put more space between them, but the bed is behind her and the door, her only escape route, is blocked by Greyson. Her eyes are wide with fear as she sizes him up, and I can tell she's recognizing she isn't safe. He's twice her size. She's so small, and no one knows they're upstairs. She tells him one more time that she isn't interested in going further, but when she motions toward the door, he blocks her. What happens next is almost too horrible to watch, but I have to.

Ingrid backs up, her arms thrusting into his chest, but her hands are minuscule compared to his. He takes her wrists and forces them behind her back. The muffled sound of fear escapes her throat, but the music downstairs is loud and nobody can hear her. Ingrid frees one of her hands and slaps Greyson across his unshaven face, but it isn't any use. He catches her wrist again and whispers something in her ear, and though I can't hear what he says I know by the look on her face that it's repulsive. With force, he pushes her down on the bed. She opens her mouth and inhales sharply to scream but he pushes her head into a pillow and drowns her out, so I start yelling for her, but nobody can hear me except Ash.

I flail my arms and try to jump on top of Greyson, punching with all my might, but my fists slice right through him like they did before. Ash pulls me into his arms, and I stifle a sob as Ingrid cries out again for help. She lands a few good kicks into his ribs and for a second I think she's going to get out from under him, but rage seems to empower Greyson and he grunts, pushing her down again and holding her in place with one arm. He unzips his pants with his free hand, and I hide my head in Ash's neck, horrified, tears leaking out of my eyes. I want to leave, run, scream, punch a hole in the wall, anything, but I can't. I can't leave Ingrid here alone, but I can't help her either. All I can do is watch; be the witness she so desperately needs.

I swallow the bile in my throat, lift my head and look back at the bed. Greyson rips Ingrid's skirt from her body as if it were a piece of tissue paper and though she kicks and wriggles and tries to roll away, she can't escape his heavy grip. I'm sobbing big, sloppy tears into Ash's shirt, feeling helpless, when I hear the faint yet distinctive sound of someone coming up the stairs. I'm used to the sounds of this house and know how the third step from the top squeaks, but Greyson, both unaware of this and oblivious to anything that isn't himself, doesn't notice. He's struggling with Ingrid putting up such a fight, but she can't manage to get away and if she doesn't get away soon, things are going to get as bad as they possibly can. I look at Ash, searching for an answer to this nightmare we've walked into, but he isn't paying any attention to me; he's looking through the closed door, at the person who came up the stairs.

It's him! Memory-Ash is standing in the hallway before his bedroom door, completely sober and extremely troubled.

Yes. *Yes.* Finally, someone who can do something. He cocks his head and walks up to the closed door that stands between him and what's going on inside my room. *His* room. My heart is nearly pounding out of my chest and I'm willing him to hurry up, to turn the handle, to *stop* it. He puts an ear up to the door and, presumably, hearing the sounds of muffled cries, he puts his fingers on the door handle.

Memory-Ash turns the knob and the whole world stops. Some part of my brain recognizes that another set of footsteps are now creeping up the stairs–these ones deliberate. Taylor emerges on the landing and follows the noise coming from my bedroom. Memory-Ash has the door open now, finally seeing what I do. He's so focused on what's happening in front of him that he doesn't hear Taylor sneaking up behind him. She clearly doesn't realize that the scene in front of her is a struggle, she just hears the dull grunts and sees the obvious–that her boyfriend is in bed with another girl. Taylor runs away from the room in tears just as Memory-Ash bursts into the room. My Ash looks from Memory-Ash, to me, to Greyson and back again, as if he's suddenly remembering a haunting dream he had long ago, one he couldn't quite piece together until this very moment.

Memory-Ash throws his body into Greyson, and though Ash can't weigh more than a hundred and sixty pounds, the shock is enough to send Greyson flying to the floor. While Greyson is trying to figure out what is going on, Ash throws a blanket to Ingrid, whose skirt has been ripped and cast aside on the bedroom floor.

"Ingrid, *go!*"

A terrified Ingrid drapes the blanket over her shoulders and runs out of the room, tears streaming down her cheeks and fear in her sallow, almond eyes.

Ash stands defiantly in front of Greyson, who is back on his feet and glaring at him.

"What the hell, man!" Greyson says angrily.

"What were you trying to *do to her?*" Memory-Ash yells, though he already knows the answer.

"It isn't what it looked like," he scoffs, daring Ash to challenge him. "She wanted it. She practically *begged* me."

"Get out of my house. Right. Now," Ash growls. "Get out of here before I call the police."

Greyson tries to maintain a glower, but a glimmer of uncertainty escapes onto his face.

"Dude, you're such a little prick, you know that?" Greyson's voice is higher than usual. He's trying to laugh it off, to make light of everything. "Just stay out of it."

After a few moments of tense silence, Greyson grabs his jacket off of the four-poster bed and walks out of the room, pushing Memory-Ash into the wall as he passes him.

"I'm out of here. This party sucks ass anyway."

As soon as Greyson is out the door and down the stairs, Memory-Ash sprints across the hall to check on Ingrid. He finds her crouched in the corner, crying silently. At the sight of Ash kneeling down to comfort her Ingrid backs violently into the wall and whimpers. I want to help her so badly, wishing more than anything that I could transport myself into this moment and hold her, but I can't. In this moment, reality has never felt further away.

Memory-Ash retracts his hand from Ingrid gently, careful not to make sudden movements.

"It's okay, you're safe now," he says, and she whimpers something in response, shivers wracking her small body like a storm. "I am going to go get my phone and call the police. Stay right here, please. You're safe here, I promise."

She doesn't verbalize an answer, but I can see the outline of her head nodding vehemently in the shadows. Ash gets another blanket from the hall closet and places it over her trembling body, and, although the circumstances are grim, I cannot help but feel a surge of love for how compassionate he is with her. I wrap my arm around Ash's torso, but he does not return the embrace. His eyes are locked on Memory-Ash, following him through the corridor and down the stairs. He looks almost shell-shocked, as if he's just witnessed an explosion, or feels one coming.

"Rafa," he begins, trailing off. "I think something bad is going to happen. I can feel it. I think…"

I press my lips to his shoulder and feel that he's the one trembling now. I don't know what could possibly be worse than what we just gave witness to, and I pray to any god that will listen that he's wrong.

Chapter 38

Ash frees himself of me and walks phantom-like down the hallway. I quickly match his pace and take his hand, allowing him to lead me. We follow Memory-Ash into the kitchen where the party is still going on and the music is loud and everyone is wasted. Memory-Ash picks his phone up off of the table and searches for a quiet corner that doesn't exist, weaving through drunken party goers until he finds his way to the back door. He steps outside into the cold in just his white t-shirt and joggers and walks toward the pool, which is illuminated against the dark November sky. We follow in his footsteps and, though I can feel the ground beneath my feet, my steps do not crunch and the frost where I step remains untouched. I'm here, but I cannot leave a mark on this world.

I stand, hand in hand with Ash, and watch Memory-Ash dial 9-1-1. The air is so still that I can hear the phone ringing as if it were held up to my own ear. It rings once, then twice, and I wonder if this vision, this memory, can change the present. If somehow Greyson will be taken out of the picture and Ingrid will be okay and Ash will just stay alive.

But just as I finish the thought, I hear footsteps pounding into the earth behind me, causing the hair on the back of my neck to rise. A large figure looms against the backdrop of the night sky, closing the space between us with a vengeance. I step out of the way, but my Ash doesn't and Greyson walks right through him, barreling toward Memory-Ash with loathing in his eyes. I look to the sky, to the constellations, and wonder which of them is supposed to protect the innocent. Even if I could remember the name, it wouldn't matter–the stars aren't out. The night is black.

I feel as if I could wake up at any moment, and none of this would exist outside of my head. I look at Ash, who's fixated on his former self, and feel as if I'm sinking to the core of the Earth. Somewhere, deep down, I know what's about to happen, and I think that Ash does too. Just as the dispatcher answers the call, Greyson reaches Ash and knocks the phone out of his hands and right into the water, where it sinks and goes black before our eyes.

As terrifying as Greyson is, Memory-Ash doesn't look shaken. My Ash, on the other hand, is white as a ghost. I can feel his pain the same way I can feel my own, perhaps even moreso, and it kills me that I cannot take it from him. I can handle almost anything; the loss of my little brother, the separation of my parents, a TBI, sprained wrist, and four staples to the head, but I cannot bear to see the ones I love in pain. I look at the pool, I look at Greyson's face, and I look at Memory Ash, except he isn't just *Memory Ash*—he's my Ash, too.

"I told you to keep your nose out of my business," Greyson growls, slurring his words and squinting his eyes until they're angry little slits. Ash doesn't say anything but stands his ground and looks at Greyson head-on.

"You know, you've always been a little bastard," Greyson continues, and I start to feel dizzy.

"Greyson...you were..." Ash begins, unable to formulate the words.

"Yeah, so what if I was?" he asks boldly. "What, are you going to do, *tattle* on me? Is this fucking kindergarten? Did I steal your favorite crayon?"

"You can't just get away with something like that," Memory-Ash replies, and I feel my Ash's body tensing up, a loaded gun ready to fire. "I'm going inside and I'm calling the police, so I suggest you get the hell out of here before they come."

"No," Greyson says under his breath, like a cat waiting to pounce, crouching for the kill. Memory-Ash ignores him and starts to walk toward the house, leaving the defunct phone in the pool's depths. I see what Ash doesn't, the look in Greyson's eyes, and it sends me into a panicky spiral.

"Ash," I plead, "I want to go home now. I don't want to be here for this. I can't be."

"We have to know," he says *"I* have to know what happened to me. How I became this shadow of who I used to be." He pulls my head into his chest and holds me while we watch what happens next with terrified, unmovable eyes. It's like watching a movie you already know ends tragically and trying to wish characters into making different decisions along the way. I want to rewind, or write to the directors, or just turn the damn thing off.

"NO!" Greyson shouts, and before I can blink, he's on top of Memory-Ash, wrestling him to the ground. They are dangerously close to the water's edge, and I close my eyes as Greyson punches Ash in the ribcage repeatedly. My Ash winces too, clutching his side, and when I touch the skin beneath his shirt it's already hot and swollen. *The bruise.*

Greyson is muscular and drunk and high off anger like some sick, deranged creature from a horror film. He continues punching Memory-Ash in the gut and my Ash falls to the ground, gritting his teeth in agony. I sink down with him and hold his head in my lap, but I'm no match for Greyson's fists. Both Ash and Memory-Ash writhe on the ground and I'm filled with a hatred so intense that I jump to my feet and scream at the top of my lungs, begging Greyson to stop, but he can't hear me and probably wouldn't stop even if he could.

"Rafa," pants Ash, reaching for me. "It's no use. It's...no use."

Greyson is on top of Memory-Ash, his massive weight crushing the body below him.

"I told you to mind your own *business,"* Greyson says, slugging Ash another time in the ribs. My Ash moans and I can feel hot tears fill the corners of my eyes. They're not from sadness, or even anger at this point. They're from the unmistakable feeling of helplessness I have–the inability to do anything to help the ones I love.

"You still don't get it, do you?" Greyson continues. "You're just going to have to learn the hard way."

Greyson heaves Ash into the water, and I watch as his body sinks to the bottom of the deep end and then floats back up to the surface, his normally tousled hair now flat and clinging to his forehead. He surfaces and gasps for air in the frigid water, but Greyson places both of his massive hands on the crown of Ash's head and pushes him down. They both struggle as my curses pierce the air around us. Ash gasps for air beside me and clutches his throat, choking on the memory. Greyson holds Memory-Ash under the surface for thirty seconds, then sixty, then what feels like hours. I scream and curse and only stop when Greyson removes his hands and lets Ash bob up to the surface like a fishing buoy or half-drowned dog.

Memory-Ash coughs and sputters and I pound my Ash's back, who finally has a moment of relief. At first, I think the torture is over, that all of this will finally end, but Greyson keeps Ash in the water from the mouth down, panting.

"Now listen," Greyson slurs. "Repeat after me: Ingrid was asking for it. She got embarrassed when I rejected her."

Ash sputters, shivering in the icy water.

"No," Memory-Ash says defiantly, spitting at him, and for once I wish he wasn't so noble. Greyson sneers at him, shrugs, and plunges Ash's head under once again, this time for even longer. My Ash kicks on the ground as if he's seizing, his shirt riding up to reveal a blue bruise spreading over his ribs like toxic sludge. Greyson holds him under for at least a minute, and when he finally releases his grip, Ash surges into the air and gulps at it desperately, like a diver who ran out of oxygen thirty meters down.

"Now, say it. Tell me *exactly* what you saw up there."

Ash coughs and blows water out of his nose, beginning to panic. Even so, he won't say what Greyson wants him to, though I'm begging him to in vain.

"Just say it." I plead to no one. "Just say it."

"Suit yourself," Greyson shrugs, as tears roll down my puffy face. "I can do this all night long. I've got nowhere to be."

Ash starts to yell but is quickly drowned out by an assault of water. His struggling body glows in the lights, thrashing and distorted beneath the surface. Memory-Ash is fighting for his life, and my Ash is slowly slipping away, too, retching on the ground beside me. I hold his head, still uselessly begging Greyson to stop. Memory-Ash kicks underwater while my Ash kicks on the ground in my arms, and Greyson plunges his head even farther down. A minute or two passes, but it feels like a lifetime. A hundred lifetimes. And then, all at once, the kicking stops from both Ash in the water, and Ash on the ground beside me, his body now as cold as the frozen earth.

Greyson releases his grip on Ash, but instead of exploding upward to gasp for air like last few times, Ash's head just floats to the top. It bobs in the water, his body gliding gently underneath. Greyson looks confused for a moment, but the confusion is quickly replaced by realization. He pushes Ash's head into the water again and lets up, as if asking for a re-do. Ash's lifeless head rolls around on the surface, and Greyson pulls him up so that they're eye level. He looks at Ash's face in disbelief, then all around the yard to make sure he's still alone.

"C'mon," he says, hitting Ash's swollen cheeks with the back of his hand and swearing. "Come on. Wake up. Wake *up*!" He slaps Ash harder and harder, but no spark returns to his cold eyes. Greyson curses again. Disbelief and panic flood his face, as if he hadn't ever considered what happens to a human when they don't have access to air. He places Ash's body back into the pool and it floats into the center, his lifeless face turning slowly toward the surface. Greyson looks at his hands, and then to Ash, and then to where I'm crouched, and though I know he cannot see me I get the sense that he knows he isn't alone. He is a frenzied animal, but this time he's the one feeling hunted. It's probably the first time in his life he's been the prey and not the predator.

He takes his hands out of the water, inch by inch, as if afraid that if he moves too suddenly someone might see what he's done. Then Greyson takes his beer, sucks the rest of it down, and tosses the empty can into the pool next to Ash. He wipes his hands on his jacket, as if that will cleanse them of the deed, and backs away. When there's a safe distance between him and the pool he just stands there, panting, looking from his hands to the body and back again.

Chapter 39

I scream. I scream so loud I think the sky might curdle like milk and rain down around me like tears from a mourning God. I sob, I hyperventilate, I send myself into a debilitating panic. I run to the pool but can't bring myself to look at his swollen, lifeless face. Ash, destroyed by a monster, the empty beer can floating next to him. If I didn't know any better, I, too, would think it looked like the scene of a tragic accident. I run back to my Ash, who is just barely clinging to life. He's coughing and choking and holding his neck, the way he did at the clearing that first night. His face is as blue as the bruise on his ribs, and veins are popping out of his neck like giant fissures.

"Ra-fa," he manages to spit out. "You have to find a way to stop him."

"Ash, I don't know how, I can't, I—"

"I–love you."

He forces out the words with the last bit of strength he has, and after that he says no more. His body goes limp, and knowing I cannot help him, I kiss his beautiful head the way I kissed Ollie's on that cold surgery table. I am not going to lose another person I love. Not again, not like this. I feel strength growing from my anger and let it fill me like rain in a dry riverbed.

"I love you, too." I push his hair from his forehead. "I am going to figure this out." I wipe the last of my tears, gathering myself together, and by the time I get to my feet there's a small, pale figure coming toward the pool, wide-eyed and quivering.

"Ingrid!"

She looks right through me, staring at the drowned boy in the water.

"What have you done?" She asks softly, as if asking a child how he spilled his juice. "What have you *done?*"

For a moment I think she's talking to me, but then I realize Greyson is still standing in the darkness gaping at his treacherous deeds in disbelief. He burns a hole through Ingrid with his eyes, and I can see the wheels turning in his brain as he tries to find the path of least resistance.

"You're not going to get away with this," she asserts bravely. "I'll...I'll..."

For a moment Greyson looks stunned and almost frightened, like he might start to cry, but the glimmer of humanity is fleeting and quickly replaced with anger.

"You'll WHAT?" he roars, the paralyzed, scared Greyson retreating, making way for this aggressive one. "You'll call the police? Do you have any proof? No. You don't. Look at him. The idiot couldn't hold his alcohol and tripped and fell into the pool drunk. That's all I see, and that's all anyone else is going to see. You don't have proof of anything." He emphasizes 'anything,' and I see Ingrid flinch. He walks up to her and she freezes like a deer in the headlights of a truck, unsure if they're about to be lethally struck. She must know she can't outrun him.

"If you say *one single word,*" he warns, his voice so low and menacing that even I recoil. "I will *end* you. And then I will tell everyone what a rotten little *whore* you were, and I will upload all of those classy little half-naked photos you sent me and that's how everyone will remember you."

Ingrid opens her mouth to speak, but Greyson cuts her off.

"Speak a single word, and I swear, I will end you with my own two hands. I am not afraid to do it, and if you don't believe me, just go for a swim with him." He jabs a thumb in the direction of the pool and Ingrid goes white, her bare legs shaking in the moonlight.

Finally, it's all coming together, like tectonic plates shifting into place. I understood why Ingrid hated him, and tonight only solidified her reasons, but I could never figure out what put Greyson so on edge around her. Sure, he could squash her like a bug, but she knows something that could ruin him. You can bounce back from a bad reputation. You can't bounce back from what he did to her. You can't bounce back from *murder.*

Ingrid opens her mouth as if to speak, but her mouth hangs open and no sound comes out. She flattens her brows and squints her eyes in disdain and for a moment I think she's going to eviscerate him. She opens her mouth again, but once again no words come out and her expression fades to hopelessness. I can almost see the cogs turning in her brain as she realizes she is completely powerless.

"Not. One. Single. Word." Greyson repeats, Ingrid growing smaller with each syllable he utters. He takes a step toward her and she takes a step back. His shadow swallows her and he takes another step forward. Ingrid takes two steps back, and it's as if he's leading her, both of them entangled in a grotesque dance.

The dance leads them halfway up the yard, Ingrid halfway to the cover of a room full of intoxicated classmates. She breaks free from his invisible grasp and at first, I think she's running back to the house but instead she sprints around the old stone home, down the driveway, into the street and out of sight. Greyson shakes his head, runs a hand through his hair, and then turns to go back to the house, rejoining the party like nothing ever happened.

With Ingrid and Greyson gone and Ash laying lifeless both in the pool and beside me, I feel so desperately alone. I try to yell to the sky but my throat is too numb, and all the escapes me is little more than a whimper. I have never been so wholly and thoroughly alone in all of my life. Except, I'm not alone at all.

At first, I think my wet eyes are playing tricks on me, as I peer into the thicket and away from the dim lights of the pool. My pupils dilate in response until my irises are slim motes of green, straining to see through the night. For a second I think that maybe a deer is watching me, but, creeping closer, I can tell the eyes are human. I inch nearer, praying whoever it is won't run away before I can get a good look, but the body is so motionless that I have little to worry about.

I can see the chest of the figure rising and falling raggedly, and the faint outline of a girl clutching an evergreen tree so tightly her fingers have begun to bleed. By the look on her blank face, stunned and terror-stricken, and by the way her breath catches in her lungs, I can tell that she saw the whole thing. Her blonde hair is caked to her face with cold sweat, and my heart stops as I recognize the figure, her lie finally making sense.

It's Taylor, and she knows what Greyson has done.

Chapter 40

I wake up alone next to the pool and everything from the memory is gone except the tears which still burn my cheeks like acid. My chest and abs hurt from crying and my lungs ache for air, and I search the grounds but don't see Ash anywhere. I cry out for him. I yell his name at the top of my lungs but he is nowhere to be found. Maybe nowhere at all.

"For God's sake, Rafa, *what* is going on?"

For a disoriented moment I think it's Taylor yelling at me, but she's disappeared too. The voice is Mom's, and she is frantic.

"Why are you out here? It's near freezing out and—"

"Mom," I begin, holding out a hand to stop her, trying but failing to contain myself. "Mom I need you to listen to me. Ash Gable, the boy who lived in this house—in our house—he didn't drown by accident. He wasn't even drunk. Somebody *killed* him. He was murdered right here, in this very place one year ago."

I get up and point to the spot where just minutes ago I watched Greyson hold him under the water until the life left his body. Mom is looking at me like I am insane, but I don't care. I am hysterical and I have every right to be.

"Rafaela, what on Earth...?"

I recognize the expression on her face; concerned and even a little afraid.

"Mom, please, if you have ever trusted me, if you have ever *believed* me, believe in me now. We have to go to the police." I can feel myself starting to break but instead of crying I get angry. I can feel the rage boil up inside me like hot water starting to bubble over a blue flame.

"Rafa, I want to believe you but you aren't well. You-"

"NO. This *isn't* about the concussion. It was him, right here. He-he drowned Ash. It wasn't an accident."

"Who? Drowned? What are you talking about?"

"Greyson Kohl. From school. He killed Ash!"

"Greyson? Wasn't he the one who fundraised for the memorial? I saw the newspaper clippings, the ones about all of this. That doesn't seem likely." She says, trying to reason with me but I am so far beyond reason I don't even hear her.

"It was all a ploy. Of course he would do everything he could to make it seem like he cared about Ash. They weren't even *friends!*"

"This isn't a movie, Rafa."

"You're right, it's worse. Ash-he was in so much pain."

"You talk like you know him." She's challenging me, she doesn't believe anything I'm saying.

"I do, Mom, I do. I can't explain it, but he was right here, just a moment ago. I could see him; I could feel him. He was as real as I am, as real as you are. Touch my arm. Feel my skin. He's as real as that. He has a heartbeat and a smile and a voice and– "

"Honey–please. Slow down."

"No." I go on, "We have to call the police. We need to report this. Call the–"

"Rafa he's dead. That boy, he died a long time ago. He died when...He died when Ollie died for Christ's sake." She's raising her voice now and even though I can tell it's out of fear and hurt it startles me into submission. "Come on, let's just go inside; get you warmed up. I'll make you some tea and–"

"*Ugh* you are not listening to me!" I'm raising my voice now too. I'm hot with anger at Greyson but I'm directing it at her, because she's the one who isn't taking me seriously. I am begging at her feet like a prisoner. I want to shake her. Anything to make her believe me. I look around. Where is he? Ash would know what to do.

"You know what? You stay here." Mom says, her face still flooded with concern. "I will be right back. Just, stay here, okay?"

I nod compliantly and as soon as she thinks she is out of earshot she unlocks her iPhone and begins dialing. I don't need to sneak up on her to know she's calling the doctor, possibly even an ambulance, so I stand up while her back is turned and just start running. When I am twenty yards away, I hear her call my name but she's too late and I am too fast. She calls to me from across the yard and then down the street and before I know it, I am out of earshot, my legs carrying me down the road faster than they have ever carried me before. I know where I have to go. Mom can have me institutionalized for all I care, but not until I prove that Ash's death was not an accident and until I am sure no one else will be hurt by the wolf disguised in preppy chino pants, a nice smile, and a letterman jacket.

Chapter 41

I keep running. I don't take the roads, because I know Mom will be out looking for me in the car. I cut through neighbors' lawns and jump over fences and run through dense patches of trees until I am clear on the other end of this small town. I have never been to Ingrid's house before, but I ask her if I can come over and luckily, she replies quickly and with her address.

She lives in the village, not far from me at all. Her street is narrow, probably only wide enough to allow one car to pass at a time. The sidewalk leading up to her house is broken, and her house is small but quaint. I run right up to the door and press the doorbell three times in a row, desperate to talk to her before Mom tracks me down.

I get lucky, and Ingrid opens the door. She looks alarmed, and I realize I probably look like I've just been through a hurricane.

"H–hi." She says timidly, still surprised by the sound of the voice she hasn't used in almost a year.

I burst through the door and hug her, hard. The events I now know took place in my home are burned

into my memory, and all I want to do is make them go
away.

"We need to talk. Can I come in?"

She opens the door to let me in. The house smells
faintly of leftover takeout and is messier than I expected it
to be.

"Are your parents' home?" I ask, as she leads me
through the kitchen and into her bedroom on the bottom
floor of the split-level home.

"No. Why?"

"Good."

She closes the door behind us and searches my
face, sensing how anxious I am.

"What's the matter? Did something happen?"

I don't know how to tell her any of it delicately,
so I just charge full speed ahead with the truth. Well, most
of it anyway.

"Look, I know this isn't going to make any sense,
but I know what happened at my house last year. In my
room and in the pool."

Her face pales. "You mean...?"

I don't let her finish, because I don't want her to
have to say any of it ever again if she doesn't want to.
"Yes. All of it and more. I know what happened at the
pool, with Ash and Greyson. I know his death wasn't an
accident at all. I know…" I struggle to even get the words
out, thinking about what Greyson did to Ash. "I know–"

"Greyson killed him." She says quietly, looking at
her hands which are fidgeting in her lap. She looks
ashamed, and I realize this is probably the first time she
has talked about what happened that night with anyone.

"Yes."

"How do you know?"

"I saw it. Everything. It was like a dream, but it wasn't. It was like a memory that I lived, but I can't explain it in a way that will make sense, you just have to trust me."

She nods.

"I saw the party. And Greyson, I know what he did–what he tried to do–to you. I saw him take you upstairs. I saw Ash push him off of you and hand you the blanket. I saw Greyson drowning Ash in the pool. I can't explain how or why I saw it, I just know that I did."

"But ...how is that possible? How can that be?"

"I know this is going to sound crazy, but I've been talking to Ash. I have been seeing him."

She looks at me as if I'm speaking Mandarin. I go on, because of all the people in the world she is the one person I need on my side.

"After my accident, I started...*seeing* him. But it isn't just seeing him, I can talk to him, I can touch him" I touch Ingrid's hand "I can feel him the way I feel you right now. At first, I wasn't sure it was even real–wasn't sure *he* was real–but some things happened that I don't have time to explain now but I promise that someday I will, and I just know he is real. He's the reason I know what happened to you, and to him."

"Rafa, Ash is dead."

I try not to let my frustration surface in my expression. Hasn't she been listening to what I just said?

"He's not dead." I say, "I don't know what he is, but he's not dead."

"So what, is he a ghost?"

I know he isn't a ghost, but I also know that "ghost" might be easier to grasp than "boy stuck between Earth and oblivion," so I go with it.

"Sort of. Maybe. Yes."

Her face is difficult to read, and she looks skeptical.

"I hate to be this person." She says in a low voice. "But how do you know...you know...that you aren't hallucinating when you think you see him?"

I think about my next words carefully, but she keeps going before I can respond.

"You have to admit that the timing isn't great. You have a TBI–a bad one– and then you just start seeing this person we all know died a year ago?"

I don't even address what she's saying because I know she's right, I know what it must sound like, and I have no tangible proof that he's real other than the story of what I saw.

"I saw him, that night and I saw you. I know you were wearing black skirt and tights and I know Taylor was angry that Greyson was paying attention to you. Your hair was longer and blonde. I saw Greyson rip your skirt and throw it on the floor, and I know Ash knocked him to the ground when he found you. I saw everything, Ingrid. How could I possibly know any of that if what I am saying isn't true?"

She nods her head and averts her gaze, and I keep going. "I know he–Greyson–was angry at Ash for stopping him, but even more angry for seeing him for who–what–he truly is; a predator. He tried to scare Ash

273

into keeping his mouth shut, but then things went too far. And I know…" I look at her again and pause. "I know the reason you stopped talking is that he told you if you spoke *one single word* about that night, he'd kill you. And I know you believed him because…because you saw what he was capable of."

There is a single tear rolling down her cheek, but I know she's damming up a whole river of them. She doesn't say anything for a very long time, as if she's wrestling with the right thing to say.

"I know, it's a lot to take in." I say, and then I ask if she believes me, because I have to know.

"I don't really have a choice." Ingrid replies. "There is no way you could know any of that otherwise. Unless concussions cause psychic visions, too."

I try to hug her again, relieved that someone is finally taking me seriously again, but she pulls back and turns her face away from me and it stings.

"You must think I'm horrible," she begins "I know you must think I am weak, and you would be right. I am weak. I'm-"

I stop her.

"No, you aren't. You're a victim of assault. You were scared and traumatized, anyone would be."

"But I got out alive and didn't tell anyone what I saw. I didn't go to the police when they ruled Ash's death an accident even though I knew the truth. I didn't tell anyone anything. Every time the memory of him-of that night…" She shudders "every time it creeps up on me, I push it out of my head and tell myself it wasn't real. That I never felt Greyson's hands on me. That I never saw him put them on Ash. I pretend the whole night does not exist. I should have done something, I should have *told* someone, and now it's too late."

She looks so ashamed, so broken, and a surge of determination flows through the blood in my veins.

"Maybe not." I say.

"No, you don't understand. There was evidence. The skirt, the bruises on my arms, the motive, but now it's all gone. I could have gone to the police the night it happened. I told myself that keeping quiet was the only way I would survive, but now I know I was just a coward. I didn't want to relive that night. Not then, not ever. I didn't want my parents to see the pictures. I was a coward and lives were ruined because of it."

"You're *not* a coward." I say defiantly. "Ingrid, you're the strongest person I know, and I mean it." I put my hand on her shoulder and this time she doesn't recoil. "He is a monster, and we are going to take him down, once and for all. You and I."

"But how?" She asks, a small glimmer of relief in her eyes. Relief that she is no longer the sole keeper of this secret.

"There was another witness," I say. "Someone else who saw what he did."

"Rafa, you can't claim yourself as a witness. No matter what you saw. You were in Boston when it happened and that will be pretty easy to prove. They will think we're both insane."

"I'm not talking about myself." I say.

"You're wrong. I wish you weren't, but it was just me out there that night. Me and Ash and...*him*."

"No," I say "There was someone else. In the woods. Someone you wouldn't have seen."

"Who?"

"Taylor. She was hiding in the woods, but she saw the whole thing. Better yet, she heard the whole thing. She can corroborate your story!"

"What makes you think she will help us? Even if she knows we know, what makes you think her mindset will change? She's clearly decided to keep what she saw to herself."

Ingrid raises a valid point. Why would she come forward now, after all this time? And what was it that kept her quiet; fear, loyalty to Greyson, or something else?

Chapter 42

Three hours later I'm sitting in a hospital bed with crossed arms arguing with Mom and Dr. Sepir. Try though I did, I couldn't talk Mom out of making me come back to the hospital. I protest that I'm fine again and again, but at this point neither of them believes a word that comes out of my mouth.

"Have you started the antidepressants?" Dr. Sepir asks, and I want to lie but I know I have to tell the truth about this.

"No" I admit. "But only because I don't need them."

"*Rafaela!* You *told* me you would." Mom looks so disappointed in me it cuts.

"I don't need them, Mom. I'm not depressed!"

"Nobody thinks you're depressed." The doctor says calmly. "Antidepressants work for all sorts of wonky brain issues. Something's misfiring up there and we're just trying to figure it out."

"Honestly Rafa, I'm about this close to sending you back to Boston to live with your father. I don't know what to do with you anymore. You won't listen to me, you won't listen to the doctors, but you'll sit in the backyard talking to someone who died a year ago and even though you have a TBI you refuse to even consider the idea that you might be hallucinating." She throws her hands into the air, exasperated.

"No!" I practically shout. A month ago, I wanted nothing more than to return to my old home and to live with Dad, but now I can't imagine leaving Esko. Leaving Ash.

"I want to stay here. I want to stay...with you." This isn't exactly the truth but I'm desperate, so I use it.

"I have no patience left with you." She says, and though her voice is calm I can tell she is at the end of her rope.

"Give me the meds." I say, holding out my hand. "Give them to me right now and I'll take them right in front of you. They're in my bag."

Mom digs the orange bottle out of my bag and hands me a little green pill, which I swallow dry right in front of them. I open my mouth and wiggle my tongue around so they can see that the pill has disappeared down the hatch.

"Happy?"

Mom looks from Dr. Sepir to me and rolls her eyes. "I don't understand you, my beautiful daughter."

"I know." I say. Nobody does. I don't know why I bother asking if I can go home now, but I do.

"Absolutely, two hundred percent out of the question. You are staying here until you stop talking to people that don't exist. That way I can keep an eye on you. And when I can't, Dr. Sepir and the other nurses will.

I am tired of you risking your recovery and your life and I'm not having it anymore. Consider my foot down."

She hands me a hospital gown and puts my chart in the rack at the end of my bed.

"Mom," I plead. "There must be people who need this bed more than I do. Dr Sepir?"

De. Sepir looks thoroughly uncomfortable being forced into the middle of an argument between his patient and chief nurse, who also happen to be mother and daughter.

"Actually Rafa, with the amount of injury you have sustained over the past couple of weeks, your ongoing delusions, and your refusal to follow doctors–and nurses–orders, I'm referring you for a CT scan, an EKG and an MRI tomorrow."

He looks at Mom, who gives him an eye, then he looks down at his tablet. "*But,* it looks like we won't be able to get you in for those until the day after tomorrow, so we will admit you for the next two nights and then go from there."

"Perfect." Says Mom, avoiding eye contact. "I'm going home to get some sleep, and Rafa, I swear if you leave this room, I will have you moved upstairs to the locked ward. You may not like it, but I refuse to let you hurt yourself any further. You are a risk to yourself whether you want to believe it or not."

As frustrated as I am, I don't fight her on it. I know how things look to her. But I have a plan, and soon, hopefully, I can prove to her that I am not delusional.

She lets me keep my phone in case she needs to get in touch with me, but of course I'm not to use it for anything other than communication with her or Dad, who has been "notified of my irrational behavior and will be checking in soon." I let her kiss me on the head and as she turns to leave, I grab her hand.

"Mom, wait."

She pauses and lets me hold on.

"I'm sorry. I'm sorry for everything."

She nods her head curtly, tells me she loves me, and latches the door shut behind her on the way out. As soon as she's out, I pick up my phone and tap on a number in my favorites.

"Are you ready?" I type, already knowing what Ingrid will send back. Luckily, we had enough time to devise a plan before Mom tracked me down.

Chapter 43

Ingrid shows up an hour later wearing all black.

"I'm ready." She says, her voice having grown in fortitude. She hands me some clothes that she stole from my bedroom while Mom was still here (I told her where to find the spare key, because there is no way I'd be able to fit into anything of Ingrid's. Her clothes would look like doll clothes on my body). I slip into black leggings and a hoodie, pocketing my phone.

"Is she coming?" I ask, crossing my fingers.

"She said she was." Ingrid replies. I don't know how she convinced Taylor to meet us at the hospital this late at night, and I don't ask.

"Yes!" I squeal. "Good job. I don't know how you did it, but good job."

She takes a little faux bow.

"Have you seen...Ash?" She asks timidly, trying to believe the things I've told her, though I can tell she's still struggling to. Either way, I appreciate her effort to appease me.

"No," I say, biting my lower lip. I haven't seen him since the lapse into his memory, which I have to remind myself was just a few hours ago even though it seems like a whole other lifetime. "But I'm not worried. He'll come back. He always does."

She nods, and together we make a Rafa-sized lump in the bed with two hospital pillows and my gown.

"This has to work. We won't get another chance, because I'm pretty sure my Mom is going to have me committed after this."

We crack the door and slip out, careful to do so only when the night shifts look away. The hallway to our left is dark, so we tiptoe into it and slither into a stairwell. Ingrid pulls a map out of her back pocket, and I turn on my phone's flashlight so we can figure out where we are going.

I shine my light on the hospital map and nearly jump out of my skin when I realize we aren't alone anymore, but my fright is quickly replaced with a warm seed of joy that sprouts in my stomach and spreads into my chest like the arms of a tree.

"Ash!" I throw my arms around him. He flinches, and I pull back.

"Careful," he says, wincing and holding up his shirt to reveal the massive bruise on his ribcage which isn't magically healed like it is when we're in the clearing. "Fresh wounds, or something like it. It's been bothering me since...well, you know."

I touch the skin around his wound gently with my fingertips, and it's boiling hot. He pulls his shirt back down, covering up the ugly bruise and draws my chin upward with his hand.

"Hey...are you alright?" He asks, searching my eyes.

"I will be," I answer, "as soon as Greyson is locked up and this is all over."

"Ahem….Rafa." The bubble Ash and I had been living in pops as Ingrid clears her throat, reminding us we're not alone.

"So this is weird." She asserts bluntly, studying us, though she can only see me. "I gotta say...I can see why your mom is concerned"

For some reason, I need Ingrid to believe me. I don't mind being invalidated by Mom and Dr. Sepir and everyone else in the world, but she is the one person I want fully on my side. We have been through so much and I need her to understand.

"Okay," I say, getting an idea and turning my back to her. "Hold some fingers, and I'll tell you how many you're holding up."

She looks at me quizzically, not seeing where I am going with this.

"Just, play along."

"Alright," She concedes. "I'll play."

I give her a moment to hold up a random number of fingers which I cannot see, then look at Ash, who is facing her. He holds up three fingers.

"How many am I holding up?" She asks, and I can tell she thinks she's going to stump me.

"Three." I say.

"Lucky guess." She says, but I can tell she is at least mildly impressed. "Again."

I look at Ash, and he holds up one finger.

"One." I say.

"Again." She says, and she makes me guess the number of fingers she's holding up ten or eleven times until she is finally satisfied. I fire off the answers, two, zero, ten, five, seven; again and again, each time answering with the correct number thanks to Ash's help. When I turn around, she's beaming in disbelief.

"I don't understand it," She says "but I can't deny it either. Either you're a psychic, or you aren't making this up."

"Thank *God,*" I say. An ocean of relief washes over me as I realize I finally have someone in this world on my side.

"I feel crazy for even doing this," Ingrid says, turning to the space next to me. "I never got a chance to say this but, thank you, Ash. Thank you for...for saving me that night."

She holds up her hand, trying to find him in the dark air. He holds his hand up to hers and even though neither of them can feel it, for a moment their hands find each other, and they touch.

"He says you're welcome, and he's sorry." I say, speaking the language between worlds. We all stand in silence for a minute, and I have to remind the group that we don't have a lot of time. We fill Ash in on the plan, and though he can't do much he is coming along for moral support, and because he and I don't want to be without each other if we can help it.

We go down two flights of stairs and enter another dark hallway. A few lights are on, but for the most part the floor is asleep. We jut across another hallway, then slip into a spacious room labeled "Surgery Waiting Area." We look for a discreet corner near the back of the room, and find Taylor already waiting for us at a round table with three empty seats. We make our way to her past anxious looking families, some holding hands, some sleeping, some crying quietly, and sit down at her table, careful to keep our heads and our voices low.

Taylor looks up at us from eyes hidden under a mint green baseball cap.

"What is this about?" She hisses, her teeth whiter than any I've ever seen, and her eyebrows recently threaded. She looks from Ingrid to me, but I'm the one who speaks.

"We know."

"You *know?* Well, gee, thanks for clearing up my confusion."

She's on the defensive and if we're not careful, this is going to get ugly. She looks over her shoulder as if she hears footsteps but finds nothing but a gaping, black window.

"We know you were there that night. In the woods."

"I don't what you're talking about." She says, averting her eyes in the direction of the door, searching for an escape. "And I'm not going to entertain it. *She* told me that this was about Greyson and some other girl." Taylor nods her head toward Ingrid, who's watching her intently. "Coming here was obviously a mistake."

Taylor gets up to leave, and Ingrid jumps from her seat, putting her body between Taylor and the exit, showing her hand.

"Stop." She says. It isn't a request, but a command.

Taylor finds her seat in shock from hearing a voice she hasn't heard in over a year. Ingrid sits back down and adjusts her sweater, as if she didn't just pause time with one word.

"Well, it is about Greyson and another girl." I say "It's about Greyson and Ash and you and I and Ingrid and everything that happened that night. I know you were there, Taylor. I know you saw everything. I know you were hiding in the woods when Ash died." I read her expression, trying to figure out if she's going to crack, then add, "When he was murdered."

A shiver runs through the room at the word, and I feel Ash tense up beside me.

"You don't know what you're talking about." She says, in a low growl. "You were still in... Providence...or wherever when it happened."

"Boston," I say, correcting her. "And you admit, something happened?"

"Uh, news flash, Rafa, somebody *died*. Everybody knows that. It's not really a secret. Not that Esko can keep a secret to save its pathetic life."

"But not everyone knows *how* he died. Only Ash and Ingrid and Greyson. And you. And now *me*."

I hope the *and now me* will elicit a response, and it does. I don't think we'll be able to crack poised, stoic Taylor, but we may be able to crack unhinged, off-guard Taylor.

"Don't you think if I knew something, I'd have said something to the police? Look, I know you probably

don't like me very much but I'm not a terrible person."
She snaps, becoming noticeably more agitated by the
second.

"Sometimes good people do things they shouldn't
do. Sometimes they hide things out of fear." I say, looking
to Ash. "Out of fear of a person, fear of not being taken
seriously, fear of losing someone we love… lots of
reasons."

She looks down at her white trainers and shifts
uncomfortably in the waiting room seat. She collects
herself, takes a deep breath, and tucks *unhinged Taylor*
safely back in her pocket.

"What do you mean *fear?*" She asks, "what do I
have to be afraid of? You think I'm afraid of my own
boyfriend?"

I can't tell if she is asking a question, or hoping I
have an answer, but either way I see another opportunity
to provoke her even further and take it.

"If Greyson is your boyfriend, then why has he
been pursuing me practically since I got here?"

Ash's jaw clenches audibly beside me, just the
thought of Greyson uprooting his calm demeanor.

"I'd hardly call that pursuing." She retorts coolly,
keeping her footing in the slippery back-and-forth we're
engaged in. "He was just trying to be welcoming. He felt
sorry for you because you didn't have anyone. He pitied
you. He talked about you to me, *laughed* about you. Said he
could practically smell the self-consciousness on you."

I shift uncomfortably this time, remembering how
alone I felt a few weeks ago, and how, had she been

talking about anyone other than Greyson Kohl, she might have a point.

"That's how it goes. A girl gets a little attention from the popular guy and starts making up stories to herself. *But he smiled at me, that* must *mean he wants me.*" She continues ignorantly.

She is not just sparring with me now, and rage flutters in my chest at the way she's taunting Ingrid. Bringing what happened to Ingrid into this is heartless, nothing short of cruel.

"Do you ever think that he likes that, Taylor? That maybe he *thrives* on the attention he gets from self-conscious girls; girls who would do anything for him, even if it meant sacrificing themselves and their integrity like lambs to the slaughter?"

Taylor flinches at this, and I can tell I've struck a nerve. She doesn't say anything, so I keep going.

"The sad thing is, we should be on the same team. I feel sorry for you that you can't see it."

"What do you want from me?" Taylor snaps, raising her voice so a few of the waiting room patrons turn around and glare.

"I want you to admit what you know, that Greyson is a monster, and I want you to admit that deep down, no matter how tough your exterior is, you're afraid of him too."

"I'm not. Afraid. Of him."

Before I retort, I think about Ingrid, and what I know Greyson is capable of. I think about how battered down Taylor always acts around him, how the strong, confident girl in front of me turns to rubble the second she thinks she's done something wrong in his eyes, and I connect the dots. She isn't just an obsessive girlfriend; that's not her. No, she's manipulated, hurt, kicked, like a helpless puppy into submission by an abusive master.

"I know what he's capable of." I say, meeting her eyes, forcing her to look at me. "Taylor, I know this isn't easy to hear, but Greyson– he didn't cheat on you with Ingrid–"

I look at Ingrid, and she nods, consenting to what I'm about to tell her.

"He *assaulted* her."

Taylor peels her arms off the table and pulls back, as far away as she can possibly go without disappearing through the window.

"That's not true," she says, looking from me to Ingrid, her voice growing weaker. "That's–that's a lie. You're just trying to get to me."

I look at Ingrid and nod my head, and she looks afraid again, as if the whole world will crash down around her if she opens her mouth but she does it anyway.

"It's true." Ingrid says, head down, pink bangs covering her eyes. Taylor looks as if she's just seen a ghost, and even though Ash is sitting directly across the table, I know the shock is from Ingrid finding her voice.

"But why-why would he do something like that? Why would he need to?"

She doesn't want to believe it, but I can see the truth saturating her like slow drips from a leaky tap. Deep down she knows what we are saying isn't as far-fetched as she wishes it were.

"Think about it." I say. "Guys like that don't do those things because they *need* to. It isn't even about sex. It's about power. It's about control. It's about bending another human being to their will."

Taylor cringes at this and I can tell she is connecting the dots too, even if she doesn't want to.

"It's true." Repeats Ingrid, force blossoming in her words. "I don't want it to be, but it is. He forced himself on me and Ash walked in on it. He stopped it." She gulps, looking toward the empty chair at the table where Ash sits, struggling to get out the next words. "If it weren't for Ash, Greyson would have succeeded. He would have broken me, the way he's broken you."

Taylor stands, then sits back down. She rubs her legs with her palms and breathes heavily, as if she's locked in a hot car, struggling to get enough air.

"No." She says, trying to sound resolute but her voice cracks with uncertainty. "No. It isn't like that. He was drunk. He got carried away. It happens; it happens sometimes with me too. He doesn't *mean* to. He doesn't…" but she can't finish her sentence because she's never realized how wrong it all sounds when she puts a voice to the story she's been telling herself.

"Taylor," I say softly. I hold out my hand to her but she recoils at my touch. "It doesn't matter if he *means to*. You aren't his to take. If someone gets behind the wheel of a car drunk, or texts and drives, it wouldn't matter if they *meant* to hit someone with the car, the point would be that they did. *Meant to* has nothing to do with it."

I stop there, because I can tell she's processing some things she may not have admitted to herself, painful things that would have been easier left buried with Ash's body, deep beneath Esko's innocent exterior.

"Think about it. Greyson did what he did to Ash because Ash knew, and he was going to call the police. That's why Greyson killed him."

"He didn't mean to!" She shouts, drawing more attention. "*He didn't mean to.*" She repeats, this time in little more than a whisper. "He was just trying to scare him. It was just like the stupid hazing they do with the freshman on the football team. It wasn't supposed to end in that way, okay? He just wanted him to keep quiet, he didn't mean to kill him. I watched his face when Ash didn't take a breath. He's not a murderer."

I'm about to speak, but Ingrid takes the words from me, rightfully so. They're hers to take.

"Ever notice how every time Greyson doesn't *mean* to do something, someone gets hurt?"

Or worse, Ash adds, rubbing his wounded ribcage.

Taylor knits her brows with her fingers, and though I expect her to keep defending Greyson, she begins to cry quietly. Mascara-soaked tears drip down her nose and collect on the table in an ebony puddle, and we all wait for her to speak.

"I-I didn't know, Ingrid. I swear I didn't. I saw what happened to Ash but nobody knew I saw and I thought I could bury it. I thought it was just some stupid hazing; I didn't know. I didn't know Greyson did that to other girls too. I thought..." she sniffles, stifling a much bigger sob. "I thought he only did it to me, and I thought it wasn't that big of a deal because it only happens when he is drunk. And that stuff happens, right? It was my fault for being a tease. For acting like...like a..."

"Slut?" Ingrid says, completing Taylor's unfinished thought. "Yeah, I've heard that one, too."

Taylor puts her head on the table and cries, whispering to no one in particular. *What have I done...what have I done?* I reach out to touch her arm again, but it's like trying to comfort an injured tiger and I'm not sure if she will be grateful for the touch or want to pounce on me and rip me to shreds.

"I know it's bad," I say "but you can help make it right. You can make sure Greyson never hurts you or anyone ever again. You can make sure Ash's death wasn't..." Here, I have trouble finding my words, but I'm reminded he's still next to me by a gentle hand on my leg. "all for nothing."

Taylor looks up, a new power in her eyes I have not seen before.

"I want to help, but if he finds out..."

"He won't." I say, "And if and when he does, it'll be too late. He won't be able to get to you. Or any of us."

She nods, but I can tell she is unconvinced. Then she looks at Ingrid.

"I don't think I can do it alone"

Ingrid nods, and reaches out to take her hand. It's funny, I never pictured the two of them having anything in common. I guess in some sick twisted way, they have Greyson Kohl to thank for that.

"You won't have to." Ingrid says, her newfound voice becoming stronger with every word she speaks.

Chapter 44

After a bit more convincing, Taylor agrees to go to the police with us. By the time she concedes, it is nearly two in the morning. I know I should be exhausted but the adrenaline is keeping me alert. When we get up to leave, Taylor takes out her phone and says she'll be right behind us.

"I just need to text my stepmom. I told her I was going to Thea's house for a few hours; I'll just tell her I am staying the night."

I can't imagine my mom letting me stay out past midnight, let alone texting her at all hours to update my plans, but I guess some parents are like that. Luckily, mine has no idea what I am up to, and won't be back to work until well after I am back in bed. I've gone on stealthier midnight outings than this before and gotten away with it, so I am not worried. And besides, even if I do get caught, it will be well worth it to see Greyson get what he deserves. Mom will be understanding once I am able to finally prove everything. Hopefully.

We sneak back up to the floor where my room is, just to make sure no one suspects anything. I don't need Mom calling the police again because I've gone missing.

Ash drifts into the hallway and scopes things out, and he reports that the corridor is quiet, and the nurses are both at their stations drowning in paperwork.

"Thanks," I say.

"Who are you talking to?" Taylor scrutinizes. It is so hard to remember that nobody else can see him, though I should be used to it by now. It's too much to explain and even if it weren't, we don't have the time. Luckily Ingrid cuts me off and lies for me.

"Her head. It's the TBI. This happens sometimes, the talking to herself. You get used to it." Ingrid shoots me a look as if to say, "keep it together."

Taylor ponders me with judgmental eyes, and I laugh nervously, knowing she too thinks I have lost my marbles, but what's one more person to add to that list.

"Whatever. Let's just get out of here."

Taylor leads the way down the stairwell to the first floor, and we follow. If this were during the day, some of the women at reception would definitely recognize me, but I haven't had much interaction with the night crew, so I don't bother trying to hide. We walk out casually, as if a friend of ours just came out of surgery and now that we know they are going to be okay, we are going home to get some sleep.

Luckily the police station is just a couple miles from the hospital (one of the perks of living in such a small town) so we don't need to worry about getting a ride.

"You're not going to like, pass out or anything, are you?" Taylor asks, looking at me.

"Probably." Ash jokes, making fun of my unreliable consciousness.

"Hey!" I say, and Taylor thinks I am responding to her.

"Well...sorry!" She says, apologetic. "I don't want to deal with mopping you up off the street when you fall and break your face, okay?"

"Guys, let's just go." Ingrid says, decisively. I ask her if she's okay, and she says no, but she will be as soon as we get this over with.

The four of us walk through the dark, which is broken every hundred yards with streetlights casting yellow orbs of light onto the sidewalk. We are all eager to get this over with, so we walk quickly up one street and down the next, until we are just half a mile from the station. Our heads are down, pushing through the breeze that whips our faces with frigid air when suddenly Ingrid, who took the lead holds out her arm like a barrier and stops us.

"Wait." She says, holding her breath. There are no more streetlights illuminating us, so all I can see are three sets of blinking eyes and the occasional white puff of cold breath against darkness.

"Do you guys hear something?"

Ash and I press our ears into the night but hear nothing. Taylor doesn't seem concerned. I shrug.

"I don't hear anything." I say, but then I do. Out of the dark, I hear footsteps, heavy and foreboding. It's much too late for casual passersby, and I pray it is just a group of kids smoking weed or a couple who snuck out to get some alone time. I squint into the darkness, but I don't see who the footsteps belong to until they are nearly on top of us. I hear a small sob form in the back of Ingrid's throat as we both realize who the faceless footsteps belong to.

"Hello ladies," Greyson condescends. I can smell the stench of beer on his breath. My fight or flight instinct begins tingling, just like it did the day I got to Esko, but I know he can outrun all of us to I stay put and let Ash pull me into him with a strong arm around my waist. There are a million questions running through my mind, but the most prominent one is how the hell Greyson found us.

"Out for a midnight stroll?"

"What are you doing here?" I demand, looking at him through eyes watering from the cold.

"Watch it, Rafa" Ash says protectively, warning me.

"I think you know," He sneers, looking directly at me. "After all, you organized this little soiree, didn't you?" Ash steps in front of me and I can feel fear starting to grow inside me. *Little soiree.* He knows what we are doing. But how?

And then it hits me. I think about Taylor, texting her "stepmom" before we left the hospital. I should have trusted my gut; I knew there was something wrong with it. I look at her accusingly.

"You?" I ask, "You told him?"

She looks ashamed and opens her mouth but doesn't speak.

"No." Ingrid says, her voice singed with betrayal. "You wouldn't...you couldn't." She can't imagine how Taylor could betray her after the moment they shared in the hospital, but as Taylor walks over to stand next to the monster, I know it must be true.

"Greyson," Taylor pleads, "there has to be some explanation. Just, explain what really happened, so we don't have to go to the police. Tell us your side. I'm sure this is all one big misunderstanding. We can all figure this out, right guys?" She looks from him to Ingrid to me, passing right over Ash. I feel anger coursing through my veins in the form of hot, feverish blood. How can she be so naive?

"People don't die over misunderstandings," I say, glaring at the both of them. Taylor tries to take Greyson's hand, but he pulls away and gives her a look of disgust like he's angry with her even though she's the one stupidly trying to help him. Taylor looks like a kicked puppy again, I almost can't believe it, but as I put two and two together, it makes perfect sense.

I think about how she follows Greyson around, admiring him like he is some kind of Adonis. I think about how she told us he takes advantage of her but doesn't *mean* to; how she defends him even though he hurts her again and again. I think about all of the times I've seen him reject her publicly, and how she just keeps going back to him no matter how many times he puts her down. Even now she stands, pleading with Greyson, begging him to be the person she believes he is. I actually feel sorry for her. She isn't a bad person, she's just completely dependent on an emotionally abusive guy and doesn't even know it.

Greyson looks to Taylor and says something inaudible, and as he is distracted, I whisper to Ingrid.

"Run. I'll distract him, you go get the police."

"I can't leave you with him," She hisses, her words laced with fear.

"You have to. It might be our only chance. I'll be okay." But even as the words slip off of my tongue, I wonder if they are true.

"Rafa–you have to get–"

"The phone, I know. Now go!" I hiss under my breath, Greyson closing in on both of us.

She backs away slowly, then takes off into the night.

"Hey!" He shouts, and starts after her, and I do the only thing I can think to do. I throw my entire body into him, kicking out his ankle and tripping him. He falls face first but catches himself, his phone tumbling out of his jacket pocket and onto the ground. He's too distracted to realize, and when he gets to his feet and lunges at me again, I'm already diving to the ground a few feet to the left. I grab his phone and smash it onto the pavement, killing the device and freeing Ingrid from his blackmail.

Triumph surges through my body, but it only lasts a moment before I realize all I've done is stab an angry bull, and I am no matador. He looks from me to the phone, which is now in three pieces, a dull growl forming in his throat.

"What the hell, Rafa!"

He gets up slowly and purposefully, and I don't know what is coming but I know it's not going to be good.

"Run, Rafa!" Ash says, pulling me to my feet, desperation in his eyes. "I can't help you like this; you have to *run*."

Except I can't run, because if I change my course now, he'll run after Ingrid who may not have made it to the police yet and God only knows what he will do to her. All I have to do is distract him for another minute, just long enough for the police to arrive.

"I can't," I say to Ash, and I stand my ground. "Ingrid!"

Greyson walks toward me, and Taylor grabs at his arm in an attempt to stop him, but he pushes her to the wet ground and she whines, holding an arm that smacked the pavement too forcefully not to hurt.

"What makes you think this is any of your business, huh?" He asserts angrily. "What did I tell you about Ash? Didn't I tell you that he died because he couldn't keep his nose out of other people's business?"

"Rafa, please." Ash begs, creating a fruitless barrier between me and my drunken adversary. "Please get out of here. *Now*."

"No!" I cry, ignoring Ash and staying put even as Greyson looms over me. "That's not true and you know it. He died because *you killed him*."

The lights in his eyes flicker and go black, and he's so close to me I can feel the heat radiating from his body.

"What did you say to me?" His beer breath stings my face. Ash is cursing at Greyson and Taylor is crying in a puddle, too beaten down to know what to do.

"I said," I begin, my body flooded with panic but my voice calm. "Ash is dead because *you* killed him. You tried to assault Ingrid, and he knew about it, and you killed him to keep him quiet. And you threatened to kill Ingrid, too."

I have never seen anyone so enraged before, but I can't tell if he is angry with me or with himself. I don't know if he has ever confronted what he's done; if this is the first time he's had to hear it out loud.

"YOU." He shouts, and lunges. I dart out of the way, and he misses me by the narrowest of margins. I am suddenly filled with a strength I have never felt before.

"What are you going to do to me?" I shout back. "You're a coward, you can't even admit to yourself what you've done. You've already taken Ash from me and hurt my best friend irreversibly, what are you going to do? Kill me, too? Go ahead and do it, then you'll rot in jail. I'd love to see you try to make my death look like an accident."

I don't know why I'm saying the things I'm saying, but I hate him so much I can't help myself. He's never been held accountable for anything in his life and I am going to make him feel the things he's done if it is the last thing I do.

"Ha!" He says, "You're joking, right? Everyone knows you're insane and probably depressed! Poor Rafa, with her dead brother and divorced parents and broken face and invisible boyfriend. Nobody would be surprised if you suddenly decided to off yourself! Heck, if I were you, I probably *would* off myself."

His words sting, but I'm not going to let him get to me. I would sooner take a thousand cuts from him than let him ever touch Ash or Ingrid again.

"Admit it." I say, ignoring him. My voice is low and coarse. "Admit you killed him."

"You are crazy." He glowers, glowing with white-hot anger, the only light coming from the screen of Taylor's phone against the backdrop.

"Better that than a murderer. Now admit it. Admit you killed Ash. I mean, what's the harm. I'm crazy, right? So just admit it."

He circles me like a ravenous hyena, but I stand my ground because I can just hear the start of sirens in the distance. Greyson is too drunk to notice the wails, so all I have to do is keep him here for another minute, then we'll be saved.

"You're off your meds."

"You know what the worst thing about you is, Greyson? It's that you don't hold yourself accountable for anything. You go through life, not caring who you hurt, or why, as long as it's to your benefit. I bet you aren't even capable of admitting what you did to *yourself*."

He stops pacing and considers what I've just said. "What did you say?" He demands.

I stand unwavering in my stance. "I said that you can't even admit a wrongdoing to yourself. You're weak, and because you're weak, you'll never be a good person. You'll never do the hard thing, the right thing."

"You're wrong."

"You can't even admit what you did to Ash. I don't know if you're in denial or just a complete psychopath."

"Shut up."

"Admit it." I demand.

"Rafa—"Ash warns, but I keep going, because the sirens are getting closer and closer. Soon I'll be able to see the red and blue lights coming around the corner, and Greyson will be taken away in handcuffs.

"No."

"Admit it."

"No!"

"Coward!" I scream. "You're nothing but a coward. A weak, pathetic, privileged, coward."

"Shut UP!" He yells, but I don't let him continue.

"Coward, coward, coward, *cowa—*"

"Alright FINE! I killed him. I killed him with my bare hands, and even though I didn't mean to, I'd do it again. He was going to ruin my life, so I ruined his. That's the way life works, okay? Eat or be eaten." He snarls and continues in a frenzy. "Is that what you wanted to hear? Doesn't matter, nobody's going to believe you. Everyone knows you've lost your mind, and she's never going to go against me." He stabs his thumb toward Taylor, still on the ground, clutching her phone to her chest.

The sirens turn onto the end of our street, and then he hears them too. I lock eyes with him and smile triumphantly, knowing it is too late for him to run, but my triumph is short lived because unlike a few moments ago, now he has nothing left to lose.

At once, he lunges at me with a rock-hard arm and body slams me to the ground. Ash tries to protect me, and I feel him throw his weight on top of me protectively, but Greyson is on me in a second. I try to wriggle away on the concrete, scraping my elbows and knees in the process but he grabs me by the legs and gets on top of me, crushing my body with his. I think he's going to start pummeling me, so I cover my face instinctively but instead he gets up, picks me up like a rag doll, and throws me back to the sidewalk.

I yell for help, realizing he's probably going to kill me, too. My head hits the damp pavement, and I hear Ash say my name; my full name. Each syllable like a warm melody in my ears. Then, I feel his hands cradle my head. I've felt them like this before, on the trail. I'd always assumed it'd been Greyson who caught me, but it was Ash. It's *always* been Ash.

I nuzzle into those strong hands, and with what cognitive strength I have left, take in the bright lights and wailing sirens and Taylor, a few yards away from me on the blacktop, still clutching her phone. I hear Ash tell me to stay with him, but my energy is completely sapped.

I nuzzle into him a little closer, and then I feel and see and hear no more.

Chapter 45

I inhale and life swells within me like air being blown into a red balloon. I am surrounded by pleasant smells. Honeysuckle and fresh rain, evergreen and peppermint. The lights are bright, but not cold, not sterile or florescent. The warm hands are on me again. They stroke my cheeks and push my wavy hair behind my ears, then I feel soft lips on my forehead and open my eyes.

He's looking at me in that admiring way he always does, as if I am the eighth wonder of the world. I smile back, observing a soft lack of pain. Just a minute ago everything hurt, now I feel deliciously comfortable, as if I've just woken up from a nap on the beach, saturated in sunlight and balmy ocean air. I wonder what drugs they have me on this time.

"Hello, pretty girl." Says Ash. Thank God he's still with me. He is sitting cross-legged on the ground, my whole body cradled in his arms. They are muscular and hard, but not dangerous. They are strong and protective, yet tender at the same time.

"Hey, you," I say, and no matter how I try I cannot wipe the grin off of my face so I just stare at him, beaming like a little kid with a puppy.

"You gave us quite the scare." He says, continuing to stroke my face. I close my eyes and melt into him, not wanting the moment to end.

"What do you mean?" I ask, not all together concerned. Pain doesn't matter now, because there is none. Just the honeysuckle and rain and peppermint and pure bliss of he and I.

"You don't remember?" he asks, not judging, just musing, as if reminiscing on some pleasant forgotten time.

I shake my head back and forth, but then something comes back to me. A small figure running away in the dark, the scent of alcohol on angry breath.

"Oh...Greyson and... Ingrid."

I sit up starkly, but he holds me in place.

"Is Ingrid okay?"

"She is," Ash says, kissing my forehead, sending ripples of heaven into my bones. "She made it to the station because of you. If you hadn't distracted him, well, who knows what would have happened."

I get a warm feeling inside knowing Ingrid is safe and that by now, Greyson must be sitting in handcuffs at the police station, kissing his future goodbye.

"Taylor?" I ask, for even though she betrayed us, I can only picture her sobbing on the ground, beaten and downtrodden.

"She's okay too." He confirms. "Physically, at least. Just a sprained wrist and some scratches."

I blink, expecting the hospital to come into focus but it doesn't. All of our surroundings are drowned out by bright, clean air. It's like being in a snow-covered field when the sun is high in the sky except it isn't cold.

"Where...where are we?"

Ash strokes my hair again, lovingly, but he looks uncomfortable.

"What's wrong?" I ask. "Whatever it is, you can tell me."

"We're..." He trails off "We're where I go when I'm...gone."

It doesn't make sense at first, so I just relish in his touch for a moment longer. His hands through my hair, his arms encompassing me like a weighted blanket.

"I don't understand," I say, closing my eyes and snuggling into his chest. "But I'm glad we're together."

Then, I hear it. At first, I think I'm dreaming, and since I do, I don't open my eyes. I know it's a dream; it always is. But then I hear it again, and it's closer and stronger this time.

"*Rafa?*"

His voice drips slow and warm into my ears like honey from the tip of a spoon. Like childhood. Like fried dough with cinnamon-sugar on Christmas morning. Like home. I open my eyes and there he is.

He's just as beautiful as I remembered him to be. He has Mom's strawberry blonde hair, and Dad's soft bronze complexion. There are freckles sprinkled across his nose, which rests in the middle of two large, hazel eyes. His skin is soft, and I want so desperately to touch it, that I reach out my hands and pray he isn't an apparition.

"Ollie?" I say, hardly daring to breathe. He comes toward me on his little, eight-year-old legs and crouches down beside us. His lips are plump and pink, and he kisses my cheek, sending a thousand emotions running through me. He wraps his arms around my neck, and I breathe him in; his curly hair smelling of heaven. Maybe it is.

I wriggle off of Ash's lap and take Ollie into my arms. I hold him for a long time; an eternity, almost. When he gently pulls away, I smother his face with kisses until he starts giggling, and the sound of his laugh makes my heart throb with nostalgia and threaten to burst.

"I've missed you so much," I say. "How–are you okay?"

"I'm okay," He says, looking at Ash and smiling. "Even better now that I have a friend." Ash tousles his hair and Ollie giggles. I still can't get over how much I missed hearing that little voice.

"Ash?" I ask, incredulous. "I don't understand."

"I didn't want to tell you." He says, "I didn't think it would make sense to you at the time, and I didn't know how to explain it even if I could. I didn't want to bring up the hurt, either. Remember that night in the house by the fire, when you told me about Ollie?"

I nod my head, my hand in Ollie's curls.

"Well, after that, I sort of...found him."

I look from Ollie to Ash and then at my own skin, half expecting it to be transparent as realization dawns on me.

"Wait..." I say "Are we in... Am I?"

"Maybe." Ash shrugs. "Maybe, maybe not."

I can't say I'm surprised. If you'd ask me yesterday what my heaven would look like, I would have painted a picture of exactly this.

"If you're dead, and Ollie's dead…" I ask, unafraid "Does that mean I'm dead too?"

"I don't think so."

I struggle to understand, but I don't think I can.

"Your body is in a coma." He finishes. I know I should be panicking, but I'm not. I am completely calm and happy and warm, and everything is perfect. I look at Ollie and he looks happy too, just like I always try to remember him.

"I don't understand." I say.

"You aren't meant to." Ash replies. Nobody is, not even us." He looks at Ollie and they share a smile. "Humans are always searching for the science of things. For concrete evidence and definitions and step by step guides on what to expect for everything. This…this next life…it just isn't something that is meant to be understood."

"How do you live with that?" I say, looking at my two favorite people.

"We don't," Ollie says "That's kind of the point, silly."

He pokes my nose and I can't help but laugh, though I have so many questions.

"We don't worry here," Ash says, "We just…are."

I try to wrap my brain around it.

"Are we floating?" I say, realizing there doesn't seem to be any ground.

"Do you feel like you're floating?" He asks, looking down at me with his beautiful blue eyes.

"No," I say, "but..."

"Here," He says, lifting me to my feet. "Take a step."

I oblige, and even though there is no ground beneath my feet, he's right. I don't fall or float.

"It's not oblivion," He says "It's so much more. It's everything and nothing all at once."

I should be crazed with uncertainty-induced anxiety, but I'm not. I lace my fingers through his and take Ollie's hand on my other side. The three of us stand, hand in hand for some time and I revel in the moment until Ollie chirps up.

"Think of something," He says. "Think of anything in the world that you want."

Being that I already have the things I love most, I'm not sure what to wish for. I am a little hungry, so I close my eyes and think of a chocolate milkshake. When I open them, there is a little cafe table with three chairs and three Instagram-worthy milkshakes; one vanilla, one strawberry, and one smothered in chocolate sauce. I pick up the latter and take a sip.

"Oh my god, that's *delicious*" I say, and Ollie picks up the pink one and takes a gulp. "Wait–Ash, are you a *vanilla* guy?"

He flashes his eyes at me and sips from the pearly white drink. "So what if I am?"

"I wish you'd told me sooner. It's just that, well, that's kind of a deal breaker for me."

I take another sip of my chocolate shake and we all start to laugh as if this is the most natural thing in the world.

"Alright, the milkshakes are nothing. Now think of something *big*," Ollie says, holding out his arms. Think of anything in the world. In the whole wide universe!"

I close my eyes and think. There is only one other thing I could want in this messed up world, and that's to be a family again. To have Mom, Dad, Ollie, and me all under one roof. To once again feel that pleasant nostalgia, but not the massive twinge of sadness that comes with the memories every time I think about them.

I can't really describe what happens next. It isn't as if Mom and Dad appear out of thin air, but I can feel them. I feel the warmth of my childhood, back in Boston before Ollie got sick. I see Mom and Dad sneaking kisses at the park, while Ollie begs me to push him higher and higher on the swings. I feel the morning of Ollie's fifth birthday, smell the coffee and the breakfast in the oven, and see a wriggling box on the table, squirming like only a new puppy can. I see Ollie, gathering Benny in his arms and hear his giggle as Benny licks his neck, his ears and his face. I feel their hands and their hearts in mine, and it comforts me like nothing I've ever experienced. It's like sitting the perfect distance away from a bonfire, not too close to be hot but not too far to feel the warmth. I have never felt so perfectly content, so perfectly *happy* in all of my life. I open my eyes and see Ollie and Ash beaming at me, as if they've just felt the whole thing too.

"It wouldn't make sense to anyone who hasn't experienced it." Ash begins. "People are such tangible, in-the-now creatures. When we want something, we don't just *want* it, we want our desire and time to align. We want it "now," but here there is no "now." Here, having something, and having *had* something are the same.

I nod my head because even though it doesn't make sense to me logically, even though I could never explain it in words, after feeling it just once I understand. Ollie stands next to me, playing with my long hair.

"Can I stay here?" It didn't occur to me until just now that that might be an option.

Ash looks to Ollie and then to me. I think of Mom and Dad, and how devastated they were when they lost Ollie, of how devastated they'd be if they lost me.

"You're just visiting."

I think I'm relieved at his answer, but not entirely sure. I feel torn between two worlds.

"Can you come with me?" I ask, looking to the both of them.

"It doesn't work that way," Ollie says quietly, knowing it's going to hurt.

"But what about you?" I ask, directly to Ash now. "What about…us?"

He looks at me with eyes full of gratitude. "You freed me," He says "When people die before their time and don't know why...when they can't ...*come to terms* with it, they get stuck. I was stuck halfway in between, and you freed me. And I think–" He pauses and looks at Ollie, who is still playing with my hair absentmindedly "–I think I'm needed here."

I want to argue with him, to tell him that *I* need him more, but how can I argue when Ollie looks at him the way he does? Like the big brother he never had. Knowing Ollie isn't alone or scared or in pain gives me more peace in my life than I ever thought I would have, and I wouldn't take that away from him. I nestle my head into Ash's chest, where it fits perfectly just below his collarbone and he holds me, our hearts beating in sync.

"I can't leave you." I say, turning my face up to his. He kisses me, soft and slow and I melt. A tear begins to roll down my cheek and he catches it with his lips, planting kisses all over my face. "I just can't do it."

"You aren't leaving me," He says, "Not really. Our lives are just a blink of an eye compared to eternity. And I'll be here, waiting for you."

"You'll come find me?" I ask, not sure what I mean, leaving the question open-ended enough to give me breadcrumbs of hope tomorrow if he says yes.

"I'll always find you."

I clutch him and listen to the sound of his voice, reverberating warm and velvety in his chest.

"I love you, Ashley Gable."

"I love you too, Rafaela Torres."

I breathe him in until I've memorized his scent, his rhythm, and all of the colors and textures that are he and I. When I know I have to, I let go and crouch down next to Ollie, who is snuggled into a beagle puppy who looks remarkably like Benny, though I know Benny is probably sleeping at home, drooling on the upholstery like he always is.

"You're the best person I know," Ollie says, and I feel tears stinging the corners of my eyes, threatening to rain down. "I love you, Rafa."

"I love you too Ollie," I say "And you're the best person *I* will ever know. Take care of Ash."

He smiles importantly. "I will. Take care of Mom and Dad. And Benny."

"I will. Always."

"Tell them I said hi?"

"I promise I will."

I squeeze him one last time, then turn back to Ash.

"I don't want to lose you," I say, the floodgates now opening as realization sets in. I might never see him again, not in my world, anyway.

"Do you believe in soulmates?" He asks, pulling me into him. I snuggle into his chest one last time.

"Of course." I say, "Doesn't everybody?"

"I think everyone wants to." He replies. "But I know I never did until I found you."

My heart is raring to burst, and I struggle to understand how a single moment in time can be so euphorically happy and heartbreakingly painful all at once.

"You're mine too," I say, then look up at him with sparkling wet eyes. "I can feel it."

"Well then," He begins, taking my face in both of his hands and meeting my gaze. "You can never lose me then."

I throw my arms around his neck and absorb as much of him as I can, and he leans down to whisper in my ear.

"Soulmates can never be lost. We're written in the cosmos, you and I. Remember that."

He strokes my hair one last time, kisses me, and sends a stream of warmth so strong and pleasant through my body, I drift away, weightlessly into the abyss.

Chapter 46

The next time I open my eyes, I know I am in the hospital for real. The lights are bright, but the walls are puce green and the air smells of Clorox and disinfectant. I sit up almost immediately, calling for Ash and a firm but careful hand pushes me back down gently. At first, I think it's Ash but it isn't.

"Not so fast," says Mom, sitting on the edge of my bed, her expression wracked with worry. She hands me a glass of water and I inhale large draughts until my throat revives itself. Once I'm a little less parched, I look around the room, hoping to see Ash but he is nowhere to be found. My heart drops.

"Honey?"

I remember Mom is there and snap out of my wondering daze.

"I just…" I want to ask about him, but it won't do any good, so I change the topic to something more tangible.

"You must hate me," I say, remembering all I've put her through over the past couple of weeks. "I don't even know how to explain, I–"

She cuts me off and presses a finger to my lips.

"You don't need to explain," she says. "the police told me everything. You're my warrior; you always have been, in your own way. I couldn't be prouder of you, even if you did almost give me a heart attack."

"I'm sorry I didn't tell you more, sooner," I say, "I know I should have; I just didn't think you would believe me."

"I'm sorry I made you feel like you couldn't talk to me."

I tell her it's okay, because I know there is no way she could have possibly believed me. Even Ingrid was pretending a little when she said that she did. I finger the bracelet Ash gave me longingly and ache for him. There are so many questions to ask, but all I can think about is the boy I love, so I have to force myself to focus.

"Is Ingrid okay?"

"She's more than okay, thanks to you, and she's hardly left your side since Greyson was taken into custody. She's a good friend."

"Custody?" I ask, hardly daring to believe it.

"Mmhmm. Taylor corroborated Ingrid's story. Not only that, she recorded Greyson admitting to what he did while he was going after you and turned her phone over to the police."

"Taylor...went against him?" My head feels fine, but this twist of fate is hard to believe.

"She sure did." Mom confirms. I feel all of the muscles in my body relax and I sink further into my pillow. "Greyson is not going to get away with what he did because of you three."

"Four." I correct her.

"Four?"

"Four." I say again, not caring what she thinks, then I remember something else and I can't keep it to myself. I would want her to tell me if things were the other way around. "I saw Ollie, Mom. He was with Ash. And he was beautiful; even more beautiful than you remember. He was perfectly healthy. And he was happy, so happy."

Her face crinkles into a smile and the corners of her eyes fight to stay dry. I know she's only tearing up because she thinks it sweet that I dreamed about my deceased brother while comatose. I think she wants to believe me, even if she can't. I roll to my side and let her rub my back in silence, when suddenly the door bursts open. A man with wild green eyes, bronze skin, and a head of dark, wavy hair that looks eerily similar to my own pushes his way into the room, nearly knocking over my med stand as he does.

"Dad!" I shout, practically ripping out my IV when I throw my hands in the air. He closes the space between us in mere milliseconds and has me in his arms before Mom can protest, which surprisingly, she does not do.

"Oh Rafa," He says in his gruff voice, holding me like I'm his little girl once more. "I love you so much. When Mom said you were hurt again, I got here as fast as I could. I'm sorry it took me three days, but it's awfully hard to get a ticket last minute around the holidays."

"Wait—three days?" I ask, astounded. "Three?"

Mom nods and shares a knowing look with Dad. "You gave us quite the scare. *Again.*"

I smile sheepishly, but neither one of them look angry.

"And since I can't seem to keep you under lock and key," Mom continues, "Dad is going to stay with us for a while."

I look at Dad and beam, almost forgetting to be sad.

"Really?"

"As long as you don't mind."

I throw my arms around his neck again in reply. When we pull apart, he stands up and puts his arm around Mom's shoulders and she doesn't step away. I am about to ask Dad a million questions when the doctor walks in, studying test results on a tablet.

"Well, I have absolutely no explanation for this, but you are concussion-free. Your brain shows no signs of a TBI whatsoever." He says to all of us, looking baffled.

"I am?"

"How is that possible?" Mom asks.

Dr. Sepir shrugs. "I've never seen anything like it. The human body works in mysterious ways, I suppose." A very un-doctorly answer, but it appears to be the only one he can summon.

"Does this mean she is cleared for school?" Mom asks.

"I'd recommend a few days to recover from the events of the past few days, but there is no medical reason for me to keep her on restricted activity. As long as she is feeling okay and the hallucinations stop, there is no reason she can't resume classes, homework; even light physical activity. But let's keep it light, for the time being." He gives me a scrutinizing look, as if I went looking for any of this.

Mom looks at me, her eyes almost pitying.

"Rafa, I know this isn't easy to talk about, but have you been seeing Ash lately?"

The way she says it, as though I am a child and he is my imaginary friend, is instantly painful. I dig my heels into what little solid ground I still have to stand on.

"I. Did not. Hallucinate. Him."

"Sweetheart, there's no reason to get angry at your mother." Says Dad, suddenly rushing to the defense of the woman who broke his heart just a few months ago. A jab of betrayal punches me somewhere beneath my sternum.

"You haven't even been here!" I say through clenched teeth, though I don't mean it like it sounds. I know it isn't his fault he hasn't been around, but I don't appreciate him automatically taking everyone's side but mine when he hasn't even heard my story. He recoils a bit, and guilt creeps into the back of my throat like bile.

"I'm sorry; I didn't mean it like that. It's just...can we not talk about this right now?"

Dr. Sepir jumps in again, clearly not wanting to be in the center of the Torres family tension yet again.

"I'll tell you what." He begins, addressing Mom and Dad instead of me. "Give it a few days; three, maybe four. If she doesn't have any headaches, nausea, tinnitus, or dizziness, and if the hallucinations stay at bay, then we will talk about getting her back into a somewhat normal routine."

I don't bother interjecting how wrong he is, because there really isn't any point in trying to defend myself when the whole room has already written off what I'm trying to tell them.

"Can I go home?" I ask. I'm trying to hide how hungry I am to get out of here, because right now all I can think about is getting back to the clearing to find Ash. To kiss his lips and feel his body against mine. To prove to everyone who has doubted me that the same gravity gluing me to this world is pushing down on him, too.

Chapter 47

The next few days are a blur, and I drift through them like a plastic bag floating in the Indian Ocean. Dad is staying in the spare bedroom upstairs and stays home with me while Mom is at work. He's taken time off of work, and when I ask him how long, his only response is "Don't you worry yourself with that. I'd quit my job if I had to just to be here."

I don't blame them for giving me round-the-clock care, but it makes it impossible to sneak out of the house especially for the first couple of days. Even in the middle of the night it's too risky, because Dad is such a light sleeper and I'd have to walk right by his room to get out. I search for Ash everywhere, every minute of every day. When I wake up in the middle of the night, I swear I can almost feel his arms around me but when I open my eyes, I am alone. In the early mornings, when the sun is just kissing the horizon and I'm still emerging from my dreams, I can hear his voice floating through my cracked window, but when I run to it, I find nothing but the humming of the breeze and the calls of geese flying south for the winter.

I become so fixated on getting to Ash—
possessed, even—I start jumping at the slightest sounds
and frantically looking around whenever the house creaks,
which is often. I try to disguise my obsession, but Dad
knows me too well and on the third day he asks if we can
talk. We sit down in the living room across from one
another; I on the couch, he in the puffy green armchair.
He rests his right ankle on his left knee in his signature
"Dad talk" position, and for a second I forget he hasn't
been here all along.

"You're jumpy." Though it isn't a question, it
begs an answer.

"I guess."

"How come?"

"I don't know." I say, looking down at my hands,
fiddling with my bracelet. My wrist.

"I don't buy it, mija."

He looks at me and my eyes meet his; mirror
images.

"Is it Greyson? Because he can't hurt you. He's
on house arrest awaiting trial. Indefinitely suspended from
school. And even if he wasn't, I'd kill 'im. He can't get to
you."

"I know." I say. Though truthfully, I'm terrified
of him, Greyson isn't what is making me anxious.

"Well, if it isn't Greyson, then what? You can tell
me. I promise I won't criticize or get upset."

I don't want to tell him, but at least one of my
walls is starting to crumble. He has always been
approachable, even when it comes to things I might be
afraid to talk to anyone else about. Even so, I can't seem

to get my tongue to form the words. There's a long pause, and then he speaks.

"Is it Ash?"

My breath catches in my throat and a shockwave of adrenaline courses through me at the sound of his name on someone else's lips. It is the first time I've heard it outside my own head in days. It's funny how easy it is to question something's validity when no one else will acknowledge it.

"How did you know?"

"I pieced it together. And Mom told me about the hallucinations."

"Nobody believes me." I say.

"Have you stopped to think that maybe they have good reason not to?"

His question trips me up and I lose my words, as if I have no fire left in me, or at least, no energy to ignite it. I stopped second-guessing Ash long before this, and I am not about to slide backwards into the lonely, soul-crushing depths of self-doubt again.

"I know how it sounds." I begin. "I know everybody thinks he's dead and that I'm just some poor, concussed, delusional girl. I understand why people have their opinions, but I can't deny this. It's so strong; too strong not to be real."

He looks at me quizzically, processing his thoughts in great detail before opening his mouth to speak. Not impulsive like Mom or like me.

"I've never told anyone this before, but sometimes I see Ollie."

I gape at him, speechless.

"I don't like to admit it, not even to myself, but it's true. It was worst just after he died, but it still happens from time to time. Sometimes when I wake up to go to the bathroom in the middle of the night, I think I hear him breathing from his room down the hall in the seconds before I come completely to. Sometimes I actually go to his room and look for him in bed, but of course he isn't there. Sometimes, I see him in faces of kids in the grocery store when I'm out getting eggs. It only takes me a moment to recognize they aren't Ollie, because obviously they never are and I know that, but that moment seems to stretch out for an eternity and in that eternity I really, truly believe it's him. That the heavens have somehow coughed him up and sent him back. I know it isn't real, but that doesn't make it feel any less so."

I want to close the gap between us; to sit on his lap like a child again, but I know I'm too old and too lanky to fit so I stay on my side of the room and he stays on his. He's trying so hard to understand, but what he is describing isn't the same. It's one thing to think you see someone you used to know for a second before you realize it's someone else, but Ash isn't someone I'm mistaking for another in the produce aisle. It isn't the same.

"I'm sorry, Dad. I didn't know."

"Of course you didn't! How could you? We never talked about this stuff after Ollie died. Any of it. Me, your Mom, you–we grieved alone, which truthfully wasn't very healthy."

"Why didn't we talk about it?"

"Oh, I don't know. Death is hard. Grief is hard. Being vulnerable is hard, especially around the ones you love. We all handle it differently, and never very well, in retrospect, at least."

"Mmhmm." I add, thoughtful.

"Do you think maybe you're trying to fill the gap Ollie left with Ash? Hearts and heads can do extraordinary things when they are in pain, you know."

"I don't think anything could fill that gap, even Ash. But now it's like–it's like I have two gaps nothing can fill."

"What about going back to therapy?" He continues, "Your Mom's going crazy with worry with you not letting this stuff with Ash go, you know that?"

I feel a twinge of guilt, but quickly swallow it because I'm not doing any of this to hurt anyone. I feel enough emptiness, pain, and anxiety right now. I can't add guilt to the list.

"I'm sorry, Dad. I don't mean to hurt anyone in any of this. I can't just let it go. It'd be like trying to let go of air. It's just not possible."

He nods thoughtfully. He's not angry and he's not arguing me on it. He is genuinely, sincerely trying to understand and for that I love him even more.

"Well then, tell me what I can do to help."

I'm so used to being on defense, I'm not sure how to respond, so I don't.

"I'm serious. Tell me what will help. Just say the word."

"Can you–will you just let me go for a walk in the woods to think? Just for an hour? I'll take my phone, and

I promise to be careful. I think I just need some fresh air."

"Well" he says, pensive. "If there's one thing I've noticed it's that there is no shortage of fresh air around here."

He stands up slowly, tiredly, walks to me, and plants a kiss on the top of my head over my tangled, unwashed hair.

"Let's just...don't tell Mom, okay?"

Chapter 48

Once back in the forest, my skin becomes alive, buzzing with anxiety and adrenaline. I'm not sure if it's just the soft breeze bringing the woods to life or if there really is a presence dipping into me, grazing my insides. I take a deep breath and swear I can smell Ash on the air, which sends hope through my body like waves gathering into a great swell.

I walk at first, knowing Dad will be watching from the window, but as soon as I cross the threshold of the woods I break into a run. For the first time in what feels like ages, the pounding of my feet against the ground does not trigger a throbbing in my head. There is something about the air here–so fresh and cold and clean– that makes me feel so alive. I almost feel as though I could take off into the air like a bird or a butterfly, and I imagine myself flying into Ash's arms and being cradled in his soft, warm cocoon. I run past the giant spruce straight toward the clearing, half expecting to see him sitting on the downed tree or cocking an eyebrow at me from across the pool. When I halt to a stop at the place where the forest lets up, I scan the clearing with desperate hope, and my breath catches when I see what lies before me.

The clearing is unrecognizable. Everything is dead. The tall grass, once so fluid and alive, is plastered to the earth like brown, shriveled worms dried out on the sidewalk from too much sun. The wildflowers have lost all of their petals and their bald heads sag in defeat, succumbing to the cold. The pond, which is usually a vibrant blue rivaled only by Ash's eyes, is a dull, cloudy winter grey. The bullfrogs are quiet, the songbirds have gone, and even the blue-black crows up in the trees do not caw.

It makes sense that everything is dead. It is practically winter in Minnesota, after all. Still, even a week ago everything here was alive and untouched by the changing of the seasons, seemingly immune to the cold hands of winter that inevitably grip everything but the pines. I had finally started getting used to all of the evergreens, and once you're used to them it is hard to remember that some things still must die.

I close my eyes and suck deep, cool breaths trying to calm my body and slow my thoughts which are twisting my insides like a virus. I count to ten and breathe in, then count down from ten and breathe out again and again until it forces my pulse to steady. When I finally regain control, I open my eyes.

I call his name, once, twice, three times. I pause in between, giving him a chance to emerge and say "What are you so worried about? I told you I'd always find you" but he doesn't come. Each time I call his name I am answered only by the silence of the dead clearing.

It's been a week since I saw him, longer than we have ever gone without seeing one another. When I was in the hospital and then stuck at home, I was able to convince myself that he was having trouble getting through the veil that separates us, and that if I came to the clearing everything would be okay. That I would run into his arms, our bodies colliding like celestial beings thrown out of orbit, and then back into it with each other. But now, seeing the clearing so dead and deserted, I cannot deny that overwhelming sensation that something is wrong.

I pace around the room the forest made for us, trying to feel him on the air but I just feel cold. Goosebumps erupt from my skin like a million little mountains and my breath is an icy white cloud against the transparent air. I pace back and forth frantically, calling Ash's name every few minutes until the sun starts to dip below the tree-line and shadows invade the clearing, making it look more like a lair than our secret place. In spite of my resolve to be strong, I feel a knot forming in my throat so thick it threatens to choke me, and shiny tears roll down my cheeks in hot, desperate rivers.

I have never felt more completely and utterly alone.

"Please." I plead with any god who will listen. "Please, it had to be real."

When nobody responds, I say it louder.

"It had to be real. *We* had to be real. Give me something, *anything.*"

I repeat it until I am shouting into the wind, but I am answered only with a sharp hoarseness in my lungs. I knew that Ash was finally free, and that he was going to stay with Ollie, but I never dreamed that he wouldn't be able to get back through to me, or that all of the life in our clearing would be sucked into whatever oblivion he disappears into. How can I survive off of nothing but the memory of him? How, after all we've been through, can that be enough? How is that *fair?*

I collapse on my knees in the dead grass and bury my head in my arms. I break down; practically decompose right there in the clearing, and that's when I hear something.

Footsteps coming right toward me.

Chapter 49

I squint my eyes, trying to see through the puddles the tears left behind. He walks toward me–slowly, gently–until his body lingers over me like the shadow of a giant spruce, sheltering me from the cold and the wind. He bends down and grasps my elbows, pulling me into a seated position with strong hands.

"Rafaela." He says softly, as though he were cooing to a baby. But I am not offended; I need some warmth. I sniffle and lift my eyes to meet his.

"I'm...sorry, Dad." I say, falling into him and holding back a fresh wave of tears.

He holds my head against his chest, and neither of us say anything for a long moment.

"Talk to me, Rafa." he says, wiping away some of my tears.

"He was supposed to be here. He was supposed to come."

Dad nods, encouraging me to go on.

"Please, don't tell Mom, okay? It's not like she thinks. I'm not sick or crazy or injured. No doctor is going to be able to read an explanation for this out of one of their stupid textbooks, but it was real, I swear to you it was."

"I believe you." He says, and relief seeps into my veins, warming my blood.

"Dad, I saw…" I drift off, but his eyes implore me to go on. "I saw Ollie. He was with Ash. They were together, in the same place. I saw them when I–after Greyson hurt me. Ash was taking care of Ollie, and he was holding me. And it wasn't a dream. It wasn't. Dad I–I fell in love him. I've loved him since we met, and now he's just gone. Vanished, into thin air. What am I supposed to do? How am I supposed to be okay when the new world I built for myself was just ripped away from me?"

We sit on the ground, side by side near the place Ash and I used to sit and talk.

"I don't know if this will help or not," He begins. "but let's say everything happened just the way you remember it. Let's say Ash was real–even after death–and he really is with Ollie and you really did see them."

He pauses and wipes another round of tears from my cheekbone with his finger.

"Let's agree that all happened just like you say it did. If that is the case, just think how lucky Ollie is to have someone so special looking after him. Wouldn't you want to know that wherever he is–that he isn't alone?"

I nod, having not thought of things from this perspective before.

"Losing people is hard. In this year alone, I lost my son, my wife, and sometimes it's even felt like I lost my daughter."

"Dad–" I begin, but he cuts me off.

"No, I mean it Rafa. There were nights I didn't think I would make it—thought the emptiness would swallow me whole—but do you know what kept me going?"

"What?" I ask.

"What kept me going was knowing that you and Mom had each other, and that you were safe and loved and finding a new happiness, even if that meant not being with me."

"Dad, please don't say that."

"No," He says, holding up a gentle hand and stopping me once again. "I'm not saying this to make you feel sorry for me. God knows it isn't your fault Mom and I separated. I'm just saying, try to think of it from Ollie's perspective, or even Ash's. Try to picture them together and happy and not in pain, and see if that doesn't help just a little."

I think back to the white place where I laid in Ash's arms and Ollie sat beside us, playing with my hair. I think of his round cheeks and the dimples on his face when he saw me for the first time and smiled. I think of the two of them, standing over me somewhere, watching me and waiting, and I feel my heart breaking in two and stitching itself up all in the same beat.

"It helps a little, doesn't it?" Dad asks, and I nod. And then another, darker thought hits me and I finally say aloud the thing I've been too afraid to say until now, for fear that no one will tell me I'm wrong.

"Dad what if...what if he wasn't real? What if Mom and the doctor were right, and it–he–was just a figment of my damaged brain?"

He pauses for a moment, mulling over his next words carefully.

"Was it real to you?"

"It is the single realest thing I have ever felt."

He nods and ponders again.

"You know what I think, mija? I think, it does not matter if it was real to them. If it was real to *you*, then it was real."

Chapter 50

I don't make plans to go back to school until after the Christmas holiday, and the school sends over a tutor twice a week which isn't so bad. Luckily, I am a quick learner, so I don't feel as though I am getting too far behind. I don't want to go back to school until I've completely recovered from the ordeal. Mom jokes that when I do go back, she's going to roll me up in bubble wrap each morning and Dad says he isn't sure that's not a good idea.

Mom and Dad have been getting along curiously well, and some nights I even catch them drinking wine in the living room long after I've gone to bed, giggling like teenagers who've broken their curfew. Dad doesn't seem to be in a hurry to book a flight back to Boston either, and Mom doesn't seem to want him to.

Ingrid comes over after school most days, and we talk in my room until it's time to eat and sometimes she stays for dinner too. She's doing better now, or so she says. She's talking again at school, not much but she's getting there, and she is going to regular therapy for

PTSD from the assault and everything else that happened to her over the past year.

"I'm glad you're getting help," I tell her one night while she's painting her toenails black at the foot of my bed. Her hair is longer now, more grown out and she stopped dying it, so her natural ebony roots are poking through. "I love you, you know?"

"I know." She says, smiling. "I don't know what would have happened to me if it wasn't for you. If you never came to Esko, I mean. Maybe I would never have spoken again."

I nod, imagining a world in which Ingrid never found her voice and Greyson walked free. One thing that has changed for me since everything happened is that I don't take the people in my life for granted-not ever. I'd rather have them get tired of hearing how much I love them than to disappear without ever knowing.

"I heard Taylor is going to therapy, too." She says. "Not that we're friends or anything, but she acknowledges me now, and we talk. Sometimes, anyway."

Taylor was diagnosed with something called "codependency." I make a mental note to look that up, not realizing there is a clinical term for getting trapped in terrible relationships, but it makes sense. Narcissists like Greyson gravitate toward people like Taylor, because they're easier to manipulate. Either way, I am glad she's doing better and getting help.

As for me, some days are harder than others. I haven't seen Ash again, not in the waking world, anyway. There are days when I can't stop crying; when the longing in my heart for Ash is so strong, I fear I will burst. I never take his bracelet off, though nobody else can see it, and I carry the little sculpture kindergarten-Ash made with me everywhere. Mom will never understand why I'm so attached to it, but it brings me comfort just to know I am holding something he touched. I think of him and Ollie out there somewhere, together, and it fills me not quite with joy, but with a sense of warmth that's enough to hold me together for now.

The thing that pains me the most is the uncertainty; the constant whisper of doubt in the back of my head that comes alive when the world is quiet and tells me it was all in my head. But I think about what Dad said to me in the clearing; that it doesn't matter if it was real to anyone else, so long as it was real to me, and this serves as ammunition to kill the doubts or at least force them to dance a little quieter. I think about what Ash said too; that he is still with me even when I cannot see him, and that soulmates can never be lost. Time may not be on our side, but it cannot take away that first sweet kiss or the magic in the clearing on those cold October nights or all the little things we shared in this world and the next.

All I can do is enjoy my time in this world and love the ones that remain here as fiercely as I possibly can. For now, that will have to be enough.

Rafa and the Real Boy

Epilogue

It is January third. I am going back to school today, and though I'm not sure how I feel about that, I am as ready as I'll ever be. Knowing Greyson isn't there and that I'll get to see Ingrid more regularly makes school infinitely more inviting than it had been before the holidays.

Like any other school day, I roll off the edge of my bed, throw my hair into a messy bun on top of my head, and slip into an outfit that just barely stays on the right side of the thin line between comfy-chic and loungewear. I brush and floss my teeth, rub some cream on my scars (but do not cover them up) and coat my lashes with a thin layer of mascara. Finally, I slide Ash's bracelet onto my wrist, just like I do every single morning and will do, probably, for the rest of my life.

When I get downstairs, Mom is letting Benny out and Dad is making his famous fresh-squeezed orange juice. I'm not sure exactly what's going on with them, but they seem genuinely happy and I heard them talking about selling the townhouse in Boston, so I think it's safe to say Dad isn't going anywhere and for this I am grateful.

"Morning, Dad." I say, taking a glass from him and flushing down a handful of vitamins with it.

"You ready for this?" He asks, cheerfully.

"As ready as I'll ever be."

I stuff the sack lunch he prepared for me into my backpack, along with the book I'm currently reading, my journal, and about a month's worth of owed assignments. I may have missed a lot of class time, but Mom made sure I kept up.

In typical Minnesota fashion, the January weather is below freezing and when Mom gets in from walking Benny, they are both covered in fluffy, cotton candy snow.

"You ready?" She asks, as Benny shakes his snowflakes onto the floor where they immediately turn to wet spots on the heated tile.

"Yep." I say, reaching into the closet to grab my winter coat. It's wool, almost the color of eggplant. As I pull it on, the sleeves of my sweater hike up my arm a bit, exposing the pale skin below.

"That's pretty." Mom says, though I don't know why. I've had this jacket since last Christmas.

"It's just my winter coat; you've seen it a million times," I say with a laugh.

I am about to slip my arms into the jacket, but she grabs my right arm and pulls it toward her. She studies my wrist for a moment.

"Not your coat, *I* bought you your coat, I think I know what it looks like. I'm talking about the bracelet," She says. "It's beautiful. Where did you get it?"

I look at her in disbelief and my heart skips several beats. I force myself to breathe, and when I do, I smell the faintest hint of peppermint on the air.

Acknowledgements

A special thanks to:

All of the wonderful students I've had the joy of teaching over the last seven years. You are the real inspiration.

My parents, in general, for everything, but especially for providing me with the education, love, and support that allowed me to pursue my creative dreams.

Diane Wagar, for making me believe that I could be a writer, a "real" writer, all those years ago.

Caitlin Conlon, for being a tremendous editor.

Ellie, for giving *Rafa and the Real Boy* her first test-run.

Jimmy Dillon, for the Spanish consult. (Gracias).

Valene, for not minding that I spend days at a time in front of a computer screen and for your undying love and support, always. This is also probably a good time to thank you for doing 90% of the dishes in our household.

And last but not least, thank *you,* for reading this book. You will never know how much it means to me.

xx, Emily

About the Author

Emily graduated from Siena College with a degree in English Literature and Education. She lives in upstate New York with her partner, a dog named Pepper, and a cat named Dash. When she isn't writing you can find her substitute teaching, drinking iced coffee, volunteering at farm animal sanctuaries, and spending time in Cooperstown with her family. More can be found about Emily at www.emilyjuniperpoetry.com. You can also find her on Instagram and TikTok @by.emilyjuniper

Also by Emily Juniper:

A Strangely Wrapped Gift

Things I Learned in the Night

Swim

One Day at a Time: A guided journal for mental health and wellness

Made in the USA
Columbia, SC
16 October 2020